More *praise for*

THE GHOST WALKER

"A corking good read . . . Coel's Catholic Irish Jesuit priest and his Arapaho friends and neighbors, each with their individual worldviews and sensibilities, make for interesting contrasts in this excellent mystery that focuses on the strange place Native Americans occupy in their own land. An outstanding entry in a superior series."

—*Booklist* (starred review)

"Engaging . . . Coel's series in the Hillerman tradition finds a space where Jesuits and Native Americans can meet in a culture of common decency."

—*Kirkus Reviews*

"Sharp writing and poignant characterizations."

—*Affaire de Coeur*

"The writing has grown smooth in a way that makes it clear that Margaret Coel and Father John O'Malley will both be around for a long time to come."

—*Mostly Murder*

"The *Ghost Walker* should show everyone that Coel is not a one-hit wonder. She not only tells a believable story, she invokes the power of place to draw readers into her tale. She crafts a good whodunit and throws in enough obstacles to keep the tension building . . . Sometimes a fiction writer knows her subject so well, you almost forget it's fiction. What more can a mystery reader ask?"

—*Gazette-Telegraph* (Colorado Springs, CO)

continued . . .

‹ The ›
Ghost Walker

Margaret Coel

BERKLEY PRIME CRIME, NEW YORK

THE GHOST WALKER

A Berkley Prime Crime Book / published by arrangement with the author

PRINTING HISTORY
Berkley Prime Crime hardcover edition / October 1996
Berkley Prime Crime mass-market edition / September 1997

For Margaret and Sam,
so loving.

ACKNOWLEDGMENTS

I am fortunate to live in a university town where, every time you round a corner, you meet an expert. These wonderfully erudite people have always been willing to share their expertise and to act as my guides through some tangled fields of knowledge. I thank them all, especially Professors Gene Erwin, Mancourt Downing, and John Tracy; psychiatrist Jay Haws and addictions therapist Ann C. Noonan; Fay Tracy, Karen and Carl Schneider, and Mary and Ed Kaupas.

And to those who read this manuscript and made many insightful suggestions—Karen Gilleland, Ann Ripley, Sybil Downing, Dr. Carol Irwin, Dr. Virginia Sutter, Dr. George Coel—my hat is off to you all.

We will not, however, bemoan thee as if thou wast forever lost to us, or that thy name would be buried in oblivion; thy soul yet lives in the great country of Spirits.

Jonathan Carver
Touch the Earth

‹ 1 ›

Snow had fallen all day, and now the open spaces of Wind River Reservation lay under deep powder. Father John Aloysius O'Malley gripped the wheel of the Toyota pickup and peered through the half-moon the wiper carved across the windshield. He tried to follow the depressions of the tire tracks running ahead, all that hinted at the boundaries of Rendezvous Road—tire tracks and an occasional scrub brush or dried stalk of goldenrod poking through the snow in the ditches. It was the second Sunday in January, the First Moon in the Arapaho Way of marking time: the Moon When the Snow Blows Like Spirits in the Wind.

A blast of frigid air filled the cab, and Father John glanced at the dashboard. The heater lever still rode on high, but the Arctic itself had begun to stream through the vents. The tiny needle on the temperature gauge danced in the red zone.

He felt the engine start to miss as he pumped the gas pedal. "Come on," he coaxed, startled at the sound of his own voice in the vacant cold. The Toyota slid to a stop. He flipped off the headlights, still pumping the pedal. Nothing. The engine was as lifeless as a block of granite.

He was already late for the meeting, which was why he'd taken the shortcut to Lander. Rendezvous Road angled across the eastern edge of the reservation and joined Highway 789 near the southern boundary. Now he wouldn't make the meeting at all, and how would he explain it to the bishop's personal representative, Clifford Keating, who had driven into a Wyoming blizzard to meet with the local pastors?

Father John opened the glove compartment, fished through a stack of opera tapes, two maps, a couple of pencils, and a spiral tablet and pulled out his earmuffs. His fingers felt stiff inside his fur-lined gloves as he removed his brown cowboy hat and adjusted the earmuffs on his head. Replacing the hat, he snapped the ends of his collar together, then yanked the flashlight from beneath the seat and swung out into the storm.

Cold seeped through his parka, past his flannel shirt and blue jeans, into his skin. The wind drove the snow slantwise, pricking his face with hard pieces of ice. He squinted as he groped for the metal catch and threw open the hood. A cloud of steam rose, and he jumped back, even though the warmth had felt good. He shone the flashlight over the engine, spotting the broken radiator hose still dripping water. The coffers at St. Francis Mission had enough last month for a tune-up and new hoses or for two recapped rear tires. He had bought the tires. Bad choice.

He slammed down the hood and, pushing back the cuff of his parka, turned the flashlight onto his watch. Seven-fifteen P.M. The meeting had started. Highway 789 lay a mile ahead. He might be able to catch a ride there to Jake Littlehorse's garage, another two miles west. It was hard to imagine any other fools out tonight, except for priests summoned by the bishop's delegate.

Swearing under his breath for not carrying a roll of duct tape and a jug of antifreeze, he pushed the flashlight into the pocket of his parka and struck out for the highway, snow crunching under his boots. He guessed the temperature to be at twenty below with the wind-chill factor. His feet were beginning to feel like ingots. Wyoming blizzards had it all over the storms he had known in Boston. You could freeze to death here.

He had probably come half a mile, but there was no sign of the highway. What was there to see? One white road flowing into another. Just ahead, it looked as if the snow had been churned by a tractor, with tire tracks crisscrossing one another. Somebody had started down Rendezvous Road and turned back. Smart, thought Father John. Whoever it was had probably decided to head home to a warm fire.

As he got closer, he could distinguish the tracks of two vehicles. He couldn't have missed them by more than ten or fifteen minutes judging by the deep, wave-like marks. They made a wide turn across the road and stopped at a dark, smudged area next to the ditch. Father John angled toward it. He saw the boot prints, the trampled slope of the ditch, the broken scrub brush. Four or five feet below the road lay a dark object, a log. Only logs didn't wear boots. The wind bore through Father John's parka, sending shivers along his spine.

He started down, his boots sliding in the snow. One boot hit something flat and sharp—a boulder—and he drove his foot against it, steadying himself while he extracted the flashlight. It flickered a moment, then went out. He pounded the plastic tube into his glove until a narrow, eerie beam burst over the loglike figure: the boots, the patterns in the black soles, the tops of gray socks. The figure was wrapped in a brown tarp, but hanging from the side was a strip of blue fabric with white stars and red and yellow stripes: the Arapaho star

quilt. He recognized the stillness of death. He was looking at a corpse. "Dear God," he prayed out loud, "have
mercy on his soul."

Jamming the flashlight back into his pocket, Father
John climbed to the road and started for the highway.
He was running now, gulping in icy air that punctured
his lungs like a thousand sharp needles. He sensed he
had passed from cold to numbness, the beginning of hy-
pothermia, but his thoughts were focused on the poor
dead soul wrapped in a star quilt and tarp and thrown
into a ditch. "God help him," he prayed silently over
and over, the words matching the rhythm of his boots
against the snow.

He ran past the stop sign and turned west on the highway. There were no headlights, no signs of life, nothing
but the blowing snow and the white earth slipping into
the gray sky. Strips of icy asphalt crept through the snow
in places. He felt his boots slipping. He nearly fell.
Catching himself, he slowed to a walk, breathing hard,
clapping his gloves together for warmth.

Just before he heard the motor, faint in the distance, he
sensed the slight tremble in the highway and swung
around. White pinpricks of light glowed in the darkness.
He started running back along his own boot prints. As he
ran, he pulled the flashlight from his pocket and waved it
back and forth before realizing it wasn't working.

Jiggling the switch, he ran on. The flashlight sprang
to life as he came into the far reaches of the headlights.
He circled the plastic tube in front, shouting, "Stop,
stop!" With a kind of shock, he realized the truck was
not stopping. He jumped out of the way.

A gray Chevy pickup lumbered by, its wheels throwing
clods of snow over him. He hollered after it, scarcely believing anybody would pass a man in a blizzard. Then

suddenly the brake lights came on, and the pickup ground to a stop. Father John ran after it and grabbed the tailgate. Half expecting the driver to take off, he lunged around the side for the door handle and hoisted himself onto the passenger seat as the truck started moving.

"Thanks," he managed through clenched teeth, swallowing the swear words he usually forgot he knew.

In the dim light of the dashboard, the driver looked to be in his twenties. The beginning stubble of a blond beard covered his chin and he wore a dark cap with ear flaps pulled down. He sat square-shouldered behind the wheel. "Didn't see ya," he said. "No car anywhere."

Pounding his gloves together to work the circulation back into his fingers, Father John said, "I broke down on Rendezvous Road." It was an effort to keep his tone civil. "I'd appreciate a ride to Jake Littlehorse's place." Then he added, "I'm Father John O'Malley, pastor at St. Francis Mission. You from around here?"

He knew the answer. Nobody from around here would think of leaving another human being out in a blizzard in subzero temperatures. Not unless he wanted the person dead.

"Yeah. From around here," the driver said.

Father John wondered why his companion was lying; what difference did it make? He shrugged it off. The cab was warm; the heat rising around his legs made his skin tingle; he was grateful for the ride. You didn't have to like the guy who gave you the ride.

He turned his eyes on the frozen landscape sliding by his window. The snow seemed lighter, gentler, like cotton billowing downward. Less than an hour ago, he'd been driving down Rendezvous Road, late for a meeting called by the bishop. The meeting was probably half over by now, and he could imagine the excuses Father

George and Father Edward and the other priests from
Lander and Riverton had laid out for him. "Always late.
Probably forgot. You know the Jesuits." And they'd all
have a good laugh, except for Clifford Keating, who
wouldn't be laughing. Jesuits. They were always trouble.

"So you broke down on Rendezvous Road?"

The question startled Father John. His new companion hadn't seemed very talkative, which was fine with
him. He was in no mood himself for a friendly chat. He
decided to keep the conversation light. No mention of
the body in the ditch. He drew in a long breath before
explaining he'd been on his way to a meeting when his
pickup had popped a radiator hose. He'd walked to the
highway to catch a ride.

The driver was quiet, and after a moment Father John
said, "Jake Littlehorse's is just around the curve up
ahead."

"Gotcha."

If the man were a local, Father John thought, he
wouldn't have to be told. The truck banked around the
curve, turned into a snow-crusted driveway, and
stopped in front of two squat frame buildings nestled
among some cottonwoods. The buildings were dark.
The headlights illuminated the black letters on the plate
glass of one: JAKE'S GARAGE. Father John knew Jake
lived in a couple of rooms tacked onto the back. He
could be there. "Mind hanging around a minute?" he
asked, stepping out.

The driver reached across the seat and grabbed the
door handle. As the door slammed shut, the truck
started backing up, its wheels grinding through the
snow. Metal screeched against metal as the gears
shifted. Then the truck took off down the highway.

Father John watched the red glow of the taillights a

moment before hunching his shoulders against the cold and starting down the driveway, kicking up little clouds of just-fallen snow. It swirled around his blue jeans, sifted down into his boots. In the back, the driveway widened into a kind of court. At the edge of the court stood an old truck chassis and a pile of hoods and doors and wheels, half covered with snow. Calling Jake's name, he banged on the back door. No answer. The tow truck wasn't around. The garage man could be out on an emergency.

Father John made his way back along the driveway, cold slipping over him like a sheet of ice. The nearest ranch house was at least a mile farther. On an impulse, he veered toward the front door and pounded into the silence. Then he grasped the metal knob. To his surprise, it turned in his glove. The door swung open, its hinges shrieking like owls in the night. A wave of warmth tinged with the faint odor of grease hit him as he stepped inside. He closed the door and leaned against it. He wasn't going to end up like that poor, frozen corpse in the ditch.

He knocked the flashlight into his glove until the bulb spurted enough light to make out Jake's office: the glass-topped counter with a cash register and phone on top, a couple of hubcaps and a calendar on the wall behind, and a metal chair next to the door that led to Jake's living quarters. He set the flashlight on the counter, pulled off his gloves, hat, and earmuffs, and scooted the phone into the beam of light.

He had just begun dialing 911 when he felt a hard object shoved against his parka into the small of his back. There was the sound of a rifle being cocked, then a male voice: "You move, and I'll blow you to kingdom come."

◆ 2 ◆

Jake Littlehorse was a nervous man.

Father John could hear the Arapaho gulping in air as he jammed the rifle harder against Father John's back. The buzzing noise in the phone seemed a long way off. One wrong move, and he wouldn't hear the noise that followed.

In a steady voice, he said, "Jake, it's me. Father John."

The pressure lifted from his back. "Jesus, Father." Jake's voice quivered. "You tryin' to get yourself killed? How'd you get in here, anyways?"

Father John turned around, catching the glint of the flashlight off the blue-gray rifle barrel. Slowly he replaced the receiver as Jake, still pointing the gun, backed to the wall and flipped a switch. White fluorescent light flooded the small office, which had gone hot and stuffy. Father John yanked open the front of his parka, keeping his eyes on the Indian, who leaned the rifle into the corner. He looked half asleep, black hair sprouting upward like a feathered headdress, eyes narrow slits in a fleshy brown face. He had on a rumpled green sweatshirt and blue jeans that hung below a cliff of stomach flesh. His stockinged feet were planted wide apart on the linoleum floor.

Father John said, "I thought you'd been called out.

The tow truck's not around. The front door was unlocked, so I came in."

"Truck's in the garage," Jake said, nodding sideways. "Guess I might've dozed off watchin' TV. I thought I'd locked up and you was some burglar. I got lots of valuable things here them Indians are always after." A whine seeped into his voice.

"The Toyota popped a radiator hose on Rendezvous Road," Father John said.

"Hell, how come you didn't say so?" Jake raised his head and squared his shoulders, a man about to enter familiar territory. "Hang on 'til I get my boots and coat."

The Arapaho disappeared through the door as quietly as he'd come in, and Father John grabbed the phone and dialed 911. He counted four rings before the operator's voice sounded. After giving his name, he explained he'd spotted a body in the ditch along Rendezvous Road about a half mile north of Highway 789.

"Hang on," said the operator. After a minute she was back. A patrol car and ambulance were on the way.

Father John knew the body would be hard to spot. If it hadn't been for the tracks and boot prints, he would have missed it. By morning it would have been buried in snow. It might have stayed hidden until spring. He told the operator he was at Jake Littlehorse's place, but would meet the police on Rendezvous Road.

As he replaced the receiver, he sensed a presence in the room and whirled around. Jake stood so close, Father John wondered he hadn't felt the Indian's breath on his neck. He had silently entered the office a second time, like a warrior stalking the buffalo.

"You didn't say nothin' about no body." The Arapaho's brown eyes widened into a stare. He kept his arms close to his sides, looking as frozen and stiff as the poor soul in the ditch.

Father John explained he'd seen what he thought was a body. It was up to the police to investigate.

"I ain't goin' out there." Jake shook his head. "I ain't goin' nowheres near. The ghost's gonna be walkin' around."

Father John felt a flush of impatience. "A few minutes ago you were about to blow me into kingdom come. Then my ghost would've been walking around here. Did you think about that?"

"You been a burglar, I might've pulled the trigger," Jake said. "I wouldn't've liked it none." Stepping behind the counter, he stooped over and began shuffling through cardboard boxes on the floor. After a minute he hoisted a roll of duct tape onto the counter, then swung a gallon of antifreeze next to the tape. Pulling himself upright, he said, "You can patch that hose good enough to get the pickup over here. I'll fix it tomorrow."

Father John saw the resolve in the Indian's eyes. No appeal to reason or common sense would change his mind. Arapahos believed in signs and wonders, in the mysterious and unseen. How could he argue? He believed in them, too. He picked up the receiver and again dialed 911. "Father O'Malley here," he said. "I'm going to need a ride to Rendezvous Road."

"Hang on." The operator's voice registered no surprise, as if she'd expected the call. No Arapaho wanted to go near an abandoned corpse—a corpse that hadn't been properly blessed, whose ghost hadn't been shown the path to the sky world. Without the traditional blessing, the ghost was left to its own devices, stumbling around the earth, lost and terrified, trying to find the land of the ancestors on its own. The Indians on the Bureau of Indian Affairs police force had to take their chances. That was their job, but it wasn't Jake Littlehorse's job.

The operator said, "Chief Banner's going south on 789. He'll stop for you."

Father John hung up and pushed the phone back. Nodding toward the duct tape and antifreeze, he said, "What do I owe you?"

"Seven-fifty. You can pay me tomorrow after I fix the radiator."

By the time Father John had snapped up his parka and pulled on the rest of his winter gear, yellow head-lights flashed through the plate-glass window. Scooping up the antifreeze and duct tape, he let himself out.

He got into the white patrol car with the gold BIA in-signia emblazoned on the side and settled the duct tape and plastic bottle of antifreeze on the floor next to his boots. Art Banner sat straight-backed in his bulky, dark-blue uniform parka, the beak of his cap tipped over his forehead, gloved hands curled on the rim of the wheel. The rear wheels skidded sideways as the patrol car backed out of the driveway and lurched forward. Snow billowed across the highway ahead.

"Dispatcher says you found a body on Rendezvous Road." The chief's tone was relaxed, as if bodies rou-tinely turned up in ditches on Wind River Reservation.

Father John launched into the story, stressing the fact that the body couldn't have been there long because the snow barely covered the tracks and boot prints.

"Man or woman?"

Father John was quiet, aware of the warm air floating out of the heater, holding the cold at bay. He had assumed it was a man, but it could have been a woman. Women wore heavy hiking boots. He said, "I'm not sure."

"Crummy way to end up. Dumped in a ditch on a

miserable night. Makes you wonder what the hell went wrong."

Father John sensed something else was on the chief's mind. When Father John first came to Wind River Reservation almost seven years ago, Banner was a patrolman along with other Indians—Arapaho, Shoshone, Lakota, Crow, Pawnee—on the BIA police force. A couple of years ago he'd made chief. Father John had never seen him lose his cool, not from the broken bodies he'd pulled out of car wrecks, the drunken brawls he'd waded into, or the battered women and children he'd carried into emergency rooms. There were times in emergency rooms when Father John had had to step into the corridor to get his own anger under control. But not Banner. He was always up to the job.

"You okay?"

"Yeah. Yeah." The chief shrugged. "Tell you what, John, you're lucky you don't have kids."

"You think so?" Father John couldn't imagine what it would be like to have tall sons, beautiful daughters. It wasn't something he thought much about. He'd chosen a different path. But Banner and Helen had four grown children, three daughters and a son.

The chief laughed. "Don't try that old psychology trick on me. I'm wise to the way you guys toss everything back like a baseball. Besides, you aren't even a psychologist. You used to be a history professor, right? Before the Jesuits exiled you here?"

"A high school history teacher," Father John reminded the chief, probably for the twentieth time. Banner persisted in believing he'd once held some exalted university position. Was it so obvious that's what he had wanted? To teach American history at one of the Jesuit universities? He had been on the fast track for such a position, would hold it now if it hadn't been for what he thought of as "the great fall"—the ten-year love affair he'd conducted with alcohol.

The patrol car turned across the snow-drifted highway onto Rendezvous Road. "Kids can worry you into an early grave," Banner said. "And turn your hair gray and keep you awake nights while they do it."

Father John stared at his friend. "What's going on?"

"Patrick." The chief sighed. "The girls, they're doin' okay. Their mother keeps up with them. But Patrick— well, he just got out of the army and needs a job. Problem is, he's a warrior now, and no job's good enough. Nothin' suits his dignity."

"What's he looking at?"

"Lookin'! Even that don't suit his dignity. Only thing he's lookin' at is soap operas." Banner stopped the police car behind an ambulance and another police car lined up at the edge of the road. Lights fastened on the other car's roof whirled like a kaleidoscope against the darkness: red-black, red-black. Two medics stomped up and down beside the ambulance, moving in and out of the light, rubbing their gloves together.

Banner threw open his door, and cold air blasted through the car. Before the chief could swing out, Father John grabbed his arm. "If you think it might help, I'd be glad to talk to him."

The chief nodded slowly. "Yeah. I was gonna ask you. Maybe you can light a fire under that warrior."

Just then a young policeman opened the passenger door and bent down. "You want to show us where you found the body, Father?"

Father John lifted himself out into the blowing snow and walked between the police car and the ambulance to the side of the road, his eyes searching for the boot prints, the smudged area. Banner and the policeman fell in beside him, their boots scuffing the snow. Their breath floated in little clouds. Another BIA policeman came toward them, shining a flashlight along the ditch.

"There," Father John said, spotting the packed, smudged area. "I hope I didn't disturb any evidence."

"Only need evidence for a crime," said the policeman with the flashlight.

"Dumping a body is crime enough." This from the chief.

Father John fixed his eyes on the policeman. "What are you getting at?"

"If there's a body out here, we can't find it." He waved the flashlight across the ditch.

Father John moved close to the edge. The snow in the ditch looked even more trampled, but where the body had been was only a smooth indentation, like a narrow cot.

"This the place?" Banner asked.

"Yes."

"You sure—"

"It was a body, Banner," Father John said, irritated. "Somebody's taken it."

Banner turned toward the other men. "Check the ditch on both sides, in case the body got thrown somewhere else around here."

Father John was lost in his own thoughts. There was one man who might have guessed he'd found a body on Rendezvous Road that wasn't meant to be found. As he and Banner walked back to the police car, Father John said, "You might want to talk to a blond guy, early twenties, new to these parts, driving a gray Chevy pickup."

‹ 3 ›

The body preyed on his mind all night. Father John managed to snatch only a few intervals of sleep before getting up at about five. He alternated saying daily Mass with Father Peter Roach, the seventy-two-year-old Jesuit the Provincial had called from retirement six months ago to help out at St. Francis. This morning was Father John's turn. He showered, dressed, and headed down the dark stairs. He flipped on the little light over the stove, which turned the kitchen into a blur of shadows.

After brewing a pot of strong coffee, he poured some into a mug and sat down at the round wood table, going over last night's events again in his mind. Everything about the body was unknown: the name, the face, the terrible fate that had brought it to the ditch, the disappearance. There were no explanations, only questions.

A couple of times the three-legged golden retriever he'd acquired last fall—or who had acquired him, as Father Peter insisted—struggled off the rug in the corner and shoved a cold nose into his hand, then flopped back down and resumed snoring. Father John had named the dog Walks-on-Three-Legs. Walks-on, for short. He felt a kinship with this animal who had also arrived at St. Francis Mission not quite whole.

At about six-thirty, he let Walks-on go out for a few

minutes while he filled the dog's bowl with canned meat and rock-hard chow. The quiet of the house was broken by the sounds of the dog slurping and chomping his breakfast as Father John shrugged into his parka and pulled on his gloves. Setting his cowboy hat low on his head, he let himself out the front door and plunged into the frigid morning.

The buildings of St. Francis Mission rose out of the snow around Circle Drive like a miniature village under a Christmas tree: the white stucco church, its bell tower floating among the ice-crusted cottonwood branches; the stone administration building where his and Father Peter's offices were; the cement-block Eagle Hall, half gym, half meeting rooms; the one-room guest house; the old school—the mission's first building. He'd once suggested demolishing it, but the elders had raised such an outcry he'd ended up apologizing for the suggestion. St. Francis was like the reservation itself: What was here belonged here. It was a sacred space, enclosed by four sacred spaces: the Wind River, the Little Wind River, the mountains, and the sky.

On the far side of Circle Drive stood the new elementary school with a white stucco entry in the shape of a tipi. Behind the school lay the baseball field where, his first summer here, he had marked off the baseball diamond, carefully measuring ninety feet between the bases, and had started the St. Francis Eagles. The kids needed something to do in the summer, he had told himself, but he knew he needed a baseball team to coach.

The first daylight glowed in the east, spreading fingers of pink and orange and magenta across the silver sky. Last night's snowstorm had passed over, leaving the sky clear and luminescent, a field of blinking stars. In the north was *Nahax,* the morning star, always the last to rise. Father John had the sense that St. Francis was gripped in the same winter stillness that had lain over Arapaho camps on the plains in the Old Time.

The stillness of the plains had been the first thing he had noticed when he came here, after an eight-month stint in Grace House. The silence had seemed loud then; he sometimes thought he could hear it. Yet it was unlike the noise of Boston where he'd grown up. As a kid, making his rounds alone in the early morning, tossing the *Globe* onto the little stoops of the red-brick buildings that lined the streets of his neighborhood, he had been engulfed in noise—dogs barking, engines roaring, tires squealing, a baby crying. Noise had seemed natural then, but it was silence that was natural. It was only in silence, the Arapahos believed, that you could hear the Divine drawing near.

He began the Mass as daylight stole through the side windows of the church and played across the faces of the old people at prayer. The old faithfuls, he called them. The elders and grandmothers who climbed into pickups every day, no matter the temperature, and drove thirty or forty miles across the reservation to Mass. John and Mary Red Deer were here, and old Donald Lightheart in his usual place in the first pew, and Eddie Walsh, rosary beads twisted through gnarled fingers, and five or six others.

This was their church, the Arapahos'. They had built it and painted the walls with sacred symbols: the lines and circles that symbolized the journey of life. Above the front door they had painted the figure of the crucified Christ, the staked warrior, like the warriors in the Old Time who had staked themselves to the ground so that enemies might vent their anger upon them while the people escaped. On the wall next to the altar, they had painted a yellow daffodil, so that a flower might always grace the altar, even in winter. Father John knew the Arapahos considered the Mass only one of the many ways to worship the Great Mystery, the Shining Man Above. There couldn't be too many. He offered Mass for the body in the ditch.

By the time Mass ended, daylight filled the church. Back in the sacristy, Father John removed the green chasuble he'd worn this morning—green symbolized life and hope—while Leonard Bizzel, the caretaker, placed the chalice and prayer books in the cabinet. Leonard hadn't reached fifty yet, but he moved with the deliberation of an old man. Every act received the same minute attention. "Bad things goin' on," he said.

The Arapaho had obviously skipped the preliminaries and gotten to what was bothering him: the dead body. The moccasin telegraph must have set a record for sprinting news across the reservation, Father John thought. Then he remembered Leonard's son was on the BIA police force.

"That ghost don't get a proper burial, it's gonna cause plenty of trouble." Leonard lingered on each word, as if it were an oracular pronouncement. "How come you seen the body?"

"The Toyota broke down on Rendezvous Road. I was walking to the highway to hitch a ride when I spotted it," Father John explained as he hung the vestments in the closet.

"Ghost's causing trouble already."

"A radiator hose popped."

"Ghost did it," Leonard said.

Father John retraced his steps to the priests' residence under a sky the color of blue-tinted glass. The snow sparkled in the early morning sun. He tried to push thoughts of the body to the edge of his mind by mentally ticking off the day's schedule: bills to pay, phone calls to return, meetings to arrange, people to counsel. He should call one of the parish priests to find out about last night's meeting. Scratch that idea, he decided. The bishop's representative would eventually call him with the news plus a reprimand for not attending.

What he did want to do was drive out to Joe Deppert's place to see how the old man was doing after his surgery. And Banner expected him at Fort Washakie to meet with the local FBI agent. Any report of a dead body on the reservation meant the FBI would be involved; major crimes in Indian country fell in FBI jurisdiction. But how the day went depended on when Jake Littlehorse returned the Toyota.

He could smell bacon frying as he came up the stairs to the concrete stoop in front of the priests' residence. He piled his parka and the rest of his winter gear on the bench inside the entry as Walks-on shuffled down the hallway, tail wagging, a red Frisbee in his mouth. "Later," Father John said, patting the dog's head before following the aroma into the kitchen.

Father Peter sat at the table, his head bent into the *Wind River Gazette*. The old man's frizzled white hair wrapped like a muff around a circle of pink scalp. Elena was at the stove scrambling eggs and tending wide slabs of bacon in a pan. Little dots of grease spouted into the air.

Elena had been the housekeeper long before Father John had heard of St. Francis Mission. With her round face and stocky build, the old woman had the look of the Cheyenne, or the *Shyela*, as the Arapahos called the people who had traveled with them across the plains. She had once told him how her grandfather had been a Cheyenne dog soldier. When he saw the beautiful Arapaho girl who came with her family to the Cheyenne village to trade, he had approached her father and asked permission to marry her. Her father had agreed because it was a dog soldier who asked. After they were married, they had lived with her people, and the dog soldier became one of the *Hinono eino*.

"I'll have my eggs fried this morning." Father John bent over the old woman, unable to resist teasing her a little.

She scooped the scrambled eggs onto a plate and laid a couple of pieces of bacon alongside, flashing him the kind of exasperated look his mother had turned on him when he was a kid. "Behave yourself," she said, handing him the plate, "or that ghost'll shoot his ghost arrow at you and give you a big pain."

Another second, and Elena had placed a mug of coffee on the table, scooped up the empty dishes in front of Father Peter, and sauntered over to the sink. Father John set his plate down and took the vacant chair across from the old priest, still engrossed in the *Gazette*. Father Peter was the temporary assistant at St. Francis, but temporary was beginning to look more and more permanent. There weren't a lot of Jesuits clamoring for assignments on an Indian reservation in the middle of Wyoming.

When Father John first came to St. Francis, Father Peter had been the superior. But four years ago, a heart attack had sent the old man into retirement. There he was last fall at Ignatius Center, immersed in his beloved Shakespeare, when the Provincial had called him back.

Now their roles were reversed. Father John was the superior, responsible for operating the mission and looking after his elderly assistant. A couple of mornings when Father Peter hadn't appeared at breakfast, he had pounded on the old man's bedroom door, fearful of what he might find.

Father Peter pushed the newspaper toward him. "You made the front page, my boy."

Father John glanced at the headline: PRIEST REPORTS BODY IN DITCH. Then his eyes ran down the column. It was all there: Father John O'Malley, pastor at St. Francis Mission, claiming to have found a dead body last evening in the ditch on Rendezvous Road. Chief Art Banner explaining how the police were unable to locate any body.

"Now, you wouldn't be having visions, would you?" The old priest's blue eyes twinkled, but Father John knew he was only partly kidding. Probably all the Jesuits expected him to fall off the wagon sooner or later. It had happened before.

He washed down a forkful of eggs with a sip of coffee, giving himself a moment to reply. "People will think so," he said finally, "if the body isn't found." That's what really bothered him. The fact that the body might never be found. An unknown dead person, with no one to grieve for him or remember him. No one to bury him.

"'Alas, poor ghost.'" The old priest sighed again and looked away a moment. Then, his eyes back on Father John's, he began waving a knobby finger. "You could've been dead out in that blizzard yourself."

Father John drained the last of the coffee and smiled at the old man. "Always carry emergency supplies in the winter. I believe that was the first lesson you taught me."

"Well, you might have fixed the pickup."

"But then I wouldn't have found the body."

Father Peter leaned across the table, a mixture of mirth and irritation in his eyes. "Are you saying you don't carry emergency supplies because they might keep you from finding dead bodies?"

"Sounds logical." Father John pushed back his chair

and got to his feet. He liked bantering with the old Irish priest. He reminded him of his father.

"Well, I'll tell you what's logical," Elena said, turning partly from the sink, hands submerged under billows of soapsuds. "That ghost wants to do his mischief. He's not ready to go to the spirit world yet."

‹ 4 ›

It was almost noon before Jake Littlehorse wheeled the Toyota around Circle Drive, and Father John called Banner to say he was on his way to Fort Washakie. He drove Jake the thirty miles back to the garage and, after paying him what came perilously close to the last of the mission's ready cash for January, he followed the highway across the southwestern edge of the reservation. At a junction he turned onto a narrow road that shot straight west. Every few miles, he passed a painted frame house with a propane gas tank propped on spindly metal legs in the snow-covered yard, a couple of trucks scattered about, laundry stiff on lines out back, and a TV antenna perched on the roof.

He turned north on Highway 287, which skirted the foothills of the Wind River Mountains. Stands of cedars and lodgepole pines, their branches heavy with snow, flashed by to the west. In every other direction, the plains, sparkling like a field of diamonds, stretched into the blue sky. Sunlight glinted off the hood, danced over the highway ahead. He squinted against the brightness.

It was on drives like this through the open spaces that he missed the music of his favorite operas filling up the cab. The plaintive notes of "Si, mi chiamano Mimi" and "Vesti la giubba," or the rousing rhythms of "Torreadoer en garde" lifted him out of himself. And "Nessun dorma" he loved. Sung by one of the masters, it encompassed everything beautiful in the world. But the Toyota had never boasted a working radio, let alone a cassette player, and the portable player he used to keep on the seat had been broken. There was no telling when he could afford to buy another. He tried to content himself with humming the arias, sometimes launching into a chorus and surprising himself that he knew the words.

He had driven about forty miles when he slowed down along the main street of Fort Washakie, the little community that meandered into the foothills. He set the Toyota into a vacant space in the parking lot next to the Wind River Law Enforcement Center, a one-story building with red-brick walls and a sloping red metal roof edged with snow.

Inside, several Indians lined up in front of a glass-enclosed cubicle, while other Indians, mostly young, waited in the green plastic chairs along the walls. Father John greeted a couple of people he recognized as occasional members of his congregation. The young woman behind the glass looked up and motioned him to a side door. After disappearing a moment, she opened the door, glancing about as if to make sure no one else tried to enter.

"Chief Banner's waitin' for you, Father," she said scoldingly.

Father John pulled off his gloves and unsnapped his parka as he walked down the corridor. The string of overhead fluorescent lights cast a white glare over the glass-paned doors and the beige walls. Little clouds of cigarette smoke hung in the air. Somewhere a phone was ringing, and the sound mingled with the clack of his boots on the tile. A voice with the unmistakable timbre of the chief's drifted through an open door. He rapped one knuckle against the jamb before stepping inside.

"Here you are," Banner said, swiveling around in the chair behind a desk. It reminded Father John of his own desk, piled with papers and folders awaiting his attention.

"Meet Mike Osgood, new FBI agent in these parts." The chief flung an arm toward the man in one of the wood chairs on the other side of the desk.

Osgood sprang to his feet and extended his hand. His grip was firm, despite his slight build. He looked to be about forty, with a light complexion, hair almost as black as Banner's, and eyes almost as dark. The navy blue suit with the white shirt and yellow tie knotted at the collar gave him a serious look, but he seemed relaxed and confident. "I understand we have a dead body floating around the reservation," he said.

Banner pressed a button and barked into the phone. "Sergeant Deerkill, on the double." Then to Father John, "We're gonna need a statement."

Father John hung his parka over the back of the vacant chair and stuffed his gloves into the crown of his cowboy hat. Then he sat down, balancing the hat on one knee. Just then a young policeman in the same kind of BIA uniform—light-blue shirt and navy trousers—that Banner wore entered the office. A tape recorder was in his hand. "This here's Sergeant Deerkill," the chief said.

The young man had the high forehead, the sunken cheeks, and deep-set black eyes of the Lakota. "Amos Deerkill," he said, setting the recorder on the desk and perching on the corner. He leaned forward to shake Father John's hand, then the agent's.

"We want you to tell us everything you saw last night," the chief said. "How you found the body, what it looked like, anything you can remember. Never know what might help."

Father John leaned back against the chair and began explaining how he'd been driving down Rendezvous Road when his pickup popped a radiator hose and stalled.

"Ghost made it break down," Banner interrupted. Rocking back in his chair, he peered across the desk, as if daring anyone to question it.

"Ghost?" This from the agent.

"Yeah," said the chief. "You got a body, you got a ghost. The ghost is causin' trouble already. That's why we gotta find the body and get it buried before that ghost causes any more trouble."

The agent turned toward Father John. The message in his eyes was so obvious Father John knew neither Banner nor the young sergeant would miss it: *We white men must strive to be rational.*

Father John said, "Every soul deserves the blessings of a proper burial."

The agent threw out both hands. "Okay, okay. Can we just continue?"

Again Father John started explaining, trying to recall all the details. The more he talked, the more the story began to sound preposterous. No wonder Father Peter thought he might be having visions. The FBI agent probably thought the same.

"You get the license on the Chevy that picked you up?" This time the agent interrupted.

Father John admitted he'd been so glad to get a ride, he hadn't noticed the license. He described the driver: male, early twenties, light complexion, blond stubble on his chin. Not a local.

"What makes you think so?" the chief asked.

"He drove past me. He didn't intend to stop, but something changed his mind."

Banner and the young sergeant both nodded, as if that was all the proof necessary to determine the driver came from elsewhere.

"We'll get this typed up for you to sign," the chief said as the young policeman picked up the recorder and disappeared into the corridor.

"Lab boys got two casts of boot prints out at the site. And they found something else." Banner opened a brown envelope, extracted a plastic ziplock bag, and tossed it across the desk.

The agent looked at it first, then handed it to Father John. He turned the bag slowly in his hands. Inside was a necklace strung with red, white, and black beads and yellow porcupine quills. The colors symbolized the four sacred movements at the center of life: the four winds, the four directions, the four seasons, the four periods of the day, the four quarters of the world. It might be worn by either a man or a woman. Returning the bag to the chief, he said, "Arapaho."

"Yeah. Just like the star quilt. Looks like we got ourselves a dead Arapaho. Only nobody's been reported missing on the rez lately." Banner turned toward the agent. "People usually go missin' in the summers. Mostly hikers, hunters, or fishermen who get lost in the back country and fall off a cliff somewheres."

"Dead bodies don't just appear," Osgood said. "They're always related to some event."

The chief sighed. "Weekend was pretty quiet. Two other calls last night. Truck went off Seventeen-Mile Road. Driver's at Riverton Memorial. Domestic disturbance out north. Man's in jail; woman went to her mother's. That's it. Friday night, Lander police got one call involving Arapahos. Loud party at the Grand Apartments. Citation issued to one Annie Chambeau. Saturday night, another call, same apartment. Claimed she'd had an intruder, but no sign of him."

The agent slipped a small notebook and pen from the inside pocket of his jacket. "Annie Chambeau," he said. The pen scratched the paper. "I'll talk to her. Maybe something happened at the party that led to somebody getting killed. I'll see you get a report." He glanced up at the chief.

Father John had been here long enough to understand that various law enforcement agencies navigated a maze. The BIA's territory was the reservation, but serious crimes, such as murder, brought in the feds. Something like this—a party in Lander, a possible murder, a corpse that may or may not still be on the reservation— jurisdictional lines began to blur. Something like this demanded a lot of cooperation.

"I've got other sources I intend to interview," the agent said. Getting to his feet, he strolled over to the coatrack next to the doorway and pulled on a gray overcoat. "Nobody can keep a body hidden forever. Sooner or later it's bound to turn up." He touched two fingers to his forehead in a little salute before turning into the corridor.

Banner levered himself out of his chair and swept one hand over the multicolored map of Wind River Reservation tacked to the wall behind his desk. "Truth is, that body could be anywhere in thirty-five hundred square miles. Could be up here." The chief pointed to the northwest where the Shoshones lived. "Or here." His hand ran along the southern half: Arapaho land. "Chances of finding that body, if somebody doesn't want it found, are about a zillion to one."

"What about the Chevy pickup?"

The chief shrugged. "Some white guy lost on the reservation in a blizzard." He traced one finger along the map. "He picked you up a little ways past Rendezvous Road and drove two miles down Highway 789 to Jake's garage. Most likely, he kept goin'. Could be in Colorado by now."

Father John stared at the map. He couldn't shake off the uneasy feeling about the young man who had given him a ride. The cold determination, the ruthlessness. And he had lied about being from around here.

"Suppose he'd been on his way to Rendezvous Road to retrieve the body," Father John began, sorting his thoughts out loud, searching for some logical path. "Suppose he saw me on the highway and decided not to chance turning onto Rendezvous Road. He stayed on the highway and deliberately passed me. Then he decided to pick me up in order to find out if I'd been on Rendezvous Road and had seen the body." He didn't say what was becoming obvious: Had he told the man about finding the body, his own life might have been in danger.

The chief flopped back into his chair. "The guy that dropped that body got the hell outta there. Why would he take a chance on goin' back?"

"Maybe he started to worry it wasn't hidden well enough."

Banner slowly shook his head. "The fed's off to talk to an Indian girl and other sources he says he has, as if Indians are gonna tell a white FBI agent something important. We've got a gray Chevy pickup and a driver who maybe knows about the body, but most likely never heard of it. And we got a missing body. Ghosts, John. We're chasin' ghosts."

‹ 5 ›

The Toyota rolled down Old Wind River Highway on automatic pilot. Father John rested one gloved finger on the steering wheel's rim. His thoughts were on the body, which had probably been dead close to twenty-four hours now, but no one had missed him, no one had called the police and said, "He hasn't come home. I'm worried." Nothing. What kind of life had he led to end up so alone?

The road veered sharply to the right, and Father John jammed on the brake pedal, fishtailing around the curve. The wind sent a cloud of snow across the road ahead. He gripped the wheel with both hands, holding it steady through the whiteness and out the far side into the daylight. Another half mile, and he turned into the driveway at Joe Deppert's place.

An uneasy feeling came over him as he slid out of the cab. Mounds of untrampled snow lay over the driveway and banked against the logs piled beside the wood fence. The open door of a tin shed creaked in the wind. The gray frame house looked empty, with the indoor shades pulled halfway down the front windows.

The door swung open just as he was about to knock. In the shadows stood Deborah Deppert, somewhere in her eighties, with hooded black eyes and gray hair curled around her head like a helmet. He might have knocked at any house on the reservation and found an elderly women like her, in a printed housedress with an apron cinching her waist, socks rolled at her ankles, and swollen arthritic feet in pink bedroom slippers.

"Hello, Grandmother." He used the Arapaho term of respect and remained in place outside. It was not polite to appear as if he even wished to enter the home until he had been invited to do so.

"Well, Father John." There was a note of surprise in the old woman's voice. "What you doin' out in the cold? Come on in."

He stepped into a small room with gray daylight filtering below the window shades. He waited as Deborah set the door closed behind him. The air smelled of wood smoke and some pungent medicinal odor, like camphor or analgesic. To the right was a double bed with a star quilt spread over the top. In the center of the room stood a round oak table and a couple of wood chairs, and beyond, an arched doorway that led to the kitchen.

To the left, Joe Deppert, swaddled in blankets, lay in one of two recliners that faced a black stove. Next to it sat a cardboard box with some kindling wood poking out of the top.

"How is Grandfather?" Father John whispered.

"Oh, he's not asleep." The old woman stepped over to the recliner and lightly thumped the pile of blankets. "We got company," she said.

Joe opened his eyes. "Marcus?" His voice sounded soft and spongy.

"Father John, Grandfather. I stopped by to see how you're doing."

A bony hand came out from under the blankets, and

Father John reached over and clasped it. It felt like a brittle bundle of twigs.

"We thought you was Marcus when we heard the truck drive up." There was a mixture of disappointment and fear in his eyes.

Deborah patted the top of the other recliner. "Sit here, Father. You want some coffee, don't you?"

The old woman sidled through the archway as Father John draped his parka over the back of one of the wood chairs and laid his gloves and cowboy hat on the table. Then he sat on the edge of the vacant recliner. The fire cast an uneven heat; the room was drafty and cold by the door, stifling as a sauna by the stove.

"How're you feeling?" Father John asked the old man. Two weeks ago, the doctors had removed both of Joe's big toes. Diabetes.

"Soon's I get these clunkers off, I'll be good as new." Joe yanked at the blankets to display the plaster casts. "I gotta learn to walk with no toes. Easier'n walkin' with no feet."

Father John smiled at the old man's courage. Joe knew that's what they would amputate next. "Has Marcus been coming by to help you out?" The young Arapaho was Joe's grand-nephew, the grandson of Joe's brother. Arapaho families were too close for words like nephew and uncle. Besides, Joe and Deborah had raised Marcus from about age twelve, after his parents had died.

Glancing toward the kitchen, the Indian lowered his voice. "Marcus is real good to us. Chops the wood and hauls in the logs. Does the shoppin'. Only he ain't come around all last week. I don't know what become of him."

"I can get in some logs," Father John said, nodding toward the cardboard box. Another cold snap like last night, and Joe and Deborah could freeze to death in this flimsy house.

"No need to bother yourself." Deborah padded slowly back into the room, balancing three coffee mugs on a plate. She handed one mug to Father John, another to her husband. Then she plopped down on the same wooden chair Father John had hung his parka on and took a sip from her mug. After a minute, she said, "Marcus'll be by today for sure. He don't forget us. You hear that, old man?" She scooted forward, staring at the back of Joe's recliner. "Marcus ain't the kind of boy that don't respect his elders."

Squaring herself against the chair again, as if the matter were settled, Deborah turned her eyes to Father John. "His new job he's got drivin' Jeeps to Denver takes a lot of time."

Father John took a long pull of the lukewarm liquid. It had the taste of coffee brewed hours ago and warmed over several times. It worried him: two helpless old people, isolated in a drafty house two or three miles from the nearest neighbor. And where was Marcus? In a ditch somewhere? He shivered involuntarily. Is this what it was going to be like? Every time he heard of somebody missing an appointment, not coming around, was he going to jump to the conclusion that *that* was the body in the ditch?

He forced his thoughts back to what Deborah had said. Marcus had a job. Good news. Marcus Deppert was one of the kids he'd worried about, ever since the summer, a few years back, that Marcus had played left field for the Eagles—when he'd felt like showing up. Breezy and self-confident, that was Marcus. A little too smart in the wrong things. Since then, he'd spent three years in Leavenworth for dealing drugs. He was still on probation. Father John sat back in the recliner. "Who's Marcus working for?"

"He ain't said exactly." Joe shifted a little in the recliner.

"Well, it's a good job." Deborah hoisted herself to her feet and collected the empty mugs before shuffling back into the kitchen.

The old man motioned Father John to come closer. "I'm real worried about the boy. So's his grandmother, only she don't wanna say so. I told her we should get the police, but she says no, 'cause of him bein' on probation. Could you check on him? Make sure he ain't in no trouble, *Teenenoo Hiinooni'it*?" He used the name one of the four holy old men had given Father John a few years before. It meant "Touch-the-Clouds" and symbolized the heart of his life, what he tried to do as a priest—reach toward the Great Mystery Above. The name was meant to remind him of his duty and to give him the strength to do his best.

"Yes, of course, Grandfather," Father John said. No missing persons on the reservation lately, Banner had said, but who would report Marcus missing? Only these two old people, scared of the police looking into what he might be up to.

"Where is he living now?"

"Got himself a place over in Easter Egg Village. First yellow house on Buffalo Road." The old man drew in a long breath and let it out slowly as if he were releasing a sharp pain.

"What else can I do, Grandfather?" Father John asked.

Joe reached out and grasped his hand lightly. "Don't listen to what that old woman says. We need some more logs in here."

Father John had on his parka, gloves, and cowboy hat and was out the door before Deborah had reappeared in the living room. By the time he'd knocked the snow off the logs and loaded up an armful, the old woman stood against the door, holding it open, eyes watchful and resigned. He brought in a couple more loads, filling the cardboard box, then stacking logs next to it. He offered to get them some groceries, but they both assured him they had plenty of food, and he promised to stop by again in the next day or two.

As Father John let himself out the front door, he saw Deborah had moved close to her husband's recliner, and the old man was patting her hand as if to reassure her everything would be all right.

Father John parked in front of the yellow house on Buffalo Road. The houses in Easter Egg Village clustered on top of a bluff, each small bungalow splashed in a different pastel color—pink, green, blue, yellow, violet. Some Washington bureaucrat's notion of what subsidized houses on an Indian reservation ought to look like. The sun had begun its descent behind the mountains, shooting red and pink flames across the sky. A pinkish glaze fell over the houses and the snow-covered ground.

Father John got out of the Toyota and started toward the house. The temperature was spiraling downward. It felt twenty degrees colder than when he'd left the old people forty minutes ago. The snow in front had been stomped down, pushed into little piles. Somebody had been here recently. He knocked on the door. No answer. Then he stepped sideways and peered through the window. The living room had the stillness of space bereft of human energy. A yellow-and-brown-striped sofa and a small dark chair stood against one wall. On the opposite wall was a TV on a cart, and next to it an opened suitcase, half full. Marcus was either about to take a trip or he had just returned.

Father John headed back to the Toyota and drove two blocks to the pastel green house of Ike and Mary Yellow Calf. Ike was chopping wood out front, and as soon as Father John pulled up, the Indian set the ax against a pile of logs and came toward the pickup. Father John climbed out, and the Indian grabbed his hand, pumping it up and down with the same energy he'd probably put into chopping wood. He had on the kind of faded jeans, long-sleeved plaid shirt, and down vest most of the men on the reservation wore. His black Stetson sat back, revealing a line of even blacker hair. Little beads of sweat stood out on his forehead.

"I just stopped in to see Joe Deppert," Father John said.

"Ah." Ike dipped his forehead into one sleeve, brushing away the moisture. "Been meanin' to get over there. How's Grandfather doin'?"

"He and Deborah could use some help. They're getting low on wood. Probably low on groceries, too, although they're too proud to admit it. Marcus hasn't been around lately."

Ike cleared his throat, turned sideways, and spit onto the snow. "Don't surprise me none. No damn good, that kid."

Father John was surprised at the vehemence. "What do you mean?"

"Ever since he moved into the village, people been comin' and goin' all hours at his house. Parties all the time."

"Deborah thinks Marcus found a job."

Ike shook his head. "You know how it is with the grandmothers. They love the kids no matter what. They believe whatever the kids tell 'em."

"Have you seen Marcus lately?"

The Indian's forehead wrinkled into deep lines. "Matter of fact, it's been quiet all week. Maybe him and that Rich Dolby he hangs with took their parties elsewhere."

Father John jammed his hands into the pockets of his parka. He was thinking about what Banner had said: The Lander police broke up a party of Arapahos Friday night. Maybe Marcus was there, but it was a stretch. How many parties were there on any given night? Marcus Deppert couldn't attend them all. Father John decided to talk to Rich Dolby's mother, Loretta, who worked in the cafeteria at St. Francis Elementary School. Chances were she'd know the whereabouts of her son, and he might know the whereabouts of Marcus.

"Let me know if Marcus shows up," he said, getting back into the Toyota.

Ike took the door and started to walk it closed, then paused. "Don't worry about the old people. I'll put the word out on the moccasin telegraph so folks'll know to look in on 'em. Me and the wife gotta go into Fort Washakie tomorrow for groceries. We'll get 'em a load of supplies."

"You're a good man, Ike," Father John said. "Marcus'll probably be along in a few days."

"Wouldn't count on nothin' with that kid," the Indian said, closing the door.

Father John swung the Toyota out of Easter Egg Village onto Seventeen-Mile Road and drove into the dusk. He wasn't sure when the green truck behind him first came into his rearview mirror, but now he could see it coming up fast. He kept his own pace steady, giving the truck time to pass, if that's what its driver wanted. There was no oncoming traffic, but the road was slick with snow and ice. The truck was close enough now so he could almost make out the driver. He—or she—wore aviator sunglasses, even though it was starting to get dark, and a knit hat pulled low over the forehead. Suddenly the truck was right behind him, looming in the rearview mirror, as if the driver intended to run him off the road.

‹ 6 ›

Father John stomped on the accelerator, and the Toyota shot ahead, tires yawing in the snow. He gripped the wheel and hoped the pickup wouldn't slide into the ditch on its own. The truck started gaining; he could see it was a Dodge. As he banked around a curve, an oncoming vehicle flashed into view and, as if in response, the truck dropped back. By the time a dark sedan lumbered by, the truck was a distant shadow.

Father John kept his speed steady, one eye on the rearview mirror. A drunk, he thought, getting his kicks from trying to run an old pickup off the road. He'd had a lot of experience with drunks. There were two types: quiet and rowdy. He'd been the quiet type, drinking himself into a stupor every night while grading papers on the Missouri Compromise, the Western expansion, the defining battles of the Civil War. Aviator glasses—that was the rowdy type.

Father John passed the sign for St. Francis Mission and slowed for the turn onto Circle Drive, one eye still on the rearview mirror. The road behind was dark. The truck must have turned off at Miller or Bejan Lane.

He stopped behind the white Cadillac in front of the administration building and stepped out into the hardening cold. A deep purple stain spread across the late afternoon sky, washing the snowy grounds in pale blue. He mounted the stairs and stamped his boots. The moment he stepped inside, the familiar, musty smell of the old building swept over him. Through the open door to his office partway down the hall came the low murmur of voices.

He stepped through the doorway. "Ah, the pastor himself in our midst," said Father Peter, who occupied the metal folding chair reserved for the occasional overflow of visitors. His arms were folded across his flannel shirt; his head, with its ruff of white hair, rested squarely on his shoulders. The overhead light glinted in his blue eyes.

A couple of men Father John had never seen before rose from the Naugahyde side chairs across the office. One was Father John's height, close to six feet four inches, with thick, neatly trimmed gray hair. Little blue lines crisscrossed his nose and cheeks, which had the telltale flush of too much alcohol in his past. Father John recognized the signs. The man's eyes narrowed, as if he had only a nanosecond to size up the pastor of St. Francis Mission, and he meant to get an accurate measurement.

The other visitor stood almost a head shorter, with a narrow face and gray hair that receded from his forehead. Both men wore the same uniform—dark tailored suits, shiny white shirts, dark ties embellished with miniature figures. The short man came forward, extending a thin, sculptured hand. "Clifford Keating. With the bishop's office in Cheyenne."

Father John had expected a phone call, but here was the bishop's representative in person to deliver whatever message he had delivered at last night's meeting.

"Nick Sheldon," the taller man said, extending his hand. "Sheldon, Jones and Johnson. Attorneys-at-law. We've been waiting over an hour."

Father John was taken aback. "Did we have an appointment?"

"Yes. Last evening in Lander."

"So we did." He motioned the men to resume their seats. He took his time depositing his parka and hat on the rack behind the open door, where two dark topcoats already hung. As he took his own chair behind the desk, Father Peter shot him a look that said, "Beware of vultures."

"Since you missed the meeting . . ." Clifford Keating began in a conciliatory tone.

"My pickup broke down," Father John said. Last night's meeting had slipped into the background, eclipsed by a missing corpse and by his worry over a young Arapaho who also seemed to be missing.

"Father Peter has explained," said the bishop's representative, shooting his suit sleeves over white cuffs. "We want to bring you up to date. The bishop called the meeting of pastors in Riverton and Lander. Naturally he wishes to satisfy himself that the spiritual needs of Catholics in the area will continue to be cared for. I'm happy to say we have that assurance."

"Continue?" Father John picked up a pencil and began tapping a pile of paper on his desk. He'd missed something here.

"Of course. With one less parish, it is a concern."

The picture began to take shape. The bishop intended to close one of the local parishes, probably for financial reasons, and Clifford Keating had been dispatched to make certain the other parishes could handle the overflow. The only thing still unclear was the role Nick Sheldon played.

"We'll welcome anyone who wants to come to St. Francis," Father John said. There would be few whites who would come. St. Francis was the Arapaho church.

A thick silence settled over the office, and Father John realized he hadn't gotten the entire picture. Nick Sheldon crossed one leg over the other. "It seems you haven't been informed, Father O'Malley. It's St. Francis Mission that will be closed."

Father John dropped the pencil. He remained absolutely still, aware of the sound of his own breathing. St. Francis closed? How could that be? Shock began to give way to anger, which welled inside him the way water pools in the middle of a river.

"You must be misinformed," Father Peter blurted out. "St. Francis Mission has served the Arapaho people for more than a hundred years. It will continue to do so."

"I'm afraid not, Father," Keating replied. "Mission work has changed, outlived its purpose. When you Jebbies first came here, there were pagan Indians to convert and educate. Well,"—he threw out both hands—"mission accomplished."

Sheldon added, "The Arapahos are already Catholic. Your high school closed ten years ago for lack of money. The BIA runs the mission's elementary school. And— am I not correct—your financial situation is in desperate straits. There is no justifiable reason to continue this mission."

It was all Father John could do to keep from jumping up and ordering both men out. Obviously the Jesuit Provincial, from his office in St. Louis, had decided to close St. Francis. He had informed the bishop who had sent these two saps to smooth over the details. No one had informed him. All of this going on. . . . He was so far out of the loop, he hadn't even known there was a loop.

Sheldon continued, "This decision is in the best interests of the Arapahos. My client plans to build a multi-million-dollar family recreation center on the mission site. Movie theaters, bowling alley, gymnasium, restaurants, the works. Small towns can't support such centers, which is why we prefer to build in the vicinity of several towns. That way, all the towns benefit."

"How, exactly, will the Arapahos benefit?" Father John managed, struggling to keep his anger under control. He could feel the heat in his face.

"Jobs. The center will employ Indians."

"St. Francis employs people from the reservation."

The lawyer smiled. "A caretaker, two part-time secretaries, a housekeeper, religious education teachers. A total of ten. Sometimes twelve, when you can afford it. My client will employ at least a hundred."

"Who is your client, Mr. Sheldon?" Father John was stalling now, trying to get his mind around the news. St. Francis Mission closed? Even in the worst-case scenarios, when he'd lain awake nights worrying about cutting back on staff or not making the payroll, it had never occurred to him the Society of Jesus might sell the mission.

"The Z Group. A private partnership based in California," the lawyer said.

Father John got to his feet and leaned across the desk, his hands gripping the hard wood edge. "The Arapahos will never agree to this. St. Francis belongs to them. This is where the drums beat at Sunday Mass. Where they can sign the Our Father in the Indian sign language. Where the Christian message can take root in their own culture."

The two ambassadors appeared to ignore him as they stood up and began fumbling with their topcoats. Then the lawyer met Father John's eyes. "I'm afraid you've missed the point," he said. "The Arapahos themselves have requested that we build the center on the site of St. Francis Mission. The business council will approve the plans at next week's meeting."

After they left, Father John stood at the window and watched the cherry-red taillights flickering in the darkness, aware of the sound of the old priest's breathing next to him. Softly Father Peter said, "'My mind is troubled, like a fountain stirr'd; And I myself see not the bottom of it.'"

This was not a quote Father John recognized, but he didn't want a lecture on Shakespeare right now. He walked back to his desk and sank into the chair, trying to make some sense of this. "I suppose, sooner or later, the Provincial would have informed us," he said. "In the meantime, the bishop decided to inform the other pastors, which forced Keating and Sheldon to tell us. Otherwise, we might not have heard until next week, after the business council had approved the deal."

Father Peter shuffled across the office, folded up the metal chair, and stashed it behind the door. "Not a peep on the moccasin telegraph," he said, shaking his head. "'Twas strange, 'twas passing strange.'"

"Not if somebody wanted the mission sold before the people found out about it," Father John said.

"The question then appears to be what do you intend to do about it, my boy?" The old man eyed him from the center of the office, a teacher expecting the right answer.

Father John was turning over the options in his mind. After a moment he said, "I intend to make the acquaintance of Eden Lightfoot, the new economic development officer on the reservation. Obviously he supports this, or the Arapaho business council wouldn't consider it. I'll have to try to change his mind."

But first he intended to talk to Vicky Holden. If anyone had heard about St. Francis Mission being sold, it would be the Arapaho attorney. She had the pulse of the reservation. He pulled the phone toward him and punched in her number. He knew it by heart.

◀ 7 ▶

Vicky Holden aimed the Bronco through the silent streets of the Lander neighborhood she had called home the past three years. The headlights picked out the cars and pickups parked at the curbs and turned the snow-packed streets the pale yellow color of butter.

She turned into the driveway of the brick bungalow she rented, her mind on the divorce agreement she'd hammered out this afternoon with the attorney representing her client's husband. She hadn't gotten everything Mary Featherly wanted or deserved, but sometimes the best possible agreement had to be good enough. She intended to look it over again tonight. And there were three or four phone calls she still had to return.

One from John O'Malley. Probably about this morning's article in the *Gazette*. She exhaled slowly into the quiet. The only time the pastor at St. Francis Mission called was when there was some kind of trouble. She would call him first, she decided, then scramble some eggs for dinner before getting to the rest of the work in her briefcase.

Darkness settled over the Bronco the instant she flipped off the headlights. She grabbed the briefcase and floppy black leather bag off the seat and stepped outside. Rather than walking up the sidewalk, which she had shoveled early this morning, she crossed the yard, watching the clouds of snow rise and scatter in her footsteps. Walking through snow always took her back to the times she and her brothers and sisters—cousins in the white world—had romped in the snow until they turned numb with cold and then had jostled one another around the stove in Grandmother's kitchen, giggling and laughing themselves warm. Snow made the earth fresh and new.

Just as she stepped onto the wooden porch, she heard the footsteps. She whirled about. A large shadowy figure came up the sidewalk. She was fully aware of her surroundings as if everything had been caught in a freeze frame: light filtering through the darkness from the houses across the street; shadows of cars and trucks at the curb; the porch light on next door; the muffled sounds of a TV. Would the neighbors hear if she screamed?

"Who are you?"

The man in a cowboy hat and sheepskin coat stopped at the edge of the porch. "Ben."

She leaned back, aware of the doorjamb against her spine, her heart catapulting in her chest. Her ex-husband, dropped from the sky, out of nowhere, out of the past. "You scared me," she said.

"I'm sorry." Ben placed one boot on the porch, but made no move to come up.

"Why are you here?"

"We've got to talk." He still didn't move. "I could use a cup of coffee. I've been waiting in the truck two hours." He nodded toward the street, and she felt a wave of anger at herself as her eyes followed. She had driven by the truck, but she'd been so preoccupied with her own thoughts she hadn't noticed anyone in it. She'd lived in the white world for almost eleven years, yet she still didn't have the hang of it—watch your back, stay alert.

"Just say what you have to say." Vicky felt the old wariness gathering inside her. She didn't want to be alone with him.

"It's about Susan."

She stared at her former husband. He always knew how to get what he wanted. He only had to mention one of their children, Susan or Lucas. She turned around and, after fumbling to insert the key in the keyhole, pushed the door open. She flipped the wall switch inside, and the lamp on the table sprang into life, illuminating the gray carpet, the blue-flowered sofa, the coffee table with its neat stack of magazines and her favorite pottery bowl, the dining table and chairs in the alcove beyond the living room.

"Nice place," Ben said, closing the door behind them.

Vicky dropped her bag and briefcase on the sofa, then slipped off her coat and hung it inside the small closet next to the door before facing him. He had already tossed his hat and gloves next to her things, and was pulling himself free from the sheepskin coat. She felt a kind of shock at how much he was like that sense of him she carried inside her. Just over six feet, straight as a lodgepole pine, with powerful shoulders and chest and long, slender fingers. His hair was still black, but flecked with gray now, and combed straight back until it ran along the collar of his tan chamois shirt.

Laying the sheepskin over the sofa, he smiled at her. Years in the outdoors had imprinted squint lines at the corners of his eyes, which glistened like black pebbles in a mountain stream. She knew the contours of his face better than her own—the strong jaw and high cheekbones, the noble nose of her people, the confident mouth. She had fallen in love with him the summer she'd graduated from St. Francis High School. He'd been out of high school for four years, and had been in the army and gone to Germany. He talked for hours about the outside world, a world she knew nothing about. He spun a fantastic web of words, and she got caught in the web. He was everything she wanted. She was seventeen.

She forced her thoughts to the present, the Time Being. "What about Susan?"

"What about the coffee?"

Her eyes locked with his a moment. He had driven sixty miles on snow-crested roads, in plummeting temperatures, across the reservation from the Arapaho ranch up north where he was the foreman, and had waited in the truck two hours. She could throw herself upon him and beat against his chest, but he wouldn't tell her why he was here until the time was ready.

She walked past him into the shadowy alcove. Moonlight filtered through the sliding glass doors that led to the patio, which was mounded in snow. She turned into the small kitchen and flipped on the overhead fluorescent light. A white glow suffused the wood cabinets and cream-colored countertops.

Ben leaned against the edge of the counter as she measured out the coffee grounds and poured water into the Mr. Coffee. "I was going to scramble some eggs," she said.

"Sounds good."

She felt his eyes on her as she broke the eggs into a bowl and whipped them with a fork. After pouring the thick yellow liquid into a frying pan, she dropped a couple of slices of bread into the toaster.

"Just like the old days," Ben blurted, as if his thoughts would no longer be contained.

"Don't, Ben," Vicky said, pushing the lumpy eggs across the pan.

"Sometimes at night, I lie awake in my bunk and watch the pictures in my head. You and me and the kids back on Lean Bear's ranch. They're good pictures, the way it used to be."

"You used to hit me, Ben."

Out of the corner of her eye, she saw him shift against the counter. "I try to see that, too, Vicky, but the picture's blurry. The drinking times are big black holes." He was quiet a moment, then said, "I haven't had a drink going on six years now."

"It's no longer my business," Vicky said, dishing the eggs onto two plates. She laid a slice of toast beside the eggs and, skirting around him, avoiding his eyes, carried the plates to the table. A gauzy light floated across the alcove from the kitchen and living room. Ben planted himself at the end of the table, a puzzled expression on his face as if he weren't certain which of the turns in the past had been the wrong one.

Opening the top drawer in the buffet that stood against one wall, Vicky removed two place mats, two napkins, and a handful of knives and forks, which she arranged on the table. Then she returned to the kitchen and poured two mugs of coffee.

"I just wanted you to know about the drinking," Ben said as she delivered the coffee mugs and settled into the chair across from him. The drinking. The words reverberated inside her as if he had shouted them in a mountain canyon. It was true, he had only hit her when he was drinking. If there was anything she was grateful for, it was that he had never hit the children. He had truly loved the children. Yet, that had been the hardest to accept—the fact that he had been able to control his rage around the kids, which meant his treatment of her had been deliberate. That was the Ben she must remember. Not the handsome and confident man across from her.

"Please, Ben," she said, scooting her fork under a clump of eggs. "What about Susan?"

The Arapaho took a long draw from his mug before saying, "You know she's back?" His black eyebrows rose upward, as if he suspected she did not know. "Susan came to see me last week. Drove all over the ranch lookin' for me. I was out pitching hay for the cattle."

Vicky swallowed the eggs slowly, trying not to betray the emotions boiling within her. Her daughter—their daughter—had returned to Wind River Reservation and had not called her, had not come to her, but had gone to Ben. In Susan's and Lucas's eyes, she was the one who had broken up their home, had given them to her own parents to raise, had gone away to Denver to college and law school, had gotten the court order that kept their father away.

"I guess she's not mad at me," Ben said, not in a hurtful way, but as if he'd read her mind.

"When did Susan leave Los Angeles?" Vicky heard her own voice, disembodied, calm. She could feel her heart thumping.

"Didn't say. She's here with some white man and a couple of his buddies. She wanted to know if they could rent our old place." Finishing the last of the scrambled eggs, Ben rested his forearms on either side of the plate. "Nobody's lived at Lean Bear's ranch since you took the kids and left. I only stayed long enough to close up the place. But I keep an eye on it. It's still in good shape. So

I told her, sure, but she didn't have to pay me rent. She said her friends wanted to keep everything legal. So I said, okay, and the next day she came back with a certified check for six months' rent."

As he talked on about how glad he was Susan had come back, how he'd never liked the kids living in L.A., how he believed families belonged together, the image of Lean Bear's ranch flashed through Vicky's mind. Ten miles up Sage Canyon in the foothills of the Wind River Mountains, it was the place Lean Bear had chosen for his family when the Arapahos came to the reservation a hundred years ago. Lean Bear was Ben's great-grandfather, one of the leading men of the tribe. He had ridden with her great-grandfather, Chief Black Night. It had always seemed as if invisible threads, stretching into the Old Time, had woven her life to Ben's long before either of them was born. It was to Lean Bear's ranch he had brought her after they were married.

"What are Susan's plans?" Vicky took a sip of coffee, conscious that it had turned lukewarm.

"She said they plan to start a business buying and selling Indian arts and crafts."

"In Sage Canyon? It's so far away, so isolated," Vicky stammered. Something about this didn't make sense. She saw in Ben's eyes that he had reached the same conclusion.

"I've been askin' myself why any white man wants to live like a hermit with an Indian girl," he said. "And how come his friends are hanging around?" Ben was quiet. After a few seconds he went on. "I've been worried about her, so I drove up to Lean Bear's place this afternoon, first chance I got. Nobody around. The house was locked up, and they'd changed the lock. I looked in the windows. Stuff everywhere. A real mess, not like you used to keep the place, Vicky. I'd like to go back tomorrow, but we've got to get the hay bales to the upper ranges, or the cattle are gonna be real hungry."

"I'll go there first thing tomorrow," Vicky said.

Her ex-husband looked at her a long moment, a blend of approval and gratitude in his eyes; then he pushed back from the table and got to his feet. She watched him slip on the sheepskin coat, sensing its heaviness as if it had fallen over her own shoulders, and methodically set the cowboy hat on his head, an act he performed every day. She fought against acknowledging the empty space he had left in her life.

"Let me know what you find out," he said. "You can leave a message at the ranch office."

Vicky stood up and followed him across the living room to the front door. He had more than an hour's drive ahead, in temperatures no creature should be out in. "You can stay here tonight," she said. "On the sofa," she added hurriedly.

Ben turned toward her and smiled. "Not this time."

‹ 8 ›

Vicky managed to open the door to her office while juggling her briefcase, a stack of folders, and the black leather bag, the strap of which had slipped off her shoulder and was riding down her coat sleeve. She balanced herself on one foot to close the door with the other. Ginger, her secretary, jumped up from behind the computer desk and hurried across the small waiting room, grabbing the folders before they spilled over the brown carpet.

"She barged in here and said she had to see you *now*," Ginger said, blue eyes blazing. She was a breed—an Arapaho mother and a long-vanished white father—which accounted for the combination of rosy skin and oil-black hair that hung in a single braid halfway down her back. Dressed in her usual blue jeans and a long-sleeved white blouse, she looked as if she might depart for the rodeo at any moment, but she ran the office like a war chief, causing documents and letters to material-ize out of the computer, fielding phone calls, marshaling clients through the day. Ginger did not appreciate any sudden change in the schedule.

Vicky glanced through the doorway across the waiting room to the little space that served as her private office. Mary Featherly sat in one of the rounded wood chairs in front of the desk, a yellow parka draped around her shoulders. She clasped a large red purse on her lap. Her appointment wasn't until this afternoon, and this morning Vicky had intended only to drop off some documents before driving out to Lean Bear's ranch. Susan had come to her in a dream last night, walking across the snowy fields, crying. Vicky had bolted upright and pulled the comforter around her shoulders to hold back the cold seeping into her bones. She had lain awake the rest of the night thinking about Susan at the ranch with three strangers—white men—and rerunning in her mind the old movies of Ben and her and the kids, wishing the ending had been different, for the kids' sake.

She walked into her private office and greeted her client in as cheery a voice as she could muster. After depositing her brown wool coat and black bag over the coat tree, she settled into her swivel chair and withdrew the agreement from the briefcase.

"That bastard gonna let me and the kids have the house?" The Arapaho woman looked middle-aged; her face was leathered and wrinkled, her lips were pulled into a tight line, and her black hair hanging over the yellow parka was streaked with gray. She was thirty, the mother of two kids, about to be divorced, and furious at the dreams crumbled at her feet. Vicky recognized the signs.

Patiently Vicky began to explain the different points in the agreement. Yes, Mary would have the house, but only until the kids became emancipated, at which time the house would be sold, the profits divided between the parties. It was a small house in Lander; the profits wouldn't be much. The good news was that Herman had been working for the state highway department nearly two months, and he could pay child support.

"As long as he has a job," Mary interrupted.

"Yes, as long as he has a job." That was the problem. Jobs for Indians had a way of vanishing overnight. If there was anything the *Hinono eino* needed, it was jobs.

Mary said, "That bastard should pay for all the times he drunk up everything and didn't come home, and me and the kids went hungry."

Vicky went over the points again. This wasn't about revenge; why was it always about revenge? This was about getting the best deal possible so that Mary and the kids could move into a new life. Vicky could tell by the look of resignation creeping across the other woman's face that she was beginning to understand. It was another thirty minutes before Mary got to her feet, leaned over the desk, and signed the agreement.

An hour later, Vicky guided the Bronco up the winding, snow-glazed road in Sage Canyon. She could feel the rear wheels slipping, and she steered toward the center, halfway between the jagged boulders and the drop-off into Sage Creek. The sense of place flooded over her. She hadn't driven here since the day she'd taken the two kids and fled down the canyon like a madwoman. Yet it was familiar: the rock formations washed in sunlight, the snow like downy feathers on the branches of the ponderosas, the soft mountain air.

She turned onto the white road that led to Lean Bear's ranch and hit the brake pedal. The Bronco slid in a half circle before stopping at the metal gate blocking the road. It was over five feet high, with three horizontal bars, and it hung between the posts of the barbed-wire fence Ben had set out the first summer they were married.

Vicky slammed out of the Bronco. The only sound in the mountain stillness was that of the breeze hissing in the trees. She walked along the gate, running a gloved hand over the top bar, her boots sinking into the powdery snow. At one end, metal hinges held the gate against the fence post; at the other, a large chain, secured by a combination lock. Squinting into the sun, she studied the green house that squatted in the meadow a short distance beyond. She could make out what looked like fresh tire tracks leading to the house.

Ben hadn't mentioned a gate, but no gate would have stopped him. He must have climbed over, which was what she was now contemplating. She'd climbed over fences and gates before, but not in an attorney suit. She gripped the middle rail, feeling the bite of the icy metal through her gloves, and was about to pull herself through the rails when she heard the distant thrum of an engine.

She walked back alongside the Bronco to the road. Perhaps Susan was coming, or one of the three white men. The noise swelled into the quiet. Then there was a momentary lull and a ratchety gearing down.

As she waited for what sounded like a truck to come around the bend, a crack appeared in her memory: She was driving the old pickup up the canyon and over the narrow dirt road that wound to the upper pasture, the high meadow surrounded by mountain peaks, with a creek purling among the aspens and willows. It was where Ben pastured the sheep in the summer, a cool oasis even on burning days, with grass the color of emeralds. She had stashed a basket of fried chicken and bread and jam, along with a thermos of hot coffee, in the bed of the pickup. Susan lay in a blanket in a cardboard box on the seat beside her.

Ben heard the pickup's engine and came galloping across the meadow, head bent low over the neck of the mare, like a warrior in the Old Time. He dismounted by the cabin he'd outfitted as a bunkhouse next to the old barn, and, with the mare grazing nearby, they sat on the blanket she'd spread over the grass and ate their picnic. And they'd made love there in the grass, with the baby asleep in the box beside them.

Vicky stamped her feet hard into the snow. These were not memories she wanted. Suddenly a gray truck rounded the bend and headed downhill toward her. Then it skidded sideways into the turn, spraying snow as the brakes grabbed. It was still rolling when the driver, a white man somewhere in his twenties, hopped out. He had on blue jeans, a jean jacket with a sheepskin collar, dark leather gloves, and hiking boots. Wisps of blond hair hung out from his blue cap. There was a swagger in his shoulders as he came toward her.

"You lookin' for somethin'?"

Vicky sensed the charge of hostility in the air. "I'm looking for Susan Holden," she said in her courtroom voice. "I'm her mother. Who are you?"

The young man seemed to consider this a moment, then shrugged. "A friend."

"Where is she?"

"Don't have the faintest." Another shrug.

"I'd like you to open the gate so I can see if she's at the house," Vicky said.

"She ain't at the house."

"I'm not here to play games, Mr. . . ." Vicky waited for him to fill in the blank. He said nothing.

"Whatever your name is. I'm here to see my daughter, and I don't intend to leave until you tell me where she is."

The young man hooked his gloved thumbs into his jeans pockets and regarded her through lowered eyelids. A chill crept down her spine. She was alone with this man, who might or might not be a friend of her daughter's, off a mountain road that might or might not see another vehicle before spring, and she had issued an ultimatum.

"Susan ain't here," he said after a long moment. "She probably went into Riverton to get some groceries."

Vicky looked past him, beyond the gate. What he said was not outside the realm of possibility, although Susan could also be at the house. Vicky knew she was not about to get by this white man who had planted himself like a chunk of granite between her and the gate. Her uneasiness grew. It bordered on fear. Who were these white men her daughter had brought home?

"When will Susan be back?"

"Later," the white man said. "Indian time."

Vicky drew in a long breath and started past him for the Bronco, the uneasiness approaching a kind of panic as she turned her back. She forced herself to take a deep breath. Why did she think he might grab her? Other than surliness, he hadn't shown any aggression. Still, she felt her muscles tensing involuntarily. If he grabbed her, she would fight like a mountain lion.

She flung open the Bronco door and slid onto the seat, slamming the door behind her. She felt the anger rising in her face like flames in a campfire. Backing the Bronco to where the man stood, thumbs still hooked in his jeans pockets, she rolled down the window.

"I'll be back to see my daughter," she said. "Six-thirty this evening. White time." She stepped hard on the accelerator, and the Bronco churned backward through the snow. Then she shifted into forward and squealed onto the canyon road.

‹ 9 ›

As soon as Father John reached his office, he put in a call to the Provincial. No answer. An hour later he tried again, this time connecting with a young Scholastic in the Provincial's outer, outer office. The Scholastic delivered a lecture, the gist of it being that the Provincial was a good shepherd concerned about the well-being of his flock at St. Francis Mission. Unfortunately the Provincial was tied up in meetings from now until the end of time and could not be disturbed. Father John could be assured everything would be done, however. . . .

Father John hung up.

No matter how much confidence the bishop's delegate and the corporate lawyer had exuded yesterday, Father John knew they couldn't shut down the mission overnight. Nevertheless, the wheels were in motion. He didn't have much time to try to stop them.

And there was the missing young Arapaho. Father John had found himself wide awake in the middle of the night wondering what Marcus had gotten himself into this time. What was it Banner had said? Kids gave you gray hair and kept you awake nights. That was the truth. How much worse was it when they were your own? What he kept coming back to, what bothered him the most, was that while Marcus might be irresponsible and unreliable, might take foolish chances and look for trouble, he would never abandon his old people. It was not the Arapaho Way. If Marcus didn't visit the Depperts, it was because he couldn't.

Father John picked up the receiver and tapped the number for Riverton Memorial Hospital. He had met the director a number of times, and he asked to be put through to her office. After a few seconds, she was on the line and he asked whether Marcus Deppert had been treated during the last week. She put him on hold. He waited to the purr of canned music that made him long for an aria—for real music. Finally she was back: Sorry, Father. No one by that name had been seen last week.

He hung up and tried the Lander Hospital where he knew one of the staff doctors. It was the same routine: question, canned music, answer. Marcus had not been seen there either.

He replaced the receiver, feeling an odd mixture of relief and concern. At least Marcus wasn't sick or hurt. But where was he? Maybe he'd returned home, in which case Ike might have seen him. The problem was, Ike's house was not one of the few on the reservation that had a phone. Father John called Jake Littlchorse's garage, then the gas station at Fort Washakie, and the little coffee shop at Ethete, leaving messages for Ike if he happened by.

Thirty minutes later, Ike returned the call. Easter Egg Village was nice and quiet, he reported. First time in weeks he and his wife were getting a good night's sleep. As far as he was concerned, Marcus and his drunken friends could stay away forever.

Father John replaced the receiver, the heavy feeling

settling over his shoulders like a leaden cloak. Nobody had seen Marcus Deppert for more than a week. And there was the frozen, lonely body in the ditch. Until Marcus showed up, or the body was found, Father John knew they would remain connected in his head. He wished he hadn't promised Joe and Deborah he'd keep the police out of it, even though he understood their worry. The last time the police started looking into Marcus's life, he went to jail for three years.

In midmorning, Father John pulled on his parka and cowboy hat and walked outside. Father Peter was just coming up the front stairs, leaning onto the metal railing setting one foot next to the other on each stair. The morning sun splashed across the mission grounds and warmed the air. On the western horizon, the Wind River Mountains stood out in relief against the light blue sky. The sounds of children at recess floated over from the schoolyard.

"'There is, sir, an aery of children,'" the old priest said, grinning.

"*A Midsummer Night's Dream*," Father John said as he held the front door open. He pulled the guess off the top of his head. Once in a while, he guessed right.

Father Peter laughed out loud and shook his head. "Oh, my, my," he said when he reached the top stair. "I'm afraid you must take your place at the bottom of the class, my boy. It is with despair I contemplate your knowledge of the great bard."

Father John thought about asking where, in the mighty canon of Shakespeare, the quote might be found, then dismissed the idea. The old priest, like any Jesuit teacher, would tell him to look it up. "'Tis not the will I lack," he said.

Father Peter patted his arm as he stepped inside. "And that, my boy, is not Shakespeare."

Father John sprinted down the stairs and out to Circle Drive. He was grateful to the old man who had welcomed him here after his career had careened off track and no superior at any Jesuit high school or college would return his call. He had left Grace House with the memory of whiskey still on his tongue and flown into Riverton, at the edge of the world. "You can begin again here," Father Peter had told him.

Close to where Circle Drive emptied into Seventeen-Mile Road stood the elementary school, a pile of cement blocks that probably resembled every other BIA school on every reservation in the West. Except for the entry. The Arapahos had insisted the entry resemble a tipi, with the door facing the east and the rising sun, like the dwellings in the Old Time.

He cut across the school grounds, following a path the kids had probably trampled earlier. It looked as if all the kids were on the playground. A group of boys, sixth-graders by the size of them, ran back and forth along the mesh fence, kicking up clouds of snow. One of the boys, Howard Bushy, spun around and darted past the others. A successful feint. He was hugging a basketball.

All of a sudden, he stopped. "Hi, Father," he called, running toward the fence. The other boys followed. They were all looking into the far distance. It was disrespectful for a child to look directly at an adult.

"What're you playing?" Father John crossed through the snow to the fence.

"Basketball," Howard said. His blue parka sported a gray iron-on patch across the front. Both sleeves were frayed. He had pulled a knit cap down around his ears, but his cheeks had turned rust in the outdoors.

"That a fact." Father John smiled. These Indian kids were great. No court, no hoops, just a basketball and a snow-packed playground. They couldn't dribble in the snow, but they could run and dodge and pass.

"Me and the other guys, we want to ask you somethin'." Howard wrapped one mittened hand through the wires, gripping the basketball with the other. His eyes looked beyond Father John.

"Shoot."

"Well, we was wonderin' . . ." Howard turned toward the other boys, as if for confirmation. They gathered closer, stomping their feet in the snow, looking down. "We was wonderin'," Howard plunged on, "if we could use the old gym after school."

The old gym was in Eagle Hall. Father John had kept it padlocked the last couple of winters. It was a struggle just to heat and electrify the meeting rooms in Eagle Hall, as well as the church, offices, and priests' residence. Every month it was a toss-up which bills he paid. This month he'd paid the telephone company. Next month he hoped to pay something on the heat and electric bill.

"We need a place to practice since they won't let us use the gym anymore." Howard tilted his head toward the school.

Father John got the picture. The BIA had cut back on funds, and frills such as afterschool activities for the kids were the first to go. But where would he find enough money to heat the gym even a few hours a day? And he couldn't turn a bunch of kids loose without supervision; they would need a coach. What's more, if they stayed after school to play basketball, they would miss the bus, which meant he would have to figure out some way to get them home. The problems were mighty.

"Listen, kids . . ." he began haltingly, aware they were waiting for an answer. He hated to let them down.

Disappointment descended over the young faces like a roiling cloud of dust. It would be better to tell them the truth now, rather than later, but a part of him persisted in believing in the little miracles that sometimes occur when everything seems impossible. He said, "Let me see what I can work out. Okay?"

"Okay." Howard shrugged. The kids turned back toward the schoolyard, kicking at the slabs of snow. A couple of them looked back and waved as if to wave him away.

Father John followed the fence to the white stucco tipi, the laughing, yelling voices of the children behind him. Howard and the others needed a place to play some real basketball and a coach to develop their skills, get them ready for basketball at Indian High School in a few years. Of all the problems, finding a coach would be the hardest.

For a second he flirted with the idea of coaching them himself. He liked coaching. He did a pretty good job with the Eagles baseball team, which went 22-3 last summer. But basketball? He'd only played one year at Boston College Prep, after the coach, who was also the math teacher, had pulled him aside and explained that any kid over six feet tall had a duty to play basketball. And if he didn't play, he could expect an F in math. It was another two years before Father John had topped out at almost six-feet-four, but by then he'd proved his talent on the pitcher's mound, and, he suspected, the baseball coach had warned his colleague against any more creative recruiting. Baseball was his sport. He could have pitched in the majors—that was a fantasy he sometimes allowed himself. But then, he wouldn't have been who he was.

The irony struck him as he swung open the glass door of the tipi and stepped onto the concrete floor. He was trying to figure out how to start a basketball program when, at the same time, two fancy suits were plotting to shut down the mission. He made his way along the empty school corridor, between walls draped in papers covered with crayon drawings and numbers and letters and gold stars. There was a faint odor of barbecue sauce.

The corridor led into the cafeteria, a spacious square with rows of tan formica tables glowing under fluorescent lights. Behind the metal counter at the far end, Loretta Dolby was stirring something in a large pot. The smell of barbecue sauce was so thick he could almost taste it.

"You're early for lunch," Loretta called as he walked to the counter. She was probably in her forties, but she looked older, with dark, sun-blotched skin and gray hair pulled into a knob at the base of her neck. She wore a light blue dress that hung loosely from her shoulders and flowed around her like a nightgown.

Suddenly she set the long metal spoon on the counter and came toward him. "Heard about that body."

It was a statement, not a question. Until the body received a proper burial, it would be on everyone's mind—the lost spirit wandering the earth, trying to find the afterworld.

"I seen it last night," she said.

"The body?" For a moment, he wondered if it had been found and he hadn't heard.

"The ghost." Loretta smoothed back a strand of gray hair that had fallen across her forehead. "It was out in the field back of my house. I heard it in the middle of the night, wailing like the wind. I looked out, and there it was, like a dust devil gettin' madder and madder. The police don't find the body pretty soon, no tellin' what that ghost's gonna do. The Day of the Death's gonna go too long."

Father John nodded. She meant the time the spirit spent on the earth after death, before it was sent to the afterworld. It was similar to his idea of purgatory, except the Arapahos believed the Day of the Death ended on the third day, when the body was buried. It had been almost two days now since he saw the corpse.

"Chief Banner's trying to find the body," Father John said, wondering how to bring up the fact that Marcus Deppert seemed to be missing. He didn't want to alarm her by suggesting the lost, half-mad ghost she was convinced she'd seen was Marcus. It was bad enough for a ghost to be anonymous. Its fate would seem even more terrible if it acquired a name.

"Where can I find Rich?" Father John asked.

The atmosphere seemed to change between them, as if someone had opened a door and let in a blast of cold air. Loretta pulled herself upright, squaring her shoulders and gazing steadily at him. "Rich is on the good road now. He hasn't been in no trouble for a long time, I don't care what nobody says."

"I'm looking for Marcus Deppert, and I was hoping Rich could help me find him." Father John kept his tone reassuring.

Loretta's eyes narrowed in thought. "Only time Rich ever got into trouble was with that no-good creep. He don't see Marcus Deppert no more, he promised me."

"He might have an idea of his whereabouts."

"Father John, I'm telling you, Rich don't have nothin' to do with him. Rich's doin' good for himself now. The first money he made on his new job he brought straight to me. Five new hundred-dollar bills. He said, 'This is for you, Mom.' That's the kind of son Rich is."

"I know Rich is a good son," Father John said. He meant he knew Loretta believed Rich was a good son. The only connection Rich ever had to work, as far as he knew, was three years ago when he and Marcus were peddling pot, an enterprise that earned them both a stay in Leavenworth. He wondered how Rich had come by five hundred dollars cash.

"Sounds as if he has a good job," Father John said. He was trolling carefully.

"Darn right." The woman's tone was defiant, but he sensed she'd taken the bait. "He drives Jeeps down to Denver for rich people. They buy 'em here 'cause it's cheaper. You know how rich people are. Money sticks to their hands, 'cause it's the most important thing in the world to 'em. He's drivin' a Jeep right now. So how could he know anything about Marcus Deppert or Annie Chambeau or the rest of that lousy gang?"

The girl's name rang a bell. Banner had said the Lander police broke up a party Friday night at Annie Chambeau's apartment. "Is she a friend of Rich's?" he asked.

Loretta laughed, a pinched, forced sound. "That breed's nobody's friend and everybody's friend, you know what I mean? Says she's Arapaho, but her daddy came from one of those traders in the Old Time. I hear she's hangin' around Marcus Deppert now. Birds of a feather."

Father John asked if she knew who Rich was working for, but she shrugged, as if it didn't matter. "All I know, it's a real good job."

Father John tried to sort through what Loretta had said as he walked back along Circle Drive. She may wish her son had broken with Marcus Deppert, but it looked as if the two young men had taken the same job. Chances were, they had both gone to Denver. But, then, why was there a half-packed suitcase in Marcus's living room? And who had hired them to drive Jeeps to Denver? Maybe the girl who had thrown the party, and who seemed to know both Marcus and Rich, would have some answers. He decided to swing by the Grand Apartments in Lander this afternoon.

But first he intended to pay an unannounced visit to Eden Lightfoot, the economic development director.

◀ 10 ▶

The afternoon sun slanted across the red bricks of the Arapaho tribal headquarters at Ethete as Father John nosed the Toyota into the parking lot. He climbed out of the cab and crossed the snow-patched sidewalk in a couple of steps. Large black letters on the glass door spelled the Arapaho word *Ne:hi:3ei*, the Center.

A young woman with thick black hair that flowed like a shawl over her shoulders looked up from the desk in the lobby. "Well, hi, Father," she said, pedaling her chair back a few inches, as if to welcome a conversation.

"Is Eden Lightfoot in?" Father John asked. Odors of perfume and stale coffee permeated the air. The building was designed in a V shape, with the offices of the business councilmen down one corridor and tribal offices down the other. From somewhere came the muffled sound of a ringing telephone.

"I'll tell him you're here." The young woman pedaled back to the desk, picked up the phone, and punched in a couple of numbers. "Father O'Malley to see you," she said. There was a long pause, confusion and surprise mingling on her face. Then, "I'll tell him."

Cradling the receiver, embarrassment in her eyes, she

said, "I'm sorry, Father. Mr. Lightfoot is tied up. He suggests you make an appointment for later."

"Where will I find him?"

"Third door." The woman nodded toward the left corridor. "Only don't tell him I . . ."

Father John started down the corridor. Light from the intermittent ceiling fixtures bounced off the beige walls and scattered over the green tile floor. He paused at the door with the small lettered sign reading ECONOMIC DE-VELOPMENT DIRECTOR. Tapping on the door and opening it at the same time, he called, "Eden Lightfoot?"

A stocky man—probably Cheyenne, judging by the broad, flat face—not more than thirty, rose slowly from the chair behind the oak desk. He was short, with a bar-rel chest and wide shoulders that seemed to support his head without benefit of a neck. He was wearing blue jeans and a light blue, silky-looking shirt with a black leather bolo tie clasped in silver. The surprise on his face gave way to something resembling confusion—a slip, perhaps. Recovering quickly, he lifted a pudgy hand and combed the fingers through his dark hair. "This isn't the best time, Father O'Malley."

"What is the 'best time' to discuss closing St. Francis Mission?" Father John said, shutting the door behind him. The director stood in front of a wide window that framed a view of the snow-packed plains. Light glim-mered off the top of the polished desk, which held a telephone, computer keyboard, and monitor. A series of sleek, black-framed documents decorated the wall on the right. In the center was an oblong degree with the director's name sandwiched between the words "Har-vard University" and "Masters of Business Administra-tion." A large multicolored map of Wind River Reservation sprawled across the opposite wall.

Eden Lightfoot resumed his seat and began tapping the palm of one hand against the desk. It made a flat, hollow sound. "We have every intention of discussing the matter with you as soon as the plans become definite. This is very premature."

"We?"

The director shifted his bulky frame. His hand went still. "The Z Group has created the opportunity of a lifetime. Any Indian reservation in the country would jump at it. Surely you can understand the importance of new jobs on the reservation."

The room felt stuffy and hot. There was the soft swish of air emanating from a vent somewhere. "What I don't understand," Father John said, "is why the Z Group wants to close a mission that has been part of the Arapaho community since the last century."

Leaning back in the brown leather chair, Eden Lightfoot said, "You're speaking of the past. Your own people have taught me the past is dead. We must live in the present and position ourselves to move into the future. Surely you can understand an enterprise that is no longer profitable must give way . . ."

"Profitable? A mission?"

"Perhaps the better word is productive."

"St. Francis is productive."

The director began tapping again. In a good imitation of a Harvard accent, he said, "We are speaking of economic considerations, are we not? The mission happens to lie at the edge of the reservation, close to major thoroughfares. It is the best location to attract large numbers of outsiders without the disruption of bringing them into the heart of our country."

Father John stepped over to the wall map. Sunlight washed out the tiny black letters of the northern

Shoshone lands: Crow Heart and Burris and Pavillion, Bushwhacker and Wild Licorice Road. He waved one hand in the sunlight. "Somewhere up north would be better. Tourists could stop on their way to Yellowstone Park." He moved his hand to the southern part of the reservation, near the Popo Agie River and Highway 287. "Even better. Closer to the people in southern Wyoming and Colorado."

"We don't agree on the best location," the director said.

"What about the Arapahos and the Shoshones? Will they agree when you get around to telling them?" It rankled Father John that the plans had been made in secret, that the mission would be sold before anyone realized what was going on.

"The matter will be presented to the Arapaho business council at next week's meeting," Eden Lightfoot said. "Make no mistake, Father O'Malley, it will be approved. And since the site is located in the Arapaho part of the reservation, the Shoshone council will rubber stamp the approval."

Father John walked over to the door and laid one hand on the knob. Turning toward the director, he said, "The general council will make the final decision." It was a bluff. There was no guarantee the Arapaho elders would call a general council, but at the back of his mind was something Thomas Spotted Horse, one of the four holy men, had once told him: The *Hinono eino* rule themselves. No matter what the business council decided, the elders might summon the people, just as in the Old Time, when the people had traveled across the plains to come together and decide the best road to follow.

The director got to his feet. A blood vessel pulsated in

the center of his forehead. "Ridiculous," he said, sprinkling little dots of saliva over the desk top. "The business council has been elected to make economic decisions based on the advice and expertise of professionals. This is not a matter for a general council and the maunderings of traditional old men. I'd advise you not to attempt to involve the elders."

Father John let himself out of the claustrophobic office and retraced his steps down the hallway. The receptionist glanced up, an expectant look about her, as if she'd been waiting to hear how the meeting went. Ignoring her, he strode out the front door and got into the Toyota. The pickup shot across the parking lot and out onto Ethete Road.

Even if a general council were called, he was thinking, there was a chance the people would vote for the recreation center and the promise of jobs. In that case, he would have to pack his bags and move on to another assignment, wherever that might be. He didn't want to think about it. He wanted to believe the Arapahos would vote for the mission, if they had the choice.

Eden Lightfoot obviously thought so. It was obvious the director didn't want a general council. But that depended upon the elders. Father John resolved to swing by Thomas Spotted Horse's ranch the first chance he got.

The Toyota shuddered through the icy slush that lay over the streets of Lander. The Grand Apartments, two piles of yellow bricks, three stories high, straddled a half block at the northern edge of town. A narrow alley ran between the buildings, while a small convenience store had been jammed against one corner. Sometime during the fifties, with uranium and iron ore mines at full blast, the Grand Apartments had sheltered mining engineers and their families, middle-class, white. Now they were home to white and Indian alike, old and young, most on welfare.

Father John wheeled the Toyota close to the curb and walked up the sidewalk. Jagged cracks of cement popped through the hard-packed snow. He had been here many times—to talk somebody into entering alcohol rehab, to visit the parents of a teenaged boy killed in a car crash, to try to convince some high school kid to stay in school. The people at the Grand Apartments were struggling.

The front door, gray and flimsy-looking, stood slightly ajar, its hinges loose. Inside the small entry was another door, propped open with a cement block. A tangle of wires poked from the stucco wall. Sometime in its history, the Grand Apartments had boasted an intercom.

He stepped around the cement block. The hallway was seedier than he remembered, with its trail of crumpled paper, fast food containers, and cigarette butts. A stairway hugged the wall on the right, while several doors marched down the left wall. He knocked at the first door. It opened slightly, and a shadow moved fleetingly past the crack. Then the door slammed shut. He knocked again and waited, but it was obvious the person behind the door had no intention of opening it again. Glancing down the dim hall, he counted eight doors. Assuming the same number on each floor in two buildings, Annie Chambeau might live in any one of forty-eight apartments.

He sighed and started down the hall. Before he reached the next door, he heard the scratching sound of the first door's knob turning.

"Who are you?" It sounded like an elderly woman.

"Father O'Malley from St. Francis Mission," he said, retracing his steps. The door stood open about three inches, the length of the guard chain. A small, white-haired woman in a print dress peered at him, blue eyes watery and outsized behind her bottle-thick glasses. Arthritic fingers gripped the door edge.

"I heard of you," the old woman said. "You that Indian priest. Why'd you come here?"

"I'm looking for Annie Chambeau. Can you tell me where she lives?"

The old woman leaned into the crack. "I'm a respectable widow," she began. Father John waited. Old people liked to work up to the point, clarify matters before confiding relevant information. "When I first come here," she was saying, "this was a good place. Then those people come, and the place went to rack and ruin. Loud parties, drinkin', fightin' all the time. I don't go outdoors no more, except to get groceries. I don't never open my door."

Curiosity probably compelled her to open the door often, Father John thought. Still, he could sense the old woman's fear. It was real. He reminded her about Annie Chambeau.

"You tell those people to go back to the reservation where they belong, will ya, Father?" she said. "You tell 'em they should keep with their own. Maybe they'll listen to you." She drew herself up and peered at him a moment. "Three-F," she announced. "You can take the front stairs."

He thanked her and started up the stairs. Before he'd gone halfway, she called, "Be careful, Father."

The floors grew progressively dimmer as he ascended, and the third floor was almost pitch dark. Light bulbs dangled from cords along the ceiling, but none was lit. Gray daylight filtered through a dirty window at the far end of the hall. Father John stopped at the door with the little strip of metal and two screws in the center, all that was left of the letter *F*. He rapped a couple of times.

There was a scuffing noise inside, followed by a thump, as if a chair had fallen onto a hard floor. He knocked again, the old woman's warning echoing in his ears. Another scuffing noise, then the wham of a door slamming. The front stairs. The old woman had told him to take the front stairs. Somebody—Annie, most likely—had just gone down the back.

Father John ran to the far end of the hallway and tried a door that probably led to the back stairway. It was locked. He sprinted back the way he'd come and descended the front stairs two at a time. The old woman peered through the crack in her opened door as he passed. Outside he cut across the snowy yard and turned into the narrow alley, which lay in shadow, the air washed with ice.

A young woman was coming toward him, pulling a red coat around one shoulder, jabbing her arm into the sleeve. She looked up. A mixture of shock and fear crossed her face. Suddenly she pivoted around and stumbled, reaching out against the brick wall to catch herself. Then she took off running.

"Annie, wait," Father John called, but she had already disappeared around the building. By the time he emerged from the alley, she had crossed the snow-packed space in back and was attempting to pull herself up a solid wood fence, her red coat dangling off one arm.

Father John stopped about ten feet from her. "Don't be afraid," he said calmly.

"Leave me alone," she screamed, whirling around, like a cornered animal, eyes darting for some way out. Her breath came in jabs, as if she couldn't catch it. She was shaking.

He said, "I'm Father O'Malley from the reservation. I didn't mean to frighten you. I'm looking for Marcus Deppert, and I thought maybe you could tell me where I might find him."

An expression of relief came into the young woman's dark eyes. She swallowed hard and began tugging the coat around her thin shoulders while shoving an arm into the empty sleeve. He wanted to help her, but he kept his place. He didn't want to frighten her again.

"Everybody's lookin' for Marcus," she said, gripping

the coat around her. "I'm freezin' to death. Could we get a cup of coffee or somethin'?"

Annie Chambeau had stopped shaking, but there was a little tremor in her hands as she clasped the mug of coffee and dipped her head to take a sip. She sat hunched under the red coat, which draped around her shoulders like a ceremonial cape. She wasn't more than twenty, Father John decided, and she could have been beautiful. She had the green eyes and light complexion of some distant white man who had probably come to the plains to trade whiskey and guns. From the Arapaho came the coal-black hair and high cheekbones, the graceful nose with the little arch near the top. But over it all was the gray pallor, the emaciated look of the alcoholic. He could recognize it a mile away.

They sat at a small table, next to the plate-glass window, the only people in the convenience store besides the woman behind the counter. Father John took a long pull from his mug, then asked if she knew where he could find Marcus Deppert.

"Do I look like his keeper?" the girl asked. "Some blond guy showed up at my place Saturday night lookin' for him. I thought you was him, the blond guy. He just pushed his way in. Where's Marcus, he says. Hell, how do I know, I say. So he pushes me down on the couch and starts tearin' my place apart. Tears stuff off the bed, pulls my clothes out of the closet, and then goes to the kitchen and takes his arm like this—" She made a sweeping motion over the white Formica table-top. "Throws dishes and stuff all over. Crazy-like, 'cause I didn't know where Marcus was."

The girl looked out the window. After a moment she picked up the mug again. The trembling had increased.

"Did he hurt you?" Father John asked.

Annie shook her head. "Just ruined a lot of my stuff. It might've been him come back yesterday, but I ran out the back and got away."

It might have been Mike Osgood, Father John was thinking. The FBI agent had said he would talk to the girl about what happened at Friday night's party. On the other hand, Annie could be right; it might have been the blond man again.

"What did he say while he was tearing up your apartment?"

The girl made a low *hmmmmp* sound. "Said I should tell Marcus he's a dead man."

Father John took a long breath. Marcus was in trouble, all right. "Did you call the police?" He knew she hadn't, even before the look of incredulity swept over her face, as if she were trying to figure out what planet he existed on. People like Annie Chambeau and Marcus Deppert never thought the police were on their side.

"What're they gonna do? Nothin'. Reason I know is that old witch down on the first floor called 'em. She's always callin' the police. She called 'em Friday night, too, just 'cause me and some friends was havin' a good time. I wish she would've called 'em faster Saturday night. Maybe they would've got that bastard before he took off."

"When's the last time you saw Marcus?" Father John heard the pinched tone in his voice. He didn't like the thought crowding at the edges of his mind: Did the man who wrecked Annie's apartment find Marcus and kill him? Was it Marcus's body in the ditch?

The young woman took another long sip from her mug. "Friday night," she said after a moment. "After not callin' or comin' around for a month, all of a sudden he comes to my party. I thought . . ." Annie stopped. She traced the rim of the mug with one finger. "I thought he come back. Only he didn't. He just run in and look around like he was lookin' for somebody. I said, how you been? What you come here for? He shook me off, like I wasn't nobody, like we didn't live in that apartment together all last year." Annie tucked her head down, and Father John saw she was crying.

The girl's pain filled the space between them, and he looked away, giving her a moment. Cold air moved through the window. The sun had dropped behind the mountains, making the afternoon seem flat and gray. It looked as if it might snow again. A green truck slid to a stop at the intersection and flicked on its headlights. Was it a Dodge? He couldn't tell for sure. Everybody drove a truck around here. A lot of them were green.

Annie cleared her throat and said, "We was good together. I mean, Marcus stayed clean all year, and I stopped drinkin'. We was talkin' about gettin' married. Then he went and got mixed up with that white chick and tells me it's just not workin', me and him. It was working fine 'til he met her. I just lost it, you know what I mean?"

Father John looked back at her. "I know."

Annie picked up the mug and slammed it down, sloshing coffee over the table. "You don't say that, you hear me?" she shouted. The attendant leaned over the counter and stared at them. "What do you know about what I'm talkin' about?"

It was familiar. The alcoholic's quick anger at the misperceived words, the lack of understanding and sympathy. He'd flared out like that once at his own mother, and at his superior and the counselors at Grace House more times than he wanted to remember. What did they know about the terrible thirst that controlled his life?

"Would you like to get drunk right now?" he asked.

The girl seemed to lift herself a fraction off her chair, then slumped back, regarding him, as if trying to make out whether he was taunting her or issuing an invitation.

"So would I," he said.

She continued to study him. He sensed her wariness, the way she was groping to assimilate contradictory kinds of information.

"They say it's one day at a time," Father John said softly. "That's not true, Annie. It's one moment."

The girl gulped a breath. "I didn't start drinkin' again 'til Marcus moved out. When I come home and saw all his stuff gone, I went and got a bottle of whiskey . . ." Her voice trailed off a moment. "I just felt so alone."

Father John fished through the inside pocket of his parka and withdrew a small spiral notebook and a ball-point pen. "We have a good group at the AA meetings at St. Francis," he said, flipping back the notebook cover and jotting down the information. "Thursdays. Seven P.M. You would be welcome, Annie." He ripped off the sheet and pushed it across the table.

She looked at it a moment before stuffing it in her pocket. He saw the half-heartedness in the gesture: the alcoholic wanting to toss it on the floor; the Arapaho too polite to do so.

"I'm sorry to ask you this," he said, "but Marcus could be in trouble. Do you know the name of the white girl?"

Annie swallowed hard. "Jennifer somebody. I heard she's new around here. Lives over in Riverton some-where."

White woman. Named Jennifer. Lives in Riverton. There could be a couple dozen. Father John felt as if he were slogging uphill in a blizzard with the trail disappearing in the snow.

"One more thing, Annie," Father John said. "Did Marcus happen to mention a new job?"

The girl's eyes widened. "A job? That'd be the day."

Her answer didn't surprise him. Marcus and Rich driving Jeeps to Denver, the large amount of cash Rich had on hand—this new job of theirs was probably anything but legal.

He regarded the girl a moment. From his own experience, he knew what she needed now was a friend. And it was possible the blond man would return. If he had found Marcus, he might start thinking about the fact that Annie could identify him. "Do you have anyone you could stay with? It might be a good idea for you to leave the apartment for a while."

Fear shone in the girl's eyes, as if she'd come to the same idea. "My grandmother in Rawlins," she said, then stopped. "Only she don't let me come around when I'm drinkin'. But my girlfriend's got a place over on Sweetwater. I guess I can go there."

Father John got to his feet, but Annie remained seated, huddled under the red coat, looking small and fragile. "Come on," he said, pulling on his parka. "Get some things together. I'll take you to your girlfriend's."

He held the door and followed her outside as a gust of wind swirled across the front of the store, showering them with snow. The temperature was making its usual late-afternoon descent.

While she went back to her apartment, he started up the Toyota, pushing the heat lever on high. Gradually the cold began to recede. After about ten minutes,

Annie appeared, gripping the handles of two plastic grocery bags that bulged with whatever clothes she had decided to bring.

Father John leaned across the seat and opened the passenger door. As she crawled inside and settled the bags on her lap, she directed him to take Fourth and turn right onto Sweetwater, assuring him the girlfriend would be home. "With two kids, where else she gonna be?"

He stopped in the driveway next to the small duplex, and Annie stepped out, clutching the plastic bags against the front of her coat. A young Indian with a baby slung on one hip and another child gripping her leg had already opened the front door and was waving.

"Soon's you find Marcus, you tell him something for me, okay?" Annie said, leaning back into the cab. "You tell him he messed up my goddamn life." She kicked the pickup door shut.

If I find him, Father John thought, backing out of the driveway.

❰ 12 ❱

Vicky stuffed several folders into the open briefcase on top of the file cabinet. The street lights below shimmered against the darkened window. It looked heavy and still outside, and snow was falling lightly. She didn't like the idea of driving up Sage Canyon in a snowstorm.

She sighed as she laid another folder on the bulging stack. How much work would she get done tonight? She was hopelessly behind. After she'd gotten back from Lean Bear's ranch this morning, she'd spent the rest of the day trying to catch up, disoriented, Susan hovering in her mind. It was after five now, almost time to leave. She had told the man at the ranch she would be back at 6:30, and she meant to be on time. The office was quiet. Ginger had left fifteen minutes ago. As Vicky closed the briefcase, she heard the soft crush of footsteps in the waiting room. She whirled around.

A man filled up the doorway, in a navy blue parka and jeans, his arms at his sides, his left hand gripping the crown of a brown felt cowboy hat. "I wasn't sure you were still here," Father John said.

Vicky exhaled a deep breath. "John O'Malley. You scared me to death."

"I seem to be good at that today—scaring women to death."

Vicky sank into the leather chair behind her desk and motioned him to one of the barrel-shaped chairs on the other side. "I tried to get back to you this afternoon," she said. And here he was, as if summoned by a phone ringing into the emptiness of his office across the reservation. She was immensely glad to see him.

Father John stepped into the office and took the chair, anchoring his cowboy hat on one knee the way her grandfather used to do. His hair was a rusty color, with a touch of gray at the temples. His eyes were pale blue, shot through with lights, and he had little laugh lines at the outer edges. He smiled easily, which made him seem even more handsome. He was smiling now, and she had to remind herself once again that he was a priest.

"I understand you've found another body in a ditch," Vicky said.

"Only one, as far as I know."

"You found Walks-on," she reminded him.

Father John's smile widened. "Oh, yeah. But he wasn't dead."

"More dead than alive. If you hadn't gotten him to the vet as fast as you did, he'd be chasing Frisbees with his ancestors. Has he noticed yet he has only three legs?"

"He hasn't mentioned it."

Vicky leaned into the soft back cushion of her chair, the polite exchange of pleasantries over. Now for the purpose of his visit. He never called unless it was important, unless someone was in trouble. She was certain this had something to do with the body on Rendezvous Road. She asked, "Have the police found the body?"

Father John thumped the fingers of one hand against the crown of his hat. "Not yet. And it seems Marcus Deppert is missing."

Vicky clasped her hands over the blue mat that occupied the center of her desk. It didn't surprise her, Marcus Deppert being in trouble. "Is there a connection?"

"I hope not," Father John said. "But I'm not having much luck tracking him down." He told her about the white man who had gone to Annie Chambeau's looking for Marcus and about the jobs Marcus and Rich Dolby had supposedly taken, driving Jeeps to Denver.

Vicky was quiet a moment. She had never heard of anyone ferrying vehicles out of the area. "I suppose Marcus's grandparents don't want the police involved." She saw by the look of surprise in Father John's eyes she'd guessed right. He was the only one looking for the Arapaho.

Ordinarily she didn't have much sympathy for people like Marcus Deppert who raised hell, made drunken spectacles of themselves, and generally confirmed all the stereotypes she and every other Indian had to fight everyday. It was the great white denial that every group had its Marcus Depperts, that all Indians weren't like him. But this white man didn't see a disreputable Indian. He saw somebody in trouble, who might need help, who might be dead. She found her own attitude toward the young Arapaho softening.

"I can ask around," she said. "See if anyone knows anything."

"Good." Father John nodded.

She held his eyes a moment, wanting to tell him about Susan, but she sensed there was something else he was worried about. She waited.

After a few seconds, he said, "St. Francis Mission is about to be sold."

She moved forward in her chair, a reflex. "You must be joking." She saw immediately he'd never been more serious.

"The Z Group from California intends to develop the mission into a recreation center. Movies, bowling alleys, something for everybody."

"I can't believe the Jesuits would sell the mission," Vicky said. It was unthinkable. Wind River Reservation without St. Francis? It was her own great-grandfather, Chief Black Night, who had marked out the land for the mission, who had ridden all the way to Omaha to ask the Jesuits to come and teach the people.

Vicky saw the anger in Father John's eyes. This had hit him even harder than it hit her. She said, "I haven't heard a word. Not one bleep on the moccasin telegraph."

"It's the new economic development director who's behind it," Father John said. "He would like to sign, seal, and deliver the deal before anyone finds out."

"It's a matter for all the people," she said. She knew the truth of this in the smallest fiber of her being.

Father John nodded. "I intend to talk to Thomas Spotted Horse about the possibility of calling a general council."

Vicky leaned back against the soft cushion, the shock of the news still reverberating through her. At least this was a man who would not pack his bags and move on, not without putting up a good fight. But it would be tough. A recreation center meant jobs, and God knew the reservation needed jobs. But the price? What price were the people willing to pay?

She pulled a yellow legal pad out of the drawer and

flopped it onto the desk. Removing the pen from the bubble-like wooden holder she'd bought for herself when she graduated from law school, she started writing. "Z Group, out of California," she said. "I'll see what I can find out. And one of my law school friends worked with Eden Lightfoot at the Cheyenne agency before he came here. She may have some insights into our new director of development. I'll also call a couple friends on the business council to see what they think about this."

Glancing up, Vicky caught the flicker of hope in Father John's eyes. "It may not help."

"It can't hurt," he said, getting to his feet.

A kind of heaviness came over her as she saw him turn to leave. She stood up, pushing back her chair. The gliders screeched against the plastic mat that protected the carpet. "Susan's back," she blurted.

He turned and faced her again. He didn't say anything.

"She's staying with three white men at Lean Bear's ranch where we used to live." Vicky stopped, then hurried on, telescoping a part of her life she didn't like to think about. "She's been here a couple weeks, and I just found out."

Father John never took his eyes off her. "Is she okay?"

"I don't know. I drove up there this morning, but she wasn't around, or so one of the men told me. I informed him I'd be back at 6:30 sharp." She glanced at her wristwatch—a white habit she'd acquired, which she hated. She would have to drive like Mario Andretti to make it.

"Would you like me to go with you?" he asked, his voice calm, strong.

Vicky turned the offer over in her mind. Yes, she

would like him to go with her. She shook her head. "This is something Susan's father and I have to handle."

Father John smiled, and she sensed his disappointment, his understanding that this was a family matter in which he had no part.

Vicky had buttoned her brown wool coat, flung a scarf around her neck, and switched off the light when she remembered her briefcase. She stepped in the darkness to the file cabinet. Grabbing the briefcase off the top, she glanced out the window just as Father John walked under the streetlight toward the red Toyota pickup, his cowboy hat pulled forward. Tiny dots of snow, like a light rain, fluttered around him. He looked so alone she could have wept.

She watched until he disappeared inside the cab. Until the Toyota nosed away from the curb and drove into the shadows of the street. Suddenly headlights flipped on at the corner. A green truck churned through a U-turn and accelerated after the Toyota.

‹ 13 ›

Snow swept lightly across the Bronco's hood and glistened in the headlights, and the wipers swung in intermittent half-circles to brush away the flakes. Vicky tried to shake off the notion that the green truck was following Father John by concentrating on the road climbing ahead. Crazy, she thought. Who would be following him? Anybody who wanted to talk to Father John O'Malley could find him at St. Francis Mission any day of the week. But for how long, how long?

The Bronco swung into the long curve before the turnoff into Lean Bear's ranch. Vicky tapped on the brake pedal, scanning the road for the black faces of ice that showed here and there through the snow. She turned right, then stopped at the metal gate, glancing at the little green light on the dashboard. Six-twenty-nine. The bozo from this morning knew she'd be back and had made sure the gate was closed.

She switched off the ignition, grabbed the floppy black bag next to her, and slid into the icy outdoors. Moonlight filtered through the clouds, casting gray shadows over the snow. She heard the soft swish of the wind in the ponderosas. She pulled the wool scarf under her chin, set the strap of her bag firmly over one shoulder, and trudged to the gate. The chain was thick enough to discourage a herd of buffalo from attempting to break through. Fresh tracks packed the snow on the other side, and a dim light glowed from the house.

Suddenly Vicky had a sense of someone watching her, as if she were surrounded by ghosts. She glanced about, silencing her own breathing, half expecting the white man to step out from the trees. No one. She turned back to the gate. About a foot and a half separated each of the three horizontal bars. She had climbed hundreds of gates like this, sat on the top rail for hours watching her father and grandfather brand the new calves, slid off the rail onto the back of her own pony, and raced across the earth. But not in a suit, coat, hose, and dressy leather boots.

She tossed her bag over, then grabbed the middle bar and scrunched down, pulling her upper body through the narrow space. She twisted around to bring her right leg over the lower bar, then the left. Snow slid inside her boots; she felt as if she'd waded into ice water. She picked up the bag and started down the driveway, walking in the hard-packed tracks.

A wave of memories washed over her as she approached the house. She remembered the plywood siding she and Ben had installed one summer and painted the color of green apples. The old pickup she had loaded the kids into the day she had decided to leave. And the memory she hadn't experienced, only imagined: Ben coming through the front door and finding her and the kids gone. The pictures dissolved into a jumble of black-and-white images, like an old movie reeling itself out.

She pounded hard on the front door, her glove muffling the sound. She yanked it off and pounded again. The static noise of a television mingled with the hiss of the wind. She waited a moment, tried the doorknob, and was surprised when it turned in her hand. "Susan," she called, stepping into the small living room. The odors of cigarettes and stale food met her.

The room was a contrast of light and shadow: the shaft of light from the kitchen; the greenish light flickering off a television set; the shadows everywhere else. Slowly a figure began to uncurl from the sofa against the opposite wall. "Mom? What're you doin' here?"

Vicky set the door in place, a mixture of relief and terror welling inside her. This child-woman in rumpled sweats with long black hair plastered to the sides of her head, with circles under her eyes so dark even the dim light couldn't conceal them—this was her beautiful daughter.

Susan stretched one hand toward a small table, groping among empty beer bottles, ashtrays overflowing with cigarette butts, and Styrofoam fast food boxes. She fingered a pair of glasses and slipped them on. Her eyes loomed large and accusing behind the wire-framed lenses.

"Are you okay, honey?" Vicky's voice rose over the noise of the television. ". . . your question, please. Would you care to guess? . . ." *Jeopardy*. She crossed the room and lowered herself onto the sofa, close to her daughter. The old black-and-white TV, the table, the sofa—all as she remembered, smaller, perhaps, more haggard-looking. The detritus of her old life.

"Yeah, I'm okay." Susan flopped both bare feet onto the linoleum floor and attempted to sit up, then slouched against the back cushion. "I was takin' a nap." Her words came slowly, as if she had formed them through wired jaws.

Vicky's stomach twisted into knots. The signs loomed like billboards on the interstate. Not just the lethargy and fogginess of marijuana, but something else—another kind of drug, which she was at a loss to identify.

"I was surprised to hear you'd come back," she managed.

"Yeah, well, I was gonna call you, but . . . no phone. Didn't we used to have a phone here? Yeah, it was on the kitchen counter next to the toaster. You used to talk to Grandmother while you smeared jelly on our toast. See, I remember." Susan brought one hand up to her forehead. "Did you take the phone?"

"Susan, you're sick. Let me help you."

Her daughter shook her head, like a child in a temper. "No, Mom. I'm tellin' you, I'm fine." She pushed herself to her feet. "Look, you want some coffee or something?"

Vicky nodded and followed her daughter into the kitchen. Dirty plastic dishes, more empty beer bottles and Styrofoam boxes, papers, and stacks of catalogues spread over the countertops and the yellow Formica table. A door on the left opened onto a dark hallway that led to the two bedrooms. The house felt hot and close, as if there were a shortage of air. She dropped her bag onto the clutter on the table and unbuttoned her coat, letting it slide back loosely around her shoulders.

Susan mechanically filled two mugs with tap water and shuffled along the counter. Stopping in front of a cluster of jars, she opened one and spilled instant coffee crystals into the mugs. Vicky pushed some papers and dirty dishes out of the way so Susan could set the mugs on the table. Tiny black specks floated in the brownish liquid.

"I didn't come here to argue," Vicky said, taking one of the two chairs at the table.

Susan slid onto the other. "So why'd you come?"

Vicky began again. "Your father said you and three men plan to start some kind of crafts business. If I can help you—"

"You can't." Susan's eyes blinked behind her glasses.

"We've got things figured out, okay? We're gonna get the moccasins and beaded stuff that people make around here. And we're gonna advertise in catalogues." She drew a catalogue from a pile and set it next to an open Styrofoam box with pieces of wilting lettuce still clinging to the sides. "Everybody wants Indian stuff. We're gonna make a lot of money."

Vicky took a sip of coffee. It was tepid and bitter. This idea sounded so good, so possible, except that Susan was stoned on something. Her hand shook as she lifted her mug. "Your friends are from Los Angeles?"

"You mean, are they white? Yeah, so what?" After a moment, Susan added, "My friends know all about starting a business. One's a real professor." Still the shaking. Little drops of coffee ran down the sides of her mug.

"So why do you need them?" Vicky asked. "You're the one Our People will trust. You're the one who can go to their homes and contract for the crafts. You could run the business yourself." Then she added, "Once you were clean."

"Don't bug me, Mom." Susan got to her feet, gripping the edge of the table so hard her knuckles blanched. "Maybe you better go away and leave me alone. You're real good at that."

Here it was, the blow Vicky realized she had been waiting for. Susan and Lucas never forgot she had left them, even though no one else on the reservation ever mentioned it. It was traditional for Arapaho grandparents to help raise the grandchildren. What had kept the moccasin telegraph buzzing for years was that she'd left Ben. And for what? To go to school and become a white woman, to become *Hisei:ci´:nihi,* Woman Alone.

Vicky pushed her chair back and walked around the table. She placed an arm around Susan's thin shoulders.

"Please come home with me. Just for a few days. You can clean up, get some food in you. You'll feel better. I'll bring you back."

The girl shrugged off Vicky's arm. "I don't need your help. I got Ty. He's here for me, and I can count on him. Me and Ty, we're gonna get married. So, please, just go."

"You heard what she said, Mom." The male voice came from the living room, and Vicky swung around as the man she'd met earlier came through the kitchen doorway. He seemed larger here than he'd appeared outdoors: six feet tall, with a thick neck, and shoulders and forearms that filled out the sleeves of his down jacket. His blond curly hair was matted in places, as if he'd just removed the knit cap he held in one gloved hand. A light stubble covered his cheeks and chin like a rash. He was about Susan's age.

Two other men followed him into the kitchen and lined up next to the counter. One was also in his twenties, thin and dark-haired, in blue jeans and a thick jean jacket. Susan sidled toward him, and he draped one arm over her shoulders, a gesture of ownership. The other man was short and heavyset, with a round face partly hidden by a dark beard streaked with silver. He had brown curly hair and pebble-like eyes that looked out from plastic-rimmed glasses. He could be her own age—forty-two—too old to be hanging out with kids.

"Who are you?" Vicky demanded.

"This is Ty," Susan said. Then, nodding toward the blond, she added, "This here's Gary." Another nod. "And that's the professor I told you about."

"What'd ya tell her?" Gary said, his tone sharp.

"Nothin'." Susan leaned into the dark-haired man.

Vicky stepped between Gary and the couple her daughter had become. "Susan, please come with me."

"She said no, Mom." This from Gary behind her. "So I'll just walk you out to your Bronco."

Vicky sensed that even if Susan wanted to leave, Gary would not allow it. Her daughter was a prisoner. The question mark was the dark-haired man with his arm slung over Susan's shoulder. How did he fit in? "I'll be back," Vicky said, not taking her eyes off Susan's. Did she imagine it, or was there the smallest flicker of gratitude?

Vicky edged past Gary and the professor. Grabbing her bag off the table, she strode to the front door. There were footsteps behind her. "I don't want your company," she said, letting herself out. She hurried across the yard and down the road, aware of Gary's boots crunching the snow. She made herself breathe deeply. The bastard was trying to scare her. When she reached the gate, the footsteps stopped.

Vicky glanced back. "Are you going to open this, or do I have to crawl over?"

Gary stood about ten feet away, arms folded, a dark shadow in the moonlight. He didn't move.

She tossed her bag between the top and middle rails, then leaned down, grabbed the middle bar and propelled herself to the other side more quickly and easily than before. Retrieving the bag from the snow, she straightened upright and walked to the Bronco.

She got in quickly and turned on the ignition, sending the wheels into a whining spin. Framed in the rearview mirror was the white man, leaning over the gate, raising one hand and saluting her. The old guilt tightened its grip, like some creature attempting to drag her into its dark hiding place. She was leaving Susan again. Oh, God, who was she leaving her with this time?

Vicky drove down the canyon and across the reservation to the Arapaho ranch, scarcely aware of the falling snow, as if she were outside of time. She parked in front of the massive log cabin and ran up the stairs to the porch that extended along the front. Snow piled over the folded aluminum chairs stacked next to the wood railing. Here was where the cowboys sat on summer evenings, smoking and rocking back on the thin chair legs, boots propped on the railing.

She pounded on the wood door. In a moment it swung open and canned television laughter, mixed with the guffaws of male voices, floated toward her. In the doorway, silhouetted by the light indoors, stood Ben's cousin, Nate Holden, shorter than Ben and broader, dressed in blue jeans and a plaid shirt. "What do *you* want?"

"I'm looking for Ben," Vicky said.

Nate stepped back, bringing the door with him. He didn't ask her in. Behind him was the cavernlike main room with log walls two stories high, the upstairs balcony that led to the bunkrooms, the sloping wood ceiling, and the plank floors strewn with faded Navajo rugs. There was a wedge of shiny pine cabinets visible from the kitchen.

She stepped sideways to get a view of the living area. Three Arapaho men sat on a Naugahyde sofa, arms folded, legs outstretched, boots dug into a rug. A couple of other Arapahos occupied two upholstered chairs. There was a vacant chair, its seat crinkled and sunken, probably from the weight of Nate Holden. A television rested on a metal cart against the wall, and a cloud of cigarette smoke hung in the air. She felt a kind of longing; she could use a cigarette right now herself. "You satisfied?" Nate said, watching her. "Ben ain't here."

The others had turned toward her, as if Ben Holden's ex-wife showing up at the Arapaho ranch at 9 P.M. promised more entertainment than any *M*A*S*H* rerun.

Vicky said, "Where can I find him?"

"He want to see you?" Nate's hostility was so thick she could almost touch it. Ben's family had never forgiven her. It was a wife's duty to stay by her husband.

"Ben's watchin' a couple sick calves at the upper range," volunteered one of the Indians on the sofa. He looked about twenty. Perhaps he'd grown up with Susan and Lucas.

Of course. On more than one occasion, Ben had stayed up two nights running to tend a sick animal. "Thanks," she called out as she turned and started down the porch stairs. The young man hollered, "His cabin's up the road about six miles. Can't miss it."

Little eddies of snow scudded into the headlights, and Vicky gripped the wheel as the Bronco climbed through a tunnel of cedars and aspens. She had never been to the upper pasture of the Arapaho ranch. She hoped it existed, that the young Arapaho hadn't done Nate a favor by sending her up a mountain in what could turn into a blizzard. She shook off the thought.

As the Bronco came out of a long curve, she saw light flickering like a campfire through the cedars. After another half mile she spotted the cabin itself, a smaller version of the bunkhouse she'd just left, with light glowing in the windows. Beyond the cabin loomed the shadow of a barn. As she pulled up, she heard a door slam. A figure emerged from the darkness into the stream of her headlights. She knew by his walk it was Ben.

"Never thought I'd see this night," he said, opening her door. He wore the sheepskin coat and tan cowboy hat she remembered from the night before. A line of snow lay along the brim.

"Ben, we've got to talk about Susan."

"Too damn cold to talk outside," he said. She felt the pressure of his gloved hand on her arm as he guided her out of the Bronco and toward the cabin. He walked a little ahead, his boots packing the snow. Stepping onto the wooden stoop, he bent down to grip the metal handle set low on the door for people in the Old Time, shorter people. He motioned her inside. "This is where I've been hanging my hat lately," he said.

Vicky took in the cabin at a glance: combination stove, sink, refrigerator, and cabinet against one wall; card table and two folding chairs in the center of the plank floor; two chairs with wads of gray stuffing poking from the cushions; cast-iron stove that gave off a hissing, crackling noise and flooded the room with warmth. The bed stood against the far wall. Spread across the top was the blue-and-white star quilt Ben's grandmother had given them on their wedding day.

She stared at it with a kind of shock, as if she had unwittingly touched an electric wire. The star quilt: No true Arapaho home could be without one. Its lines and circles and stars were a reminder that all creation is alive, even the sky and the earth, and that all creatures are meant to live in harmony. She swallowed hard against the sense of the past welling inside her.

Crossing the room, Ben lifted a log out of a wood box, opened the stove's little metal door, and tossed the log onto the fire. "That should keep us plenty warm." Then, glancing back at her he asked, "You had supper yet?"

Vicky shook her head. She'd intended to get a bite before driving out to Lean Bear's ranch, but she hadn't had time after John O'Malley's visit. She laid her coat and bag over one of the chairs, suddenly aware of the hollow feeling in her stomach.

Ben shucked off the sheepskin coat and hung it over a wooden peg on one wall. He set his hat on top. In two steps he was at the stove, flicking a match while pressing one of the small black knobs on the stove front, lighting the burner under a metal coffee pot. Then he lit the burner under a large pan. "How about some stew?" he asked.

"Your recipe?" Vicky asked.

Ben laughed. Plunging a spoon into the stew, he said, "The cook down at the bunkhouse sent it up. Didn't want it on her conscience, my starving to death. I've had a couple of sick calves on my hands. Haven't had a chance to eat yet." Still stirring the stew, he looked at her and smiled. "Must've been waiting for you."

"Ben . . ."

He nodded. "This is about Susan. But we can get some grub in us first." He ladled the stew into two pottery bowls and placed them on the table. Then he filled two mugs with coffee and set them next to the bowls. In an instant he produced plastic spoons and knives, half a loaf of bread in a plastic bag, and a tub of margarine.

Nokooho. The word sprang into Vicky's mind as she sat down. Out of the natural order. In the eleven years she'd been married to Ben, he had never waited on her. Warriors did not wait upon women. Warriors rode out and slaughtered the buffalo, and brought the carcasses back to the village for the women to butcher and preserve and tan and dry, to cook and to serve. Warriors did not perform the undignified tasks of women.

"Surprised you, huh?" Ben took the folding chair across from her, looking pleased. He could always read her thoughts, sometimes even before she had them in focus. But he hadn't read her intention to leave him, hadn't even suspected.

Steam curled out of her bowl, which was filled with lumps of meat, potatoes, and carrots in brown gravy. It smelled of sage. After the first few bites, she began to feel warmer, calmer. Ben was eating, too, and she was aware he hadn't taken his eyes off her. "You saw Susan?" he said finally. The time was ready.

Vicky set her spoon next to the almost empty bowl. "She's on drugs again, but I don't know what she's using."

Ben seemed to consider this as he spread a yellowish glob of margarine onto a slice of bread. After a moment, he said, "Stop blaming yourself. If Susan's got herself screwed up again with drugs, it's not just your fault." He laid the knife across the top of the opened margarine tub and regarded her a long moment. "It's my fault, too, Vicky."

Vicky heard the catch in her own breath. She could hardly believe what she had just heard. She had been carrying the guilt alone, a heavy burden. And now he had stepped up to shoulder his share. She felt the years fall away, and in the forty-six-year-old man with gray mingled in the black of his hair she glimpsed the young warrior with soft black eyes, so handsome she hadn't dared hope he could ever notice her, the man she had crawled out of her bedroom window on summer nights to meet, the man she had run away with and married.

Vicky switched her eyes away. The cabin felt smaller, the heat from the stove oppressive. She would not be drawn into the circle of his charm. She forced herself to focus on the present. "Discussing who's at fault won't help Susan. We have to get her away from Lean Bear's ranch."

"Are you suggesting we kidnap her?" Ben set the slice of bread on the table.

"You could evict the white men."

Ben shrugged. "On what grounds? They've paid six months' rent. In any case, they would have thirty days to leave. Longer, if they took the eviction notice to tribal court. You know that. You're the lawyer. And what if they did leave? Susan might go with them."

Vicky sipped at the coffee still hot in her mug. Probably so. In any case, evicting the lot of them wouldn't get Susan into drug rehab, which was what she needed. "Your turn," she said, setting the mug down.

"Susan told me they're going to start a business. It could work for her. I say let her have her chance."

"Business? Don't make me laugh. Where do you think she's getting whatever drug she's on? Those three men haven't come here to sell Indian crafts. They're here to sell drugs."

Ben said, "We both know Susan would never bring drug dealers to her people."

Vicky pushed her chair back and got to her feet. She turned and stared at the window, watching the flakes chain along the edges. What was she thinking? Just because Susan had slipped back onto drugs out of her own pain didn't mean her three friends were drug dealers. Where was the evidence? She was jumping to conclusions. She almost laughed out loud thinking of the way an opposing attorney would tear something like this to shreds in a courtroom.

"Don't worry so much, honey," Ben said. There was the sound of chair legs scraping the plank floor and footsteps. In a heartbeat, he was behind her, slipping his arms around her waist, his breath warm on her neck. A rush of remembered feelings came over her: the comfort and excitement of the man who had been her husband. She tried to push them away. They belonged in the past, not in the Time Being.

"Don't, Ben," she said, turning within the little circle he'd made. Instantly his mouth was on hers, searching as if he would devour her.

She pushed against his chest as hard as she could, and he stepped back, a mixture of anger and bewilderment on his face. "You want me just as much as I want you," he said. "You want us back together."

Vicky slid sideways toward the kitchen stove, feeling the knobs against the small of her back. She didn't trust herself to move, didn't trust her loneliness. If he came toward her again, if he touched her, she might go willingly with him, just as she'd done all those years ago, and the woman she had become would no longer exist.

"I want you back, Vicky," he was saying. "Any way you can come back to me, I want you to come. You tell me how it has to be, and that's the way it'll be. Hell, I'll serve you supper every night." He nodded toward the card table. "You know you want to come back. That's why you came here tonight."

"This isn't about us," Vicky said. The strength in her

own voice surprised her. "It's about our daughter. We have to find some way to help her."

"That's right." Ben raised his voice. "The only reason Susan's got problems is because we had problems—I had a problem. But I'm not drinking anymore. Soon as we're okay, Susan's going to be okay. Once her parents are back together, she'll be able to help herself."

Vicky let his words hang in the air without a reply. It was clear to her now, his view of the world. He'd seized the chance to tell her about Susan last night, knowing she would race out to Lean Bear's ranch today, find Susan in trouble, and come here this evening. Who else could she turn to except Susan's father? Who would arrange to be at the cabin in the upper pasture alone, would have the cook send up the stew. And everything in his world would be set right. They would get back together; Susan's problems would disappear. It would be as if the past had never existed.

She stepped around him, by the little card table with the empty bowls and mugs, the margarine-coated bread, and slipped into her coat. "I know you love Susan," she said. "But this isn't the answer. The past is what it is."

A blast of cold air hit her as she opened the front door and stepped outside. "Don't go," Ben said. She pulled the door behind her, feeling as if she had stepped back from the edge of a precipice.

Vicky drove through a white world. Whiteness drifted in the air, piled onto the hood, clung to the windshield and fell away at the whoosh of the wipers. She sat hunched over the steering wheel, feeling alone and scared for Susan, willing the Bronco across the white stretches of Wind River Reservation, down Highway 789, through the snow-shrouded streets of Lander.

How easy it would be to do what Ben and his family and all the grandmothers, even her own family, would celebrate—going back to Ben. She thought about what Grandfather had once told her: "We are edge people. We live at the edge of two worlds, white and Arapaho. It is hard to remember who we are when we dwell in the edge space." *Ah, Grandfather. You don't know. You don't know.*

She parked in the driveway, aware of the tiredness seeping through her, and walked across the snow to the porch. The knob on the front door spun in her gloved hand before she'd turned the key. She stopped. She always locked the door here. On the reservation, she had never locked the door. If someone came to take your material possessions, well, that person must be in great need. That was the Arapaho Way, but this was the white world.

She had been so distracted this morning, she must have forgotten. She pushed the door open and stepped into the warmth. Even before she had snapped on the light switch, she sensed another presence, heard the quiet sounds of breathing. Her heart leaped against her ribs.

"'Bout time you got home, Mom," Gary said. He sat at the end of her sofa, boots propped on the stack of magazines on her coffee table.

❮ 15 ❯

Father John saw the shadow dart through the trees. He ran after it, up the wooded hillside of Boston College, his heart pounding. He was close, but as soon as he reached for the shadow, it darted away. The sounds of traffic on Commonwealth Avenue, the clanging of a Green Line trolley, filtered through the trees. For a moment the ringing seemed a continuation of the dream. He sat up, disoriented. Then he realized it was the phone. Marcus, he thought. They've found Marcus. It struck him it was Marcus's shadow he'd been chasing—the ghost was walking in his dreams.

He swung out of bed and made his way down the dim hallway. The phone perched on the stairway landing. He always trailed the extension cord up the stairs when he went to bed in case someone tried to reach him in the middle of the night. He went down on one knee, aware of the hard wood floor biting into his kneecap as he lifted the receiver.

"Can you come over?" It was Vicky. He heard the terror in her voice.

"Right away," he said. As the buzzing noise sounded, the frantic feeling of the dream washed over him. This wasn't about some Indian kid arrested for disturbing the peace or driving under the influence, or about arranging an adoption or counseling somebody thinking of divorce. This was about Vicky.

He could hear Father Peter moving around inside his bedroom, and he told the old man through the door he'd been called on an emergency. In a few minutes, he was dressed and out the front door. The metal gears screeched into the silence as the Toyota pickup lurched onto Circle Drive. It had stopped snowing, but a blanket of downy snow lay over the earth. Seventeen-Mile Road and Highway 789 blended into the white open spaces. The occasional track of a squirrel or coyote or red fox dotted the snow. The eastern sky was lit with bands of scarlet and plum; the sun would be up soon. He thought of what Thomas Spotted Horse had once said: Each human being faces the rising sun and the day that it brings alone.

Father John kept the gas pedal down, ignoring the occasional loss of traction and sideways slip. He could still hear the terror in Vicky's voice, and he knew he was trying to outrun his own alarm as he raced to Lander.

The Toyota slid against the curb in front of her house. Light seeped around the slats of the window blinds and fell in yellow stripes across the snowy yard. He jumped out and ran up the sidewalk.

"Thank God, you're here," Vicky said. Her breath came quickly as if she were sobbing. She still had on the dark suit from yesterday, but her hair hung loose, not clipped in back the way he was used to seeing it. There were black smudges under her eyes. She turned abruptly and walked over between the sofa and coffee table. Magazines lay scattered over the top, crowding the pottery bowl, which was filled with ashes and butts. A cigarette and matchbook lay to one side. She picked up the cigarettes and pulled one out. After fumbling with the matches, she finally managed to light up.

"I bought them yesterday, the cigarettes," she said as if he wouldn't know what she was talking about. After taking a long draw, she laid the cigarette in the bowl and began combing her fingers through her hair, pulling at it.

"What happened?" Father John felt his heart pounding against his ribs. This was not the Vicky he knew.

"I was so worried about Susan," she began, and he realized with a kind of shock she was still explaining the cigarettes. She was hysterical. "So after yesterday morning at the ranch, I bought them at the Seven Eleven. But when I stopped off at home, I threw them away. I didn't want to take them to the office. I didn't want to start smoking again. But last night, after he left, I dug them out of the bottom of the wastepaper basket."

Father John was at her side in two steps. He put his arms around her and held her close, trying to comfort her, as he would have comforted his own child perhaps, or his wife. Her hair smelled faintly of sage, and she was trembling. "Who, Vicky? Tell me. What happened to you?"

"He was here on the sofa. Gary. One of the white men with Susan. Sitting right here, waiting for me. I always lock the door. I don't know how he got in. Maybe I forgot, or maybe he jimmied the lock somehow."

"Did he hurt you?" Father John wasn't sure what he would do, how he would react, if this Gary had hurt her. He could feel the anger waiting to flood over him, an enormous black reservoir held in check by such a thin membrane of rationality. For an instant, he glimpsed the force that might drive a man to kill another human being.

"He didn't touch me," Vicky said. The trembling was quieter now, and Father John let his arms relax around her. His own relief was like another presence in the room. He wanted only good things for her, prayed that only goodness would follow her.

She stepped back and sank into the middle cushion of the sofa. Reaching toward the bowl, she crushed out the cigarette, keeping her eyes on the little trail of blue smoke that floated upward.

Father John sat down beside her. "What did he want?"

"He said if I loved my daughter—" Vicky stopped a moment, then continued, "if I loved Susan, I would leave her alone. I would stay away from the ranch. He said Susan wanted him to tell me because she didn't know how." She paused, gathering strength for the dash into the heart of it. "He threatened to hurt her."

Father John felt the anger rising in his throat. He swallowed hard, to keep it under control. "What did you do?"

Vicky moved to the edge of the cushion. "The minute that bastard walked out the door, I dialed 911, but I hung up. Before I start pressing charges, I have to get Susan away. She's sick, John. She's using drugs again, and she needs treatment. I have to make sure she's safe before I nail Gary's hide to the wall."

Father John realized she'd probably walked the floor all night, turning over all the options. If she had Gary arrested now, she might alienate her daughter. Susan came first. "I don't understand," he said. "Why would this goon show up here and threaten you?"

"Last night I tried talking Susan into coming home with me. With a little more time, I might've convinced her. But Gary and another man—Susan calls him 'the professor'—and Ty, the man she's involved with, showed up. It was pretty obvious Gary didn't want her to leave. If I don't get her away from there . . ." Vicky's voice was rising, ". . . what will happen to her?"

"What about Ben?" Father John wasn't sure why he'd asked, except that yesterday she had made it clear anything having to do with Susan was between her and Ben. He did not want to trespass where he knew he didn't belong—in her family.

Vicky got to her feet and began circling the room. "Ben believes in miracles. Susan's problems will disappear if only—" She stopped and looked at him. "I can't count on Ben. I never could. All night I've been trying to figure out how to get Susan out of the clutches of that monster, and I think I've got it figured out."

"Then let's go get her," Father John said. He was relieved she had called him, but he was also certain that, had she not reached him, she would have gone alone.

The sun hung low on the eastern horizon, like a laser shooting white beams over the snowy earth. Father John squinted against the glare as they headed north on Highway 287. Before they'd left, she had changed into jeans, a bulky red sweater, and a jacket patterned like an Indian blanket, while he'd invaded her kitchen and made himself a cup of instant coffee.

Now she sat beside him, gripping a pair of binoculars, talking about Susan. He listened quietly, allowing her thoughts to take shape, a habit of the confessional. He heard how Susan would crawl out of bed at night and crouch on the chest under the window to watch the stars, and how Vicky would find her there when she went to check on the children. How she would stay with her and hold her—Susan was so small then. And how they talked about Sister Moon and the Star Nations, the Star Men who had brought the people the sacred gift of sage, a symbol of the mysteries of the sky. All the things her grandmother had told her, she had tried to tell Susan. "But there was so little time," Vicky said. "So little time together."

Father John glanced at the woman next to him. She had the profile of her people, the high cheekbones, the fine nose with just a hint of a bump at the top, the dark, glistening eyes, the brown skin with the trace of red on her lips, the shiny black hair pulled back now into a beaded clasp. She was beautiful. "Susan will be all right," he said, hoping she wouldn't sense his own misgivings.

After a few miles of silence, Vicky blurted out, "Gary and the others are drug dealers. I'm sure of it. They're supplying Susan."

This could be, Father John thought. The idea had already started to play at the edges of his mind, but he hadn't wanted to acknowledge it. He didn't like the logical conclusion—that Susan Holden had brought drug dealers to the reservation. He said nothing as the Toyota started climbing up Sage Canyon, threading the narrow road between the mountainside and the steep drop-off into the creek. They'd gone about five miles when Vicky asked him to slow down. She had turned sideways and was staring beyond him, out his window. "There it is," she said. "The old logging road."

Father John saw the narrow cut, like a wagon road nearly lost in snow between the rock outcroppings. Easing up on the accelerator, he turned into the cut and started winding up the road. The wheels munched the snow, and the cedar branches scraped the roof. He hoped the Toyota wouldn't get stuck.

Vicky sat forward, one hand braced on the dashboard. "Just ahead," she directed.

The pickup lurched upward through the trees, groaning into the mountain stillness. "This is it," Vicky said. Before he had brought the pickup to a full stop, she was out the passenger door.

He followed her around a pile of boulders, ducking past the cedars. The wind sighed in the trees; snow sifted around them. It felt ten degrees colder. Vicky stopped, peered through the binoculars a moment, then started climbing the boulders. Standing above him like a sentinel in the Old Time, she raised the binoculars again. "Perfect," she said.

He followed her up the boulders, so slick in the snow he had to grab a branch to keep from sliding backward. She handed him the binoculars, and he bent toward her slightly to see around the branches. A small frame house with faded gray-green paint came into view. The front end of a truck was visible behind the house.

"See anyone?"

"Not a creature stirring."

"The truck's still there," Vicky said. "If I'm right, they'll leave any minute. By the time I got here yesterday morning, the truck was already gone. If Gary hadn't come back, I might've been able to talk to Susan then."

They handed the binoculars back and forth, stamping their feet, clapping their gloved hands in the cold. Father John's feet and hands felt numb. Suddenly Vicky leaned so far into the binoculars he was afraid she might tumble down. "The front door just opened," she said. "Looks like the professor coming out. And somebody behind him, but I can't tell who. He's got on a blue parka like the one Gary wore last night, but his hat's pulled down too far to make him out. They're walking

back to the truck," she said, handing him the binoculars.

Father John watched the cloud of blue exhaust burst
alongside the house. Out of the cloud rolled a gray
truck, which gathered speed then stopped at the gate. A
tall man in a blue parka jumped from the driver's side,
fiddled with the gate, then swung it open. The man
looked familiar. He got back in, and the gray pickup
spun out onto Sage Canyon road.

"What does Gary look like?" Father John asked.

Vicky shrugged. "Like a white man. Tall, muscular,
blond hair, stubbly face, as if he can't quite grow a
beard. Why?"

"Gary picked me up Sunday night on Rendezvous
Road after I'd found the body." He didn't tell her Gary
had come close to running him down first and had then
left him stranded in a blizzard at Jake Littlehorse's
garage. Vicky was worried enough about Susan.

They picked their way down over the boulders and
hurried to the Toyota. Neither spoke. Father John knew
she was probably thinking what he was thinking. If it
wasn't Gary in the pickup just now, he would still be in
the house with Susan.

◀ 16 ▶

Whoever the driver was, he'd left the gate open. Father John drove the Toyota past and stopped next to the ranch house. "Gary must have thought he'd scared me off," Vicky said.

"He didn't know you." Father John swung out of the pickup and followed her to the front door. She turned the knob and pushed the door open. As they walked in, a tall, thin-shouldered young man with dark, straggly hair lifted himself off the sofa and stumbled against the small table, sending a couple of empty beer cans scuttling across the top. He looked as if he'd just awakened and the world wasn't yet in focus.

"Susan's not up yet, Mrs. Holden," he said, deference in his tone. He had on a red shirt, ragged at the elbows, with the collar partly turned under and the V-neck exposing a dirty gray T-shirt. His jeans were smeared with grease, and he was in stockinged feet. There were holes in the toes of his black socks.

Vicky brushed past him and into the kitchen. Father John followed, watching her retreat down a dim hallway, then he stepped back to the living room. The young man looked about to go after her, but Father John blocked the way. "Are you Ty?"

"What're you doin' here?" the young man asked.

Something about the question made Father John wonder if Ty knew who he was. He switched off the idea. Even if Gary had mentioned giving Father O'Malley a ride last Sunday night, how would Ty know he was Father O'Malley? He'd never seen this young man before.

"I've come with Mrs. Holden. I'm Father John O'Malley from St. Francis."

"Oh, man, this is gettin' really squirrely." Ty staggered backward, his eyes darting about as if he expected something to materialize. He shook his head, a frantic motion. "Susan isn't leavin' here."

The jerky movements, the explosion about to erupt—Father John knew the signs. Drugs or alcohol, the behavior was the same. There was a sense of helplessness about the kid—he wasn't much more than a kid, probably in his early twenties. But the wrong word, the wrong tone, and anger would burst forth like a bronco out of a chute.

He kept his voice calm. "Susan belongs in treatment. Her mother wants to help her."

"I been lookin' after her. Me and Susan, we're gonna get married. You think I don't care what happens to her?" The young man's tone rose; his fists clenched at his sides.

"Of course I don't," Father John said. "I'm sure you love her."

Ty's fists relaxed a little, and Father John felt the tension begin to evaporate.

"I been helpin' her cut back, but last night, after her mom left, she got pretty stoned, you know? Like, man, she passed out on me. I got scared she was gonna stop breathin' or something, but she come out of it, and this morning she wanted another hit 'cause, you know, she's feelin' pretty sick. I say, no way."

"What's she on?" Father John decided to take a chance on the dissolving tension. Any information might prove helpful.

"Pot." The young man shrugged.

"Anything else?"

Ty ran one hand through his hair. "Just pot."

"Where does she get it?"

"Hey, man, what is this?" The tension rolled back between them. "You think I'm her supplier? She was smokin' out in L.A. before I met her. She brought her stash with her. I been tryin' to get her off it."

Sure, Father John thought. *You're on it yourself, whatever it is.* Just then a shuffling noise sounded, and Vicky came into the living room, one arm around the thin shoulders of a young woman in green sweats, a younger version of Vicky herself. The girl looked dazed, as if it were an effort to place one foot after the other. The small suitcase in Vicky's other hand scraped against the wall, and Father John took it from her.

"You shouldn't be goin' nowhere, Susan," Ty said, a rising panic in his tone. "Gary's gonna go crazy if he finds you gone."

Susan turned blank eyes on the young man and leaned against her mother. Father John slipped his free arm around the girl's waist to keep her from listing sideways as they made their way to the front door. He'd seen enough drug overdoses in enough emergency rooms to know by the raspy sound of her breathing that the girl was in trouble. It would be a race to the Lander hospital.

As he pulled the door shut, Father John caught a glimpse of Ty watching them. The young man was capable of serious resistance, yet he was letting them take Susan away. He must care for her, and Father John was glad for that. Not since he was a kid back in Boston had he had to fight somebody off, and it wasn't something he wanted to do again. But if Ty had tried to stop them, he would have had no choice.

Father John and Vicky sat on the small sofa outside the emergency room of the Lander Community Hospital, waiting for the stocky, middle-aged nurse to appear through the swinging door and deliver another of her intermittent reports. They'd given Susan a shot of Adrenalin. They'd taken a urine sample, but the lab report wouldn't be back for a day. Susan claimed she only smoked some pot, but they knew that wasn't true. The girl was scared. A good sign. A psychiatrist was on the way to talk with her. Maybe she'd tell the truth. It would be easier to help her if they knew the truth.

"What do you think it is?" Vicky interrupted.

"The symptoms—respiratory depression, nausea, diarrhea—point to some type of opiate."

"Opiate." Vicky spit out the word. "You mean heroin."

"I'm afraid so." The nurse nodded before retreating behind the swinging door.

Father John placed his arm around Vicky's shoulders. The trembling was there again. He said, "If Gary and the others have brought heroin to the reservation, Banner needs to know."

"What are you saying?" Vicky jerked away. He was surprised at the intensity in her eyes. "The police would swarm all over Susan. She's too sick to handle that now."

"Vicky," Father John began, "this could be about more than drugs. This could be about murder. There's a dead body out there someplace, and Gary could be involved."

Vicky was shaking her head. "You're saying Susan might know about a murder? No. You're wrong. I know my daughter. She might use drugs, she might even be on heroin. . . ." Her tone rose until she was almost shouting. "But she would never be involved in murder. Don't you see, those men have used her to get on the reservation. She thinks they're going to start a legitimate business. She doesn't know anything about what they're doing."

Father John leaned back against the sofa and regarded her. This wasn't the best time for logic. She was too upset to think clearly. He reached out and took her hand. "Okay," he said.

They waited, mostly in silence, until the nurse reappeared. Susan's heart rate and blood pressure were stabilizing, but they were going to admit her to the psych unit for twenty-four-hour observation. After that, well, it depended upon whether she would agree to long-term treatment. Her mother could see her for a few minutes.

Vicky pushed herself up from the sofa. Before she disappeared through the swinging door, Father John took her hand again. He extracted a promise she would call 911 if she even *felt* Gary's presence nearby.

◀ 17 ▶

Highway 287 slid ahead like a conveyor belt, asphalt-streaked where the morning's traffic had worn away the snow. Light gray clouds dipped among the Wind River Mountains, but the stretch of milk-white plains glistened like fireflies in the sun. Father John missed the sounds of his favorite arias floating around him. He would have liked *La Bohème* now, or perhaps *Faust*. He drove absently, one finger on the rim of the steering wheel, his thoughts three years back when he'd looked up from his desk one morning and saw Vicky in the doorway.

"You don't know me," she had said. She was wrong. He knew her immediately, this striking Indian woman in a blue suit, holding a briefcase. The grandmothers had been clucking for weeks over the return of the *hu:xu'wa:ne'h,* the lawyer. They called her *Hisei:ci':nihi.* Woman Alone.

He had worked with her ever since, not for any grand notion of justice on an Indian reservation, but for the occasional fragment of justice for the man in the drunk tank, the kids lost in the bureaucratic maze of social services, the girl injured by a drunk driver. He had never expected such a gift, to have a woman like her at the edge of his life. Just to know she walked the earth at the same time and in the same place as he did was enough for him, and he was grateful. In different circumstances— But he couldn't imagine that. In different circumstances, he would not be the man he was.

He hadn't expected the gift of his priesthood either. It was an unfolding that had begun when he was an altar boy serving the early morning Mass at St. Marys. As the bell jangled through the apse at the elevation of the host, the sense had come over him of God's presence in the world, and of the priest, holding the host high, witnessing that presence.

A "calling," the church called a vocation to the priesthood. He had tried to stop up his ears. When he looked into the future, he had seen himself with a wife and a bunch of kids. He'd had girlfriends from the age of twelve, most of whose names he'd forgotten. He'd never missed a prom or a frat party, and senior year at Boston College he'd met Eileen. The thought of her was still charged with pain, not because he'd loved her, but because he'd allowed her to love him when he knew he had been called elsewhere. The day he'd told her he was entering the Jesuit seminary, she'd become hysterical, had begun pulling off her clothes and screaming he was a fool. He'd been in the seminary three months when she and his brother Mike ran off to New York and got married. He never thought of Eileen without uttering a prayer for forgiveness.

Absorbed in his thoughts, Father John nearly missed the turn onto Plunkett Road. He hit the brake pedal, which sent the Toyota into a skid. Heading toward the ditch, he steered into the skid until the pickup straightened itself.

At the top of a rise, he spotted Ike Yellow Calf's pickup backing out of the Depperts' driveway, which meant Marcus was still missing. It was time to bring the police in on this. Why was it every time he mentioned the police to an Arapaho lately, he met a wall of resistance? If the old people still resisted, he resolved to tell Banner himself and take the responsibility.

Father John parked in the snow-packed tracks vacated by Ike's truck. Newly chopped logs had been stacked against the fence and, most likely, piled beside the old people's stove. The kitchen cabinets were probably full. Ike was a good man, in the Arapaho Way. He was generous and thoughtful of others.

Inside, the house looked much the same, with Deborah hovering around and Joe propped in the recliner, the outsized casts pointing into the circle of heat. Color had seeped into the old man's face, but worry still lodged in his eyes. In both old people Father John sensed an attitude of resignation. They'd heard about the body by now. They'd probably heard stories about the ghost walking around. They would have put two and two together.

When Father John told them it was time to notify the police, they nodded, as if they'd already come to that conclusion. As he stood to leave, Joe grabbed him by the sleeve. "It might be some time before the police get around to lookin' for the boy. You keep tryin' to find him, okay? His grandmother and me, we gotta know what happened to him."

He had almost convinced himself he must be paranoid, thinking a green Dodge truck was following him, but now he wasn't so sure. There it was in the rearview mirror, staying with him down Plunkett Road and through the turn onto Ethete Road. As far as he knew, the only man upset with him right now might be Gary, the white man with the stubbly beard who didn't want Susan Holden to leave the ranch. But he and Vicky had taken the girl only this morning, and the truck had been shadowing him for two days now. Besides, Gary drove a gray Chevy truck.

As he turned into the main street of Fort Washakie, the truck fell back, and by the time he nosed the Toyota into the parking lot of the Wind River Law Enforcement Center, it had disappeared. He got out and crossed the pavement, slick with melted snow that had re-formed into ice. The sky had turned pale blue, with traces of snow clouds floating past the early afternoon sun.

The lobby was almost empty: two Arapahos waiting on the metal chairs, thumbing through magazines. Father John caught the clerk's eye behind the glass enclosure and mouthed "Chief Banner." She nodded and disappeared. After a moment she opened the door, and he slipped past. The corridor felt damp and smelled of wet wool and floor polish. Banner's voice floated toward him.

Father John stopped at the open door, waiting for the chief to finish his phone conversation. ". . . Couple of DUIs, disorderly, the usual. We'll fax over what we got," the chief said as he alternately picked up and dropped a file folder on top of a stack of others on his desk.

Banner replaced the receiver and waved Father John to a chair. "I've been leaving messages all over the rez for you," he said.

The office felt warm and close as Father John sat down. "You found the body?"

Banner gave a little shake to his head. "Almost three million acres on the rez, all snowed under. The fed says he needs an airplane and infrared to search for the body, but nobody's got that kind of budget. That body's not gonna turn up 'til spring."

If not the body, then what was on the chief's mind? Father John shifted in the chair as Banner pulled a yellow pad from under the pile of folders and clicked a ballpoint. "I understand you talked to a girl named Annie Chambeau yesterday."

Father John felt a flicker of surprise. The moccasin telegraph often turned out to be more efficient than he imagined. Banner must have heard Marcus was missing and had started looking for him. He leaned back, feeling a little more confident. The bigger the team on the playing field, the better the chance of finding the young man—or his body.

"Homicide," Banner said, tapping the ballpoint on the yellow pad.

"What?"

"Annie Chambeau caught a .32 slug in the chest last night."

◀ 18 ▶

"Coroner says victim was shot sometime between nine and midnight." Banner had flipped open the folder and was scanning the top page. It looked like a fax. "About eleven P.M., victim left girlfriend's house on Sweetwater Street and returned to the Grand Apartments, number three-F, to retrieve personal items. Victim did not make contact by midnight, and girlfriend notified Lander police. Call received at 12:06 A.M., by which time a unit had already been dispatched in response to a call at eleven fifty-five from Mrs. Herbert Skinner, resident of apartment one-A, reporting gunshots. Unit arrived at 12:10 A.M. and located victim. Perpetrator had evacuated premises. Police contact made with victim Friday night last. Victim issued citation for disturbing the peace. Contact also made Saturday night. Victim reported intruder had broken into her apartment."

"Dear God." Father John thumped his fist against the worn arm of the chair, disbelief and anger careening through him like a heat-seeking missile. In his mind's eye, he saw the girl across the table from him, hunched under a worn red coat, her hand trembling as she lifted the coffee mug, her life tangled and confused. No one had the right to deprive her of the future or the redemption it might have held, to efface her humanity, to reduce her to one among many inanimate objects—victim, perpetrator, premises.

"Girlfriend says victim met with you yesterday," Banner was saying. "Detective Loomis at the Lander PD asked me to find out what the meeting was about."

Father John had come here to report Marcus Deppert missing. That was all. He hadn't intended to tell Banner where to find the man who had driven the Chevy pickup near Rendezvous Road Sunday night, not yet. He had decided to give Vicky a little time. Now everything was changed. Now a girl was murdered. A girl connected to Marcus, whose body might have been in the ditch. And Gary might be responsible. It could have been Gary who ransacked Annie's apartment.

It was tenuous, this theory, full of holes. He had no evidence, just hunches. He felt as if he'd walked onto the mound and suddenly found out the game wasn't baseball. He wasn't sure of the rules. He drew in a long breath, then started at the beginning, explaining how he'd talked to Annie Chambeau on the chance she might know the whereabouts of Marcus Deppert.

"Marcus Deppert missing?" The chief looked up from the yellow pad. "There's no missing person's report."

That led to a side explanation on how the old people didn't want the police involved, to which Banner nodded, as if he understood and would have done the same in their position. "That boy has a history of gettin' himself into trouble. No tellin' what he's up to this time." The chief's ballpoint pen made little scratchy noises on the pad.

Father John continued. The white man who had broken into Annie's apartment Saturday night and ransacked the place had been looking for Marcus.

Banner stopped writing and resumed tapping the pen on the pad, as if it were a drum. "You sayin' there's a connection? Marcus missing. Victim murdered."

Father John hesitated a moment. "Marcus could have been murdered, too. It could have been his body in the ditch."

The chief shifted forward. "Couldn't be Marcus. Ghost is always opposite of the true person, you know. This ghost is a hell raiser, just like Marcus. It's already caused a lot of trouble. Six vehicular accidents never should've happened—hell, one guy rolled his truck in his own driveway. Plus, Grandmother Petey slipped in her bathtub and damn near drowned, and Herman Running Wolf walked into his barn and dropped through the floor five feet. Barn floor had been perfectly good. . . ." He stopped for a moment and shook his head. "Ghost that's walkin' around now was a pussycat in true person."

Father John interrupted before the chief could recount any more ghost stories. "Let's suppose the man who forced his way into Annie's apartment finally found Marcus. Then who knows what happened? Marcus ends up dead, and the man dumps his body into the ditch. The man then murders Annie Chambeau before she can identify him."

Banner pursed his lips and squinted in thought. "Makes sense."

Father John continued, "Suppose further that, after the man dumped Marcus's body, he had second thoughts and decided to retrieve it. Maybe he was afraid somebody might spot it, just as I actually did. So he was on his way back when I flagged him down."

Banner had swiveled sideways and was staring out the grimy window next to the desk. "All this supposes Marcus being dead, which we don't know for a fact since we don't have a body. And none of my boys has spotted any white man driving a gray Chevy pickup on the rez. Chances are the guy blew out of here with the blizzard, which means it wasn't him that murdered the girl."

Father John swallowed hard. He had to thread his way carefully here. "I think he's still here. His name is Gary. I don't know the last name. He and a couple of other white men are staying at Lean Bear's ranch."

The chief swiveled back square with the desk. His bushy black eyebrows shot up. "That so? Ben Holden know about that?"

"He rented it to them." Father John said nothing about Susan. He realized his instinct was to protect the girl as long as possible, just as it was Vicky's. There would be time for Banner to question her later, after she felt better. In the meantime, he could check out the three men. Maybe he'd find enough evidence to arrest them without the girl's help. He hoped so. He would sleep a lot easier if Gary were behind bars.

Banner laid the ballpoint pen across the yellow pad and leaned back, lacing his hands behind his head. "You got any evidence that the guy in the Chevy pickup is the same guy who menaced the victim?"

Father John shook his head. He had nothing. Now it was his turn to stare out the window. The afternoon sky glinted like steel, and the wind had started up, flicking a small branch against the window pane. It made a tick-tock sound, like an old clock. He could be way off base, in which case he had just implicated an innocent man in murder. The realization did not sit well on his conscience.

He said, "It's just a hunch. And there's something else. I've heard Marcus took a job driving Jeeps to Denver. It's possible he could be somewhere between here and there." He realized a part of him was unwilling to close the door on the young man's life.

"New Jeeps? Used Jeeps?" The chief started writing again.

"New, I assume," Father John said. He should have been more thorough in gathering information.

"Every gas station in Wyoming has a Jeep or pickup for sale out back. If Marcus is drivin' used Jeeps, could take us a while to track him down. But only a couple of dealers sell 'em new. The dealer over in Riverton is pretty small. Big Phil's place in Lander probably does most of the business in these parts. Owned by Phil Beefer. Remember him? He played center for the Denver Nuggets some years back. Helluva good man for a white man." The chief glanced up. "Sorry. Sometimes I forget about you being one of 'em."

Father John absentmindedly waved away the apology. Phil Beefer's name rang a faint bell, even though basketball went on around him, out there somewhere. Except for the national championships, which he usually watched so he could discuss them with the kids at St. Francis.

"Problem is," Banner was saying, "I can follow up leads on the rez, check with the Depperts and Marcus's friends about his activities. But Lander isn't my turf. Lander PD is handling the homicide investigation. All I can do is give Detective Loomis this info." The chief stopped a moment, as if to underline the next point. "If Loomis agrees there's some connection between Annie

Chambeau's homicide and Marcus Deppert's disappearance, he'll make inquiries."

"And if not, he won't spend a lot of time looking for a missing Indian?"

"Yep."

The tick-tock of the branch and the sound of a ringing telephone down the corridor punctuated the quiet. "There's nothing to keep me from talking to the Jeep dealers," Father John said.

"I can't officially instruct you to do that. 'Course, if you do it on your own, nothing I can do about it." Banner grinned, as if they had reached some kind of understanding. Then, "Lean Bear's ranch is on my turf. I'll send a couple of my boys up the canyon to talk to this Gary fellow. You never know." The chief shrugged. "Your hunch could be right."

Placing both hands on the arms of his chair, Banner leveraged himself to his feet. "I haven't had lunch yet today. How about you?"

Father John had ignored the hollowness in his stomach all morning. All he'd had today was the cup of instant coffee in Vicky's kitchen. "Name the place," he said.

"Lana's." Banner picked up the phone and tapped the buttons. "Mind if Patrick comes along? I been wantin' you to talk to him."

‹ 19 ›

father John wasn't sure how it was that Banner arrived at the cafe first. The chief hadn't left the building before Father John drove out of the parking lot. Yet there was the white police car with the gold BIA insignia on the front door parked in front of Lana's cafe as he drove up the snow-rutted driveway. The cafe, a one-story brick square, nestled against the foothills on a bluff overlooking the white plains. Dark skeletons of cottonwoods stood out against the horizon, and black smoke curled from the chimneys of the ranch houses in the distance. The afternoon sun hovered over the mountains, gripping the parking lot in frigid shade.

The neon sign over the door spelled LANA'S in bright fluorescent green. Father John stepped inside. The smells of grease and fresh apple pie enveloped him. He waved to Turner, perched behind the counter. Lana cooked and waited tables; her husband collected the money and joked with the tourists traveling through Indian country. *What's it like being half of a movie star? Better'n not bein' none. How come you looked so glamorous up there on the screen? Natural-born good looks.*

Father John walked past the vacant booths along one wall, the tables piled with dirty dishes. Four men were still at lunch in one booth, and behind them Art Banner sat across from a surly-looking young Indian with black hair, green eyes, and a lighter complexion than that of most Indians on the reservation.

"You remember Patrick here?" Banner asked as Father John deposited his parka and cowboy hat on a nearby coatrack and slid into the booth beside him.

"Welcome home, Patrick." Father John extended his hand toward the kid, who looked about twenty-two years old. He'd met Patrick once before, when he'd been home on leave from the army. His hair had been cropped close to his skull then. Now it hung almost to his shoulders. Silver earrings dangled from each ear, and a beaded medallion hung from a cord around his neck. He was wearing a black T-shirt with the sleeves rolled up.

"Yeah," Patrick said. "Like warriors get a real big welcome around here."

"Our People honor warriors. It's our tradition," Banner said, his tone a mixture of patience and exasperation.

Lana appeared at the end of the table. She was short and pear-shaped, with white frizzy hair. "What's this? Some kind of special occasion? Police chief, returning warrior, and pastor all at the same table? I think I'm gonna faint with excitement."

"Before you do, bring us three of your world-famous hamburgers and a pot of coffee," Banner said.

"I got three pieces of famous apple pie, too." Lowering her voice and glancing toward the adjoining booth, Lana said, "You want I should save 'em for you?"

"Well, somebody's got to eat 'em, I guess." Banner laughed. Then, as Lana walked away, he added, "That okay with you guys?"

"We don't get much choice, do we?" Patrick shifted in his seat, as if to locate the perfect position for the next volley.

Father John jumped in. "Tell me, Patrick. How'd an Indian kid like you get saddled with an Irish name?"

Before the young man could answer, Banner said, "His great-grandfather gave it to him. Hell, we didn't even know Helen was expectin'. One day she was washin' clothes. You remember that big scrub board your mother used to set in the sink and wash the clothes on?" Banner glanced at his son, then turned back to Father John. "She was scrubbin' away when, all of a sudden, her great-grandfather, Patrick O'Riley, was standin' in the kitchen. Dead thirty years or more, he was. So he says he sure would be obliged if she named the child after him." Banner regarded his son again. "Good thing you turned out to be a boy."

Patrick rolled his eyes and gazed at the ceiling, as if he'd heard the story so many times it had taken on a life of its own separate from his.

"Arapahos aren't the only people that got ghost walkers." Banner laughed and nudged Father John's arm.

Father John shot the chief a look of mock surprise. He couldn't deny it. As Lana delivered the hamburgers and coffee, his memory slipped to the long-ago night his Uncle Daniel came to him in a dream, tall and handsome, a black Irishman with black hair and laughing blue eyes, not a responsible bone in his body, and an endless supply of funny stories and songs. Uncle Daniel could make the sun dance a jig. He was dressed in white—suit, hat, shoes, a white coat neatly folded over one arm as if he were about to embark on a cruise. He had come to say good-bye. Father John was ten years old. He sprang awake, jumped out of the foldaway bed in the living room he shared with his older brother, Mike, and padded down the hallway to his parents' bedroom. His father's head was nestled against his mother's shoulder. He tapped his mother gently. "Uncle Daniel's dead."

Both parents sat straight up in bed. "What're you talkin' about, boy?" his father said.

Thinking about it now, it was what his parents didn't say that seemed odd. They didn't say, "That's silly, ridiculous, irrational. Go back to sleep." They got up and sat in the living room, his mother wrapped in a flower-printed robe, his father's white legs visible beneath his flannel robe. When the phone rang, his mother said, "Well, that's it, then."

No, Father John couldn't deny his people's ghosts. He had never been convinced that everything could be explained. He picked up the large hamburger in both hands and bit into it. It was juicy and delicious and made him realize how hungry he was. The young man kept his eyes down, working his way through his hamburger and ignoring both his father and Father John. Banner was right. It wouldn't be easy for Patrick to make the transition back to the reservation. He recalled what Vicky had once said. "It's hard to be one of the edge people." He understood because he also dwelled in the edge space.

"Any job prospects?" Father John asked. He was afraid he already knew the answer, but he hoped something might have turned up.

Patrick shook his head, eyes still downcast. "Maybe in the spring. BIA police say they'll have a couple openings."

"He'd be a good cop," Banner said, as if the young man weren't sitting across from them, silently chewing a hamburger and washing it down with coffee. "Trouble is, he doesn't want to take something 'til then."

"He thinks I should be a waiter over in Riverton." Patrick rolled his eyes again.

"Oh, yeah, I keep forgetting," Banner said. "Being a

waiter isn't dignified enough for warriors and basketball stars. So you're just gonna sit around 'til spring, contemplating your warrior exploits and all the basketballs you dunked back in high school."

Father John set the rest of his hamburger down on the plate. Here it was, a little miracle. He'd forgotten Patrick Banner had played basketball for Indian High School during the long run when the Indian kids had shellacked every basketball team in the state. He'd been an all-star senior the first year Father John had spent at St. Francis, but he didn't know Banner or his son then.

He wanted to grab the kid and haul him over to St. Francis right away. He took a long sip of coffee, weighing his options. Patrick needed something to do until spring. The kids needed a basketball coach. But he had no idea how he'd come up with the money to heat the gym and pay a coach. And who knew whether St. Francis would still exist come spring?

"Look, Patrick," he said, plunging in anyway, "what would you think about coaching some kids over at St. Francis every day after school?"

"You kidding me?" For the first time, Patrick's face broke into a grin.

The wind sent little puffs of snow scudding over the highway ahead. Orange and scarlet clouds floated across the western sky and dipped around the white peaks of the mountains. It was midafternoon, but there was the hint of dusk coming on. Father John was thinking it would take a large miracle to make the school's basketball team happen. Those two clowns—Nick Sheldon and Clifford Keating—had set the wheels in motion to close down the mission. Make that four clowns counting the bishop and the Provincial. And he had been so busy the last couple of days, he hadn't gotten out to Thomas Spotted Horse's ranch yet to find out if the elders might call a general council so the people could vote on whether to close St. Francis mission.

He swung right onto Plunkett Road, the two-lane trail cut by the people in the Old Time that uncoiled across the top of a ridge like a rattlesnake, snow banked in the ditches. As he started into an easy curve, he glanced at the rearview mirror. The green Dodge truck was coming up fast again.

◀ 20 ▶

The truck was on his rear bumper. Father John stomped on the gas pedal as he rounded the curve. The engine shuddered, and snow blew back alongside the cab. He didn't want to lose control, not with the snow-drifted ditches falling away on both sides. They were the only vehicles on the road. This was no drunk behind him. This was somebody who, cold sober, wanted to see him in the ditch.

The truck was still there as Father John fishtailed onto Seventeen-Mile Road. He saw the truck make the turn and start to gain on him. It looked like the same driver he'd seen behind the wheel the first time: aviator glasses, hat pulled down on the forehead. He still couldn't tell if it was a man or a woman.

Another truck appeared in the distance behind, and Father John let up a little on the accelerator. Aviator glasses wouldn't put him in the ditch with a witness close by. The truck also slowed, keeping the same distance behind. They passed Givens Road, Arapaho Road, Blue Cloud Road. The sign for St. Francis Mission loomed ahead. Suddenly the truck was coming fast, the grille gleaming in the mirror. Just as Father John began to turn onto Circle Drive, he felt a hard thump and heard a long scratching noise as his head whipped backward. He skidded to a stop in a flurry of snow and jumped out. The Dodge truck flashed past the spiky cottonwoods lining Seventeen-Mile Road.

Father John inspected the Toyota's tailgate. It looked as if it had caught a fast pitch from a concrete ball. The left side was punched in and smeared with green paint. The top of the *T* was gone. He took off his hat and ran his hand through his hair. This didn't make sense. If Aviator Glasses had wanted to run him into the ditch, he could have done so on Plunkett Road. Why had he followed him to the mission turnoff and rammed the Toyota just enough to dent it? A warning? Is that what the driver had delivered? A warning against what?

He got back into the cab, uneasiness gripping him. His neck felt as if it were locked in a vise. He was grateful the Dodge hadn't run him off the road. The Toyota wrecked . . . the idea made him shudder.

He parked in front of the administration building and climbed the cement steps, part of which showed patches of snow. He made a mental note to ask Leonard, the caretaker, to take another swipe at them. The details of running the mission, he realized, were getting away from him.

Inside, the dim light from the ancient glass fixtures along the ceiling washed over the corridor, illuminating the portraits of the Jesuits of St. Francis past that lined the walls. A mixture of kindliness and cruelty, generosity and greed, all the human conundrums, shone out from eyes framed by little round glasses. A musty odor mingled with a faint smell, like that of burning oil, and the soft hum of the furnace in the basement seeped up through the wood floor. From further down the corridor came the tap-tap-tap sounds of Father Peter at his old Smith-Corona typewriter.

Before Father John could hang up his parka in his office, the tapping stopped, and the old priest stood in the doorway. "The messages accumulate throughout the day. 'Double, double, toil and trouble . . .'"

Father John threw up both hands, palms outward, in the Arapaho sign of peace. "Any word from the Provincial?" he asked, taking his chair. Stacks of papers, unopened mail, and messages toppled across the desk.

"The Provincial?" Surprise crossed Father Peter's face. "You expected a call? Well, it would be welcome evidence he is aware of St. Francis Mission."

"He's aware, all right," Father John said. "He's about to confine it to the Jesuit archives. Students will research how once upon a time the Society of Jesus worked with the Arapahos. Some enterprising young seminarian will probably write a dissertation."

The old man slumped against the doorjamb. "'Can such things be, and overcome us like a summer's cloud, without our special wonder?'"

Father John was thumbing through the stack of telephone messages. He stopped at one with *Urgent* scribbled across the top in Father Peter's wobbly handwriting. "Nick Sheldon called?"

"Further bad news, I fear. He was quite annoyed not to find you in your office. I believe his exact words were you should call him immediately."

"If not sooner," Father John said, flipping through the rest of the stack. Another message caught his attention. "Thomas Spotted Horse came by?"

Father Peter stared at him, remembrance in his eyes. "We're old friends, you know, so naturally I thought he'd come to see me. However, it was you he wanted to see. Disappointed you weren't here. Thomas wonders if you might find time to stop out at the ranch tomorrow. You know the humble and polite way of the Arapahos.

Never would he say it was urgent, but if he drove all the way over here in that old truck of his when he can hardly see through those thick glasses, well, I would suggest to you it is urgent."

Father John set the message to one side. "Did Vicky Holden call?" There was nothing to indicate she had.

The old priest shook his head and stepped back into the corridor. Then he reappeared around the doorjamb. "You haven't forgotten about the meetings tonight?"

"No," Father John said, although he had.

"I intend to take the liturgy committee," Father Peter said as he started down the corridor. The old floor creaked under his steps.

That left Father John with the two other meetings jotted on his calendar: the high school religious instruction committee and AA. He didn't want to miss either. He saw himself darting between the meeting rooms at Eagle Hall, a juggler with two glass balls in the air, both of which would shatter if he didn't do something to save St. Francis.

Sighing, he lifted the receiver and punched in Vicky's office number. The secretary informed him crisply that Ms. Holden was out. She couldn't say when she might return. She hoped it would be soon since the pile of work, the depositions, the clients were waiting. Father John broke off the conversation, wondering what it was about his voice that inspired these uninvited confidences. Pushing back the cuff of his flannel shirt, he checked his watch. He had a little more than two hours before the meetings got underway.

◀ 21 ▶

The elevator bell rang into the hospital silence. Father John stepped between the parting doors onto the third floor of the hospital. Light from the recessed ceiling fixtures gleamed on the turquoise vinyl floor, and odors of disinfectant and floor polish wafted toward him as he started down the corridor. From somewhere came the clanking sound of a dinner trolley, but no one was in sight. Even the nurses' station ahead was empty. A couple of computer screens on the low counter blinked into the void.

The door across from the station opened, and Vicky slipped past. Keeping one hand on the knob, she closed the door silently behind her. She looked like a teenager in the bulky red sweater and blue jeans. Her black hair shone almost silver under the light. Surprise crossed her face as she turned toward Father John. "Susan's sleeping," she whispered.

"How is she?"

"She has some tough days ahead. If we hadn't brought her in . . ." Vicky lowered her face into her hands, and for a moment he thought she was going to cry.

He stepped toward her and placed one hand on her shoulder to reassure her. "Susan's going to be okay now," he said.

Vicky looked up and stared at him a moment as if willing herself to believe what he had just said. Then she slipped one hand into the front pocket of her jeans and withdrew a folded piece of white paper. "*Hoho'u h:3tone'3en,*" she said, handing it to him. "I am thanking you."

"What's this?"

"I had some time while they got Susan settled in the room. I called my law school friend. That's the unofficial version of why Eden Lightfoot left the Cheyenne agency and is now conferring the Harvard method of economic development upon us. You are up against one smart Indian, educated in one of your best schools."

Father John unfolded the paper. It was filled with lines of clear, precise penmanship, the kind some scholarly old Jesuit had insisted upon thirty years ago at the St. Francis school. "All *t*'s crossed and *i*'s dotted." He slipped the paper past his parka and into his shirt pocket. He would study it later.

"As for the Z Group,"—Vicky gave her shoulders a little shrug—"zilch."

"What do you mean?"

"I had Ginger call the California Secretary of State's office. The Z Group is listed as an assumed name under which a partnership called the Paulson Company does business in California."

"Who owns the Paulson Company?" Father John felt the sense of excitement of the researcher about to close in on a critical piece of information.

"That's just it," Vicky said. "The state has no record of any company with that name. End of paper trail."

He leaned against the wall. Nothing but shadows, specters—ghosts—everywhere he turned. "How can that be?"

"A couple of reasons," Vicky said, locked in her lawyer tone now. "The company may simply have failed to file the correct documents, or they could be lost in the computer. The clerk promised to check further and get back to us."

"In the meantime, we know nothing about Nick Sheldon's client."

"Not true," Vicky said. "We know it is a development company capable of building anywhere, simply by the fact it selected this area. We know the people have done their homework—drawn up all the graphs and charts, put all the numbers through a dance. They can probably project profits over the next couple of decades down to a few dollars. Profits are what count for them—we know that."

Father John stared past her down the quiet corridor a moment. Enough profits, he wondered, to try to scare him away from interfering with their plans?

"More bad news, I'm afraid," Vicky said after a moment. "I talked with two members of the business council. In the last couple of days, Eden Lightfoot has met personally with each member to explain the Z Group's proposal. Lobbying, I'd call it. Anyway, the council is pretty excited about the recreation center. My friends say—" She stopped, worry in her eyes. "It looks like a go."

Father John blew out a puff of air. She had confirmed his worst fears: a major development company with the financial resources, determination, and political savvy to put St. Francis out of business. It was bad news, all right, and he hadn't yet gotten to the bad news he'd come to tell her. "Vicky," he said, "there's something else we have to talk about."

*   *   *

They sat at a square table in the far corner of the hospital cafeteria under fluorescent bulbs that flooded the tables with a white light. Except for another couple, heads together, whispering, at a table across the room, they were the only ones there. A muffled shout from the kitchen, the clank-clank sound of dishes, the swish of double steel doors opening and closing sounded through the almost empty space. It smelled of onions and chicken broth.

Father John crumpled some saltines into his bowl of chicken soup, the way his father had always done. Vicky was sipping at hers. The time was not yet right to talk. After a moment she set her spoon down. "Does this have to do with the white men at the ranch?"

"It's possible." Father John kept his eyes on hers. "A girl named Annie Chambeau, Marcus Deppert's old girlfriend, was murdered last night."

Vicky leaned back against the metal chair. "I overheard the emergency room nurses talking about a gunshot victim." She shook her head. "The poor girl. There aren't many Chambeaus left. Just her grandmother. She was Maisie Birdsong. She married Alfred Chambeau, the grandson of Charles Chambeau, one of the French traders in the Old Time." Vicky paused. "Sorry. You don't want to hear another Arapaho genealogy."

Father John smiled. Arapahos were connected through the years, through the generations, their identities woven by strong, invisible ties.

"What does the girl's murder have to do with . . ." Vicky paused, as if she'd answered her own question. She looked stricken.

He hurried to remind her about the body in the ditch, Gary near Rendezvous Road. The white man who went to Annie Chambeau's looking for Marcus. It could all be connected.

Vicky was shaking her head, and Father John saw the resistance in her eyes. His theory led to Susan, to the possibility Susan could be involved. How could she accept such a theory? "Do you know for a fact it was Gary who went to the girl's apartment? Did she tell you? What proof is there Marcus Deppert has been murdered or that the body was his? What proof do you have of any connection between the body and the murdered girl?"

Silence filtered into the space between them. He had no proof. After a moment he said, "I hope I'm wrong. But if I'm right, you and Susan are in danger. Gary has already threatened you. When Susan is released tomorrow, you can take her to the guest house at St. Francis. I'll leave the key under the rock by the front door and have Elena lay in some food—"

"John," Vicky interrupted, impatience in her voice. "Gary didn't want Susan to leave the ranch. Now it's a moot point. She's gone, and there's nothing he can do about it. Besides, I'm hoping Susan is scared enough to agree to go into treatment tomorrow."

Father John reached into his parka pocket and brought out his small spiral notebook and ballpoint pen. "One of my friends—a former Jesuit—runs a drug treatment center in Denver," he said, scribbling on the paper. "This is his number." He tore off the sheet and handed it to her. "It's best you both leave the area until Banner can put together enough evidence to arrest Gary."

"What?" Vicky let the sheet of paper flutter onto the table. "What are you saying? Have you already passed this bizarre theory on to Banner?"

He was surprised at the anger in her voice. "A girl has been murdered, Vicky. A young man is missing."

The chair screeched against the floor as she got to her feet and leaned over the table toward him. "Oh, I concede these men are probably here to deal drugs. Maybe they're involved in murder, I don't know. And neither does Susan. She is not involved."

Keeping his tone calm, rational, Father John said, "She may know something that could help the police."

"No." It was like a slap. "Don't you understand how sick she is? She almost overdosed last night. She could have died. She can't handle a police investigation right now." Vicky straightened herself. "I thought you were on my side. I thought you cared about me and Susan, but obviously I was wrong," she said, slamming the chair into the table and wheeling around.

He watched her cross the cafeteria, dodging the rows of empty tables and brushing past the doorway. He was still watching as she disappeared into the elevator. Then he got slowly to his feet, relieved to see she had taken the paper with the Denver number.

He drove north on Rendezvous Road through the silver glow of evening. It might snow again tonight; the air felt heavy. In his mind he replayed their conversation. Why hadn't he seen the raw emotional space he had blundered into? He knew the force of her love for Susan—charged with guilt and regret and sadness. Why hadn't he handled things differently? He had wanted to warn Vicky, to protect her, but somehow he had succeeded only in pushing her away. It had happened so easily he was shocked.

At least she had taken the note he'd scribbled. If she wouldn't go to the guest house, maybe she would take Susan to Denver. As long as Gary was free they were in danger; he felt sure of it.

He glanced at his watch. The religious education meeting would be winding up soon, but the AA meeting would go on for a while. He would be late. It seemed to be a recurring theme in his life—missing appointments, showing up late—like the motif of an aria.

As he slowed the Toyota around Circle Drive, Father John saw the commotion in front of the priests' residence. He pulled in beside two vans with CHANNEL 7 CHEYENNE emblazoned on the sides. What looked like a tripod stood on the sidewalk, spindly black legs under a gigantic spotlight. Snow fluttered into the white light. Father Peter, hands bunched in the pockets of his black coat, stood in the circle of light while two men trained boxlike cameras on him and a woman shoved a microphone in his face.

Father John swung out of the cab. Suddenly he was in the circle of light himself, a silvery object now waving in his face, a woman walking toward him. "Here's the pastor now. Tell us, Father O'Malley, how does it feel to be the last pastor of St. Francis Mission?"

◀ 22 ▶

The woman moved closer, looking at Father John expectantly. She was bundled in a black fur coat, but her head was bare. She raised a gloved hand and brushed the snowflakes from her eyes and cheeks. Snow clung to her short blond hair. Father John recognized her as the anchorwoman on the ten o'clock news, where, he suspected, St. Francis Mission was about to become tonight's lead story.

"No comment," he said, hurrying past her up the sidewalk toward Father Peter. He took the old man's arm and gently turned him toward the front steps.

"Is it true you oppose the creation of jobs on Wind River Reservation?" The voice was shrill as the anchorwoman saw her story about to disappear into the priests' residence. "Father O'Malley, can you explain to our viewing audience why you would stand in the way of jobs for the Indians?"

He was in a surreal world, caught in blinding light with blackness beyond, searching his pockets for the front door key. Father Peter waited on the step below, a shadow at the edge of the light as Father John fingered the key and jammed it into the keyhole.

"Could it be you are only protecting your own job, Father O'Malley? Isn't it true that, given your background, it would be difficult for your order, the Society of Jesus, to place you elsewhere?"

"That is an egregious calumny," the old priest shouted.

Turning around, Father John saw the confusion and discomfort in the young woman's face. She started to speak, faltered. "Could you explain for our viewing audience?"

"I'll explain for you," said Father Peter impatiently, as if reprimanding a particularly dim student. "It's a damn lie."

The young woman blinked. "I beg your pardon, Father, but—"

The old priest cut her off. "Father O'Malley is a highly trained historian. He would be in demand at any of the fine educational establishments the Society of Jesus operates. He would have his choice of positions as chief executive at any of the Society's missions around the world. Choice of positions, young lady."

"Isn't it true Father O'Malley is an alcoholic?" Panic tinged the young woman's voice.

Father John heard Father Peter draw in his breath, as he took the old man's elbow again and ushered him to the top step. Then Father John turned back to the anchorwoman. "I am a recovering alcoholic," he said.

The old priest jerked his arm away and squared his shoulders. "As are many of your colleagues, young lady. Perhaps some of your friends. Perhaps members of your family."

The woman gasped. A stricken look came over her face as if she had been personally insulted and wasn't sure how to respond. Gently and firmly Father John steered the old priest into the front hall and closed the door behind them. "Thanks for the vote of confidence," he said, helping Father Peter out of his long coat.

The sounds of car doors banging, metal clanking

against metal, and engines turning over filtered inside as Father John hung the coat and his own parka on the rack. Then he followed the old man into the study and slumped into the worn leather chair behind his desk.

Father Peter had taken one of the blue wingback chairs on the other side. In a voice still trembling with emotion, he said, "We are up against street fighters, my boy."

Father John smiled at him. He'd always felt he could fight his own battles, and it had been a long time since anyone had stepped up to the bat for him. "What questions did she ask before I got here?"

"Questions that beg the issue. A common tactic when one's premise is fallacious." Father Peter rested his head against the chair and closed his eyes a moment. There were moments when he seemed very ancient.

"And what did you tell her?"

"*Macbeth*. Act five, scene five. 'Blow Wind! Come, wrack! At least we'll die with harness on our back.' The Bard never fails me."

"You quoted Shakespeare to them?" Father John threw his head back and laughed. The old man was beautiful. Then it hit him: All of Wyoming was about to get a good look at the priests of St. Francis Mission, one in his dotage, the other a selfish, alcoholic obstructionist.

A gurgling pipe somewhere, air swishing through a vent—the sounds floated through the silence in the house. Father John thought the old man had fallen asleep. Suddenly Father Peter's head jerked forward, his eyes opened. He looked startled.

"I find it interesting," Father John began, testing his own thoughts out loud. "The plan to sell the mission has been kept top secret. Not a word leaked onto the moccasin telegraph. Yet now it's about to be announced on the ten o'clock news."

"They have made the first strike, my boy, before you could develop any opposition. The Provincial also hopes to obtain your acquiescence by bringing public pressure to bear. Certainly he may sell the mission without your blessing, but it would look as if he were abandoning the people here. It would be what is known today as a public relations disaster."

Father John swiveled around and stared out the window at the falling snow. Pale moonlight glinted on the glass. Clever, he thought. People across the state would support anything that promised jobs on the reservation. Even the Arapahos might choose jobs over St. Francis. He pulled the yellow paper out of his shirt pocket and unfolded it. The neat, precise handwriting gave him a start. They had still been friends, he and Vicky, when she'd gotten this information for him. The information was elliptical: Eden Lightfoot; Harvard MBA; brought four companies to Cheyenne Agency; rumors of commissions from companies; no proof, but left agency under cloud; investigation pending.

Father John laid the paper on the desk. It didn't surprise him. He'd already guessed Nick Sheldon had the economic development director in his pocket. "Tomorrow I'll drive out to see Thomas Spotted Horse," he said.

"'Tomorrow and tomorrow and tomorrow . . .'" The old priest got to his feet. It was a kind of unfolding: First his head rose, then his back, then his legs. "Tonight we must attend our meetings."

Father John checked his watch again. The religious education meeting had ended, but AA was probably still going on. He lifted himself out of the leather chair. It was beginning to feel like a charade, going through the ordinary routines of St. Francis as if the mission would exist forever.

The AA meeting was almost over when he slipped past the door into the small room in Eagle Hall. Ten or twelve people, a mix of men and women, occupied the folding chairs arranged in a circle. He saw a couple of new faces. Every week brought changes. People recovering for years fell off the wagon and no longer came to the meetings; people who had been drunk for years decided to climb on the wagon and join AA. His thoughts went to Annie Chambeau. What would she have done had she lived?

He helped himself to a cup of coffee from the metal pot on a side table then took a vacant chair. The others smiled at him before turning their attention back to Clarence Little Bear, who sat forward on the edge of his chair, elbows dug into his knees. "I was like the body on Rendezvous Road," he was saying. "Hell, I was like the ghost wanderin' around, not knowin' where I was goin', only I was still alive. Barely alive," he added, emitting a short laugh. "'Til I come here to the mission, I didn't think there was no hope for me."

"Yeah." Another man spoke up. "Every time I drove down Seventeen-Mile Road and seen the church tower through the trees, I'd think this ain't no good for me or the family. I gotta do better. So one day I pulled in to the mission and took the pledge."

Father John sipped at his coffee as the testimonials went on. The words varied, but the meaning was the same. Here at St. Francis, they had found hope. *Dear God*, he prayed silently, *help me to find the way to help the mission.*

◄ 23 ►

His boots scattered the snow as Father John walked along Circle Drive. The powder rose light as air, then settled into little piles. Tiny flakes floated downward, spaced far apart, like miniature white birds circling a nest. The sky was lighter in the east where the sun glowed behind the clouds. The east: one of the four sacred directions, the symbol of hope. Despite the beauty around him, he didn't feel hopeful. Everything was spiraling downward. The murdered girl. Marcus missing. Vicky angry at him. The mission about to pass into history. He couldn't shake the feeling he had let them all down.

A stream of pickups pulled into the parking lot behind the elementary school, and Father John followed, spotting Loretta about to enter the back door. He called out, and the woman turned around, shoulders slouched. She dropped the mesh bag she was carrying. It crumpled in the snow at her feet. She was bundled in a long gray coat with a red scarf wrapped around her head, covering part of her face. For a moment he wasn't sure he'd hailed the right person.

"I'm still looking for Marcus Deppert," Father John said when he reached her.

Annoyance and disapproval flashed in the woman's eyes. "I told you, Father, me and Rich don't know nothin' about Marcus Deppert. He was nothin' but trouble for my boy. Rich is a lot better off now that he broke with him."

"Is Rich back from his trip?"

"Tomorrow," she said hurriedly. "He'll be home tomorrow for sure."

"You've heard from him, then?"

Loretta's eyes followed a couple of pickups pulling into the parking lot. "Not exactly. He said he'd be home Saturday, but he didn't show up last weekend, so I figured he must've meant this comin' Saturday. I was the one confused, is all. He'll be here day after tomorrow."

"Ask him to get in touch with me, will you?"

"Father, I told you a hundred times now—"

"Please, Loretta," Father John interrupted. "It's very important."

The woman shrugged and started toward the door, dragging the mesh bag along the snow. It made a soft, squishy noise.

"Are you okay, Loretta?" Father John asked.

She looked back. "Soon's they get that body buried proper like, I'll be okay. Ghost comes every night and wakes me up. It can be calm everywhere, but out back in the field, it's blowin' like fury, 'cause ghost's there. I went over and talked to my grandfather yesterday. He's gonna come out and bless the field this weekend, maybe give ghost some peace 'til they find his body. You oughtta come out and bless the field, too."

"Good idea," he said. The earth was sacred; all created things were sacred. What harm could there be in standing in the middle of a field to acknowledge the sacredness and give thanks to the Creator? Besides, saying a few prayers and sprinkling holy water around might give the poor woman some peace.

* * *

After trekking back along Circle Drive to the administration building, Father John spent some time at his desk, which overflowed with notes of calls to return, meetings to arrange, and letters to answer. One of the religious ed teachers had taken a job at the Holiday Inn in Riverton, which meant Father John had to find someone else to teach the tenth-grade religion class this evening. Within a few phone calls he had found a replacement. The generosity of Arapahos always amazed him. They gave what they had. Usually all they had was time.

He returned two calls, both of which turned out to be from Arapahos wanting to know if St. Francis was really closing. Then he stacked the rest into a pile and set it aside. What could he tell people? Yes, it's true, unless a miracle happens? Pray for a miracle?

He punched in the numbers of the law enforcement center. Within seconds, Banner was on the line. "Just about to call you," he said. "My boys paid a visit to Lean Bear's ranch yesterday. Made contact with three whites: Gary Rollins, Ty Jones, and Morrissey Porterfield." It sounded as if the line had gone dead. Then Banner's voice again. "And white people think Indians have funny names. Anyway, looks like we got some weirdos wanna play Indian on the rez. No crime in being weird."

"What about Annie Chambeau?"

"Said they never heard of her. Gary Rollins swore up and down he wasn't anywhere near Rendezvous Road last Sunday night when you say he gave you a ride. The other two back him up. Claim they were all at the ranch watching TV."

"You believe that?"

"Hell, no, I wouldn't believe 'em if they told me my own name. Trouble is, we don't have proof they're up to anything. Just a feeling in the gut. Another thing,

John. My boys didn't see any sign of drugs. 'Course, we'd need a warrant to search the place, but we need some evidence to get a warrant."

Susan might be able to provide it, Father John thought. If she would. If her mother were willing to entertain the idea. He had to try talking to Vicky again. He said, "What now?"

"All we can do is keep an eye on the weirdos. I passed our report on to Loomis at the Lander PD. He's gonna interview Gary Rollins based on your belief he's the guy that threatened the Chambeau woman."

The Chambeau woman. At least she had been upgraded from victim-object to human being. Father John replaced the receiver, a heaviness weighing on him. Now Gary knew the police were suspicious. The next move would be his. What would it be? To make sure no one could tie him to Annie Chambeau? To make sure Susan Holden didn't talk to the police?

The ringing phone startled him out of his thoughts. It was Nick Sheldon. Father John detected the imperious tone of a man used to being obeyed even before the lawyer identified himself. "I've been trying to reach you, Father O'Malley. I have something you will want to see. Are you free this afternoon?"

"I can be."

"One-thirty, then," said the lawyer.

Father John jotted down the address. It was in a residential neighborhood in Lander. The vultures, he thought, are circling for the kill. Next to call him would probably be the Provincial. He decided to leave before the phone rang again.

Grabbing his parka off the coatrack, he strode down the corridor and looked in on Father Peter's office. The old man was slumped in the chair at his desk, softly snoring. He let him sleep.

❮ 24 ❯

Ahead of him the Wind River Mountains shouldered into the clouds, their great blocks of granite, their ponderosas and lodgepole pines swept with white powder. Snow was falling lightly over Seventeen-Mile Road. He would miss this sacred space, the Middle Earth, a gift to the Arapaho people from Shining Man Above.

Father John turned onto a narrow road and headed north alongside the mountains for several miles, snow glancing off the Toyota's hood. Just as the road veered west, he swung into the drive to Thomas Spotted Horse's ranch. The white, two-story house and the un-painted barn stood among a cluster of cottonwoods, like the tipis in the Old Time. He parked in the wide clearing between the barn and the house and walked around to the front. Wind whistled through the leafless branches as he rapped on the door.

From inside he heard a scraping sound. Then the door swung open, and Mardell Spotted Horse stood in front of him. She was somewhere in her seventies, in a blue dress with a yellow apron tied around her wide waist, with black oxfords and brown stockings rolled at her an-kles. Her gray hair was parted in the middle and braided into two ropes that hung over her ample bosom.

"I knew you'd be along, Father," she said. "So I

baked up a batch of cinnamon rolls. Come on in. You and me and the old man gotta eat 'em."

Removing his cowboy hat, Father John stepped into the living room filled with the moist, sweet odors of a bakery.

"How'd you know I like cinnamon rolls?"

"'Cause you're a man." Mardell led the way past the sofa with a star quilt spread over the cushions, the twin easy chairs, the television on a wood table. He set his hat on top of the television and followed the old woman into the kitchen.

She pulled a chair away from a round oak table. "Sit here," she instructed. "You looked mighty handsome on television last night. And Father Peter talkin' his gibberish sure got those white people confused before you showed up. We was lovin' it." The old woman let out a hearty laugh. Then a kind of sadness came over her, like a curtain slowly falling. "It's a no-good thing, this closing down St. Francis."

He hung his parka over the back of the chair and took his seat. Cabinets ringed the walls, and the counters overflowed with bowls and spoons, jars of flour and sugar. A percolator sat on the stove. Over the sink, a block of windows faced the barn and the back fields. He guessed that the door a few feet from the sink led onto a porch.

Mardell was at the window. "Here comes the old man now. Must've heard your truck." She gave a little shake of her head. "Much slower and he's gonna be walkin' backwards."

They heard the loud bang of an outside door closing, followed by a clumping noise on the porch. Then the kitchen door opened, and Thomas Spotted Horse came in leaning on a wooden cane. He stood six feet tall, weighed probably three hundred pounds, and wore blue jeans, a tan canvas jacket, and a black knit cap. He hooked the cane on the counter then yanked off the cap and turned toward Father John. The old man's eyes bulged behind his thick glasses.

Father John got to his feet in a gesture of respect. Thomas belonged to the Big Lodge People, those entrusted to care for the sacred objects, including the sacred pipe. They were the most revered people of the Arapahos. "How are you, Grandfather?"

"Ah, *be:hi':hehi':nino*. I am an old man. But for a three-legged, I am excellent." Thomas shuffled across the kitchen and sat down heavily in the chair on the other side of the table. Mardell leaned over and began helping him withdraw his massive arms from the jacket, which she then cushioned between him and the chair.

"See that Japanese tin can of yours got a new name. Ioyota." Thomas laughed. It was a large bellow that filled the kitchen. "There's a can of white paint out in the barn, if you wanna get the old name back. But if I was you, I'd get some rich white friends to buy me a good American truck."

Father John laughed as he resumed his own seat. His friends seemed fewer and fewer these days. Nobody was rich.

Mardell swung the percolator from the stove and filled three mugs with coffee. She set the mugs in front of them, then placed a pan of cinnamon rolls and a stack of napkins on the table. After layering out three portions of rolls, she sat down next to her husband.

The warm brown sugar and frosting ran along his fingers as Father John bit into his roll. It took him back for a moment to his own home, when he was a boy. He grabbed a napkin and mopped his hands. "Thank you, Grandmother," he said. The old woman beamed.

Eat first, then talk; that was the Arapaho Way. Any other sequence was impolite. When they had finished a couple of rolls each, Thomas cleared his throat. "My grandson Lester," he began, then drew in a long breath. "Whites'll say Lester's my brother's grandson."

Father John gave a nod of understanding. There was no concept of aunt, uncle, or cousin on the reservation. Your brother's child was your child. Thomas and Mardell had no children of their own, but they were not childless.

"You remember Lester got himself elected to the business council last fall?" Thomas's gray eyebrows shot up. "Well, he come to see me yesterday to tell me outsiders wanna close down the mission. That's before we heard it on the television. Lester says that economic development fellow the council hired has been workin' with the outsiders and gettin' the plans together real secretlike. The council just found out, but the whole matter's gonna be brought up at next Tuesday's meeting. Eden Lightfoot's got a majority of councilmen lined up behind it on account of new jobs."

Father John was aware of the knobby slats of the chair against his back. Sheldon and Keating held all the aces. Now they were about to play them. What councilman wanted to take a stand against jobs?

Mardell's chair scraped across the linoleum as she got to her feet. She grabbed the coffeepot and refilled their mugs. "You ask me, not all them council members wanna see the mission disappear. Lester, for one. When Eden Lightfoot come to him to line up his vote, he got real mad. He went to school at St. Francis. He's got good memories."

Thomas regarded his wife a moment before shifting

his gaze back to Father John. "Lots of folks got good memories. So if anybody asks 'em, they're gonna say they want the mission here. Trouble is, this deal's goin' through before anybody asks 'em."

Father John picked up his mug and took another sip of coffee. He said, "What about a general council, Grandfather?"

The old man was quiet a moment. "Lester says some folks'll be agitatin' for the recreation center 'cause they think it might mean somethin' else down the road."

"He's got that bull by the horns," Mardell said as she slid back into her chair. "Folks that go on the powwow highway up to South Dakota and down to Arizona and places like that see all them fancy casinos and a lot of Indians gettin' rich. They come back here and say, 'What are we, a bunch of dumb Indians 'cause we ain't gettin' rich?'"

Father John set his mug down hard. "What are you saying? The recreation center is the first step to a casino?" It was hard to believe. The business council had turned down plans for a casino two years ago, after the elders had called the people to Blue Sky Hall and Great Plains Hall and reminded them of the Arapaho Way. Casinos were not the Arapaho Way.

Sadness showed in the old man's watery eyes. "There's Indians been tryin' to get gamblin' here. So here come these outsiders. Say they're gonna build this here recreation center. Promise all kinds of jobs, and the business council gives the okay. They put up a big building, just right for gamblin' tables and slot machines, then they tell the business council: Our figuring must've been wrong. This here recreation center's not gonna get enough business. If we want jobs, we gotta turn it into a casino and make us a lot of money to boot."

Father John placed both elbows on the table, made a double fist, and blew into it. A new picture was coming into focus. Why St. Francis? he'd asked himself a hundred times. There was nothing but open space here, miles and miles of it. The recreation center could be built anywhere, but the Z Group had targeted the mission, and now he saw why. Sheldon and his bosses didn't want just to operate a casino on an Indian reservation—a casino owned by the Arapahos. They wanted to own the casino. But reservation land couldn't be purchased by non-Indians. Except for St. Francis Mission. It was the only land here already owned by outsiders, and it could be sold to outsiders.

Father John wanted to laugh. He'd give anything to see the faces of the Provincial and the bishop when they realized they'd traded St. Francis Mission for a casino. He didn't laugh. The odds against the mission were escalating.

"There's always the get-rich-quick people," Thomas said. "They're gonna show up at a general council and shout for a recreation center, thinkin' someday it'll be a casino." The old man shook his head and exhaled a long breath. "I been out in the barn feedin' the horses and runnin' all this through my mind. The *Hinono eino* shouldn't turn into a bunch of gamblers. Us old men gotta think about the children. We gotta take the chance and call a general council. We gotta try talkin' sense to the people."

Father John locked eyes with the old man a long moment. He knew Thomas was thinking the same thing he was thinking: The last thing Sheldon or Lightfoot wanted was a council where the elders could influence the people. They hadn't come this far to be stopped by some old Indians. Still a general council was risky, and it could be dangerous.

‹ 25 ›

Downy snow sculptured the Lander streets and weighted down the branches of the box elders at the curbs. Father John peered through thin gray film deposited by the windshield wipers. The address Nick Sheldon had given him was on Martin Drive in a neighborhood of sprawling brick houses. He stopped in front of a two-story, red brick house with a portico that arched over the side driveway. Under the portico stood a white Cadillac.

Nick Sheldon opened the glass-paned front door and extended a fleshy hand. He had a strong grip. He was wearing navy sweatpants and matching shirt; the sleeves were pushed up around his forearms, which looked tan and muscular, like those of a man who knew how to relax and work hard at the same time. What passed for a smile crossed his face.

"Good to see you again," Sheldon said, leading Father John into the living room. Its decor gave it the soulless feeling of a department store: plump white sofa, black easy chairs, ornate wood desk pushed against the far wall, a couple of small wood tables with polished tops. The air smelled of some kind of chemical and stale cigarette smoke. And whiskey. He could have identified that in a field of sage.

Sheldon said, "Apologies for last night, all those TV people descending upon you. I had no idea Channel 7 was on to the story."

Father John nodded noncommittally. Sheldon was lying. The television news announcement had been perfectly planned. Enough time before next week's business council meeting to rally supporters behind the recreation center, but not enough time for much opposition to develop. Sheldon and the Z Group had hit a homer and were rounding the bases before the outfielders even saw the ball.

Sheldon had started toward the L-shaped dining area that extended off the living room, and Father John followed. "Take a look at this beauty," the lawyer said, placing one palm on a large Plexiglas case that sat on the oblong dining table.

Just yesterday Eden Lightfoot had assured him the plans weren't final, but here, in miniature, crawling over the grounds of St. Francis Mission, was the recreation center. The contour of the land, the open spaces and arroyos, the knoll that held the cemetery, the Little Wind River winding along the southern edge, and the cottonwood trees on the riverbank where Chief Black Night had brought his people a hundred years ago were all captured in the model.

The mission buildings were gone. St. Francis Church, the administration building, the school, Eagle Hall, the guest house and priests' residence, even the old school, were all replaced by an enormous building that crept across Circle Drive. *The perfect casino*, Father John thought. He said, "Bowling alleys, movie theaters, gyms, restaurants, and everything else in one building?"

"Efficiency." Sheldon slapped the top of the Plexiglas case. It made a hollow sound. "Mom bowls while Dad works out and the kids play miniature golf in the same building. No sweating in the summer or freezing to death in the winter going from place to place." He stopped and drew in a long breath. "A boon to everybody in the whole area, but, of course, the Arapahos will benefit most. The center will provide jobs and good, clean family fun. It will help to ameliorate some of the problems here, problems I understand, you're personally familiar with. Why, I heard you brought some poor drugged-out Indian girl to the hospital just yesterday."

Father John allowed the comment to float in the air, but it bothered him. How did this outsider know about Susan? He let the question drift away. He'd been here long enough not to underestimate the random wires of the moccasin telegraph system.

"I don't believe the Arapahos want this," Father John said.

"Don't want jobs? You must be joking."

"Now that the news is out, the people will want a say in the matter."

Sheldon smiled indulgently. "Ah, yes. Eden Lightfoot has informed me of your hopes for a general council. He assures me he has already spoken with some of the elders. They only wish to maintain the traditional Arapaho beliefs. They have no interest or, may I say, understanding of modern economics. Eden has assured me they will leave this matter in the hands of the business council, unless of course someone like you should insist they become involved. That would be unfortunate. Of course, any opposition on the part of the elders would eventually be overcome. But naturally the Z Group is anxious to avoid costly delays."

"I can't tell the elders what to do," Father John said, starting into the living room.

"Father O'Malley." The lawyer's voice behind him sounded calm, friendly. Surprised, Father John turned back. Sheldon had folded his suntanned arms and was rocking on his heels. "We're both men of the world here, even though you happen to be a priest. Let me be candid. In what way might the Z Group make your life more comfortable? Perhaps an extended vacation? A sabbatical, isn't that what you Jesuits call it? Relax on a warm, sunny beach somewhere. I know a great spot in Antigua. Stay as long as you like. And you could certainly use decent wheels for your next assignment. Maybe a little sporty job. I'm sure you've seen the Lexus SE 400 coupe? Beautiful."

Father John thrust his hands into the pockets of his parka. "And what do you want for all this bounty, Sheldon?"

"Well, of course, it would be nice if you could support the recreation center. But I respect you, Father O'Malley. I realize that isn't possible. We will content ourselves with the support of the Jesuit Provincial. All I ask of you is—how shall I put it—your noninvolvement. You simply do nothing."

"All of that to do nothing?" Father John smiled. "It's not enough, Sheldon."

Just as Father John was about to let himself out the front door, the lawyer said, "Let me emphasize something, Father O'Malley." A lawyer's tone now, taut, precise. "It would be most unwise of you to encourage the elders to interrupt the normal processes of this matter. Do I make myself clear?"

Outside, the cold air slapped at Father John's face. He brought the brim of his cowboy hat forward as he cut across the snowy front yard to the Toyota. There was a lot of money riding on this deal, probably more than he had realized. The Z Group didn't want any interference, and Sheldon's job was to ensure there wouldn't be any.

He'd been warned. He didn't like warnings.

Three men stood on the cement bay in front of Big
Phil's Backcountry Wheels. Shoulders hunched,
hands jammed into the pockets of tweed overcoats,
the salesmen exuded the confidence of those who work
for a thriving dealership located at the busiest intersection in town. As Father John slipped out of his Toyota,
another salesman wheeled alongside him in a large blue
van with BIG PHIL'S splashed in red letters across the side.

He slid off the seat and started toward the Toyota, his
boots scraping the snow-packed asphalt. Perhaps thirty
years old, with his blond goatee and mustache he
looked like a cowboy dressed up for the city. "Afternoon, there. You lookin' to replace that pickup, today's
your day. We got some fine deals. Couple of pickups"—
he gestured toward the rows of trucks, vans, and Jeeps
stretching around them—"Big Phil's in a piss-hurry to
move out, make room for new models comin'."

The salesman ran a gloved hand over the Toyota's
tailgate, the way he might appraise a horse. "Whoa.
Somebody clipped you real good. Major dent here.
Paint damaged."

"Is Big Phil in?" Father John asked.

"You here to see the big man himself?" The salesman's face lit up as if he'd encountered some kind of

VIP without knowing it. "Follow me." He led the way up the concrete stairs edged with metal bars, past a wall of windows, through the double glass showroom doors. They crossed the green-and-white-tiled floor, threading a path between a shiny black pickup and a red Jeep. Two men hovered over the Jeep, their voices floating through the nearly empty showroom.

The salesman paused at the doorway to a glass cubicle. "Somebody to see you," he called before heading back across the showroom.

Phil Beefer unfolded his lanky frame from the leather chair behind the desk, rising half a head above Father John, and extended a hand easily large enough to palm a basketball. Father John looked up into a long face with concave cheeks, a chin that jutted forward, dark eyes behind clear, plastic-framed glasses, a thatch of gray hair.

"You must be Father O'Malley. Saw you on television last evening," the dealer said. "Shame they're gonna be closin' down St. Francis Mission. Wife and I been to Mass there a few times. Pretty little church." Beefer craned sideways and looked out the front plate glass. "Looks like you could use a new pickup."

"That Toyota and I are stuck with each other for a long while," Father John said as he took one of the twin black leather chairs Beefer indicated. Alongside the desk stood a narrow table devoted to a computer, monitor, and keyboard. Silver-framed photos lined the walls: Beefer and a plump, smiling woman surrounded by children dressed for the sixties, seventies, eighties. Basketball teams posed for the publicity camera; young Phil Beefer stealing the ball, going for a lay-up, racing downcourt.

Folding himself back into his chair, the dealer said, "If I can't sell you a new truck, what can I do for you?"

"A young man on the reservation is missing," Father John said, unsnapping his parka and placing his cowboy hat on one knee. Warm air from the overhead vent swept across his head and face. "His name is Marcus Deppert. He's taken a job delivering Jeeps to Denver. I was wondering if he's been working for you."

Beefer's head was shaking. "We don't make deliveries out of state." Suddenly he swirled sideways and began tapping the keyboard. Tiny yellow letters and lines appeared on the black monitor. "No customers by that name."

Father John fought back his disappointment. He was about to get to his feet when the big man, still bent toward the monitor, tapping an arrow key, said, "Hold on a minute. He might've been one of those Indian guys that picked up a couple Jeeps for a customer a while back. What did you say the name was?"

"Marcus Deppert." Father John settled back in the chair and allowed himself to feel a flicker of hope.

The dealer peered at the scrolling screen. After a moment, the yellow letters stood still. "Here we go," Beefer said. "I remember now. Outfit called High Country Tours bought two red Jeeps last November. Sent two guys for 'em. Rich Dolby was one. The other was your man."

High Country Tours didn't ring any bells. "Any names with that business?" Father John asked.

"Says here the owner's name is Steve Nichols." Beefer swirled back, facing Father John. "Unusual deal. This Steve Nichols called up, said he was starting a tour business in Lander, and placed the order. Everything was done by phone. Courier delivered a certified check, and

Nichols sent two Indians to pick up the Jeeps." The big man shifted in his chair, as if uncomfortable with the memory. "Tell you the truth, Father O'Malley, I wasn't keen on releasing 'em. Those Indians looked like a couple losers. Giant hangover types, you know what I mean? I wouldn't want 'em drivin' any vehicle I owned, but they had notarized letters saying we should give 'em the Jeeps."

"Any address?" Father John heard the excitement in his own voice. Maybe the Depperts and Loretta Dolby had been right; maybe Marcus and Rich were delivering Jeeps, if not for a dealer, for some private party.

Beefer turned back to the monitor. "Post office box downtown."

"Post office box." Father John felt as if he were back in his dream—watching a shadow disappearing ahead, always out of reach. He was chasing ghosts.

Big Phil had flipped open a phone book and was running one finger down a white page. "No Steve Nichols listed." He turned to the yellow pages. "No High Country Tours either. A guy starting a new business oughtta get listed in the telephone book first thing." He shut the book and clasped his hands on the top. "Strange deal, start to finish. You think something might've happened to this Indian kid?"

Father John heard the parent's concern in the man's voice. "I hope not," he said.

"I hear nobody's found that body you saw. Hope it's not one of those two Indians. They looked like trouble for sure, but you hate to see anything bad happen to 'em. You always hope they're gonna straighten out." The big man leaned back in his chair, staring at some point beyond Father John. After a moment, he said, "Come to think of it, there was a white girl with 'em.

Nice lookin', too. I remember wonderin' what she was doin' hanging around two guys like that."

"White girl?" Father John felt another surge of hope. Annie Chambeau had said Marcus left her for a white girl.

Beefer rose out of his chair and, looming over the desk, waved toward the plate glass window. Before he could refold himself, the cowboy salesman was back in the doorway.

"You remember those two Indians picked up the red Jeeps a few weeks ago?" Beefer asked.

The salesman's face looked blank for a few seconds before comprehension crept into his eyes. "Yeah, I think so."

"Father O'Malley here would like to talk to the white girl with 'em. Dark hair. Kind of tall with a great figure. Real pretty. You paid her a lot of attention while I was squaring things away with the Indians. You just hittin' on her, or she a friend of yours?"

The salesman's eyes darted from Beefer to Father John, as if this was some kind of test and he wasn't sure of the correct answer. "I seen her a few times over in Riverton at Herb's place. Jennifer somethin'-or-other."

"There you have it," Beefer said, turning his eyes on Father John as he waved the salesman away. "Anything else I can help you with?"

Father John glanced at the basketball photos on the wall behind the car dealer's desk. "As a matter of fact . . ."

"Say no more." The dealer sat back at his desk, pulled out the center drawer, and extracted a checkbook. Grabbing a ballpoint pen from a stand that looked like a miniature basketball, he began scribbling. "I'm happy to make a donation. Might show how folks around here appreciate St. Francis Mission. How about a couple hundred?"

"I could use a thousand," Father John said.

The dealer stopped scribbling and looked up, surprise and amusement in his eyes. "That's a lot of appreciation."

Father John began explaining. The mission had sixth-grade boys who could shoot a basket across the school-yard. They had talent and potential, but no gym to play in and no coach to bring them along. St. Francis had the gym, but no money to heat it and no money to pay a coach.

"You gonna be the coach?" Beefer asked, ballpoint poised over the check.

Father John laughed. "I've lined up somebody who knows the game. Patrick Banner."

Beefer dropped the pen and swirled around. Reaching up a long arm, he plucked one of the photos from the wall as if he were snatching a rebound. "See that kid there? My youngest. Best damn center in the state. You know who stopped him from bein' high school All-American? Patrick Banner. Every match-up between Lander and Indian High School, Banner'd block him so hard he'd only get a few shots, and they were off. Or that Indian kid would steal the ball and rack up points himself. And you expect me to help pay his coachin' salary?"

"The kids would appreciate it."

Beefer leaned back and laughed, a large, raspy sound. Then he lifted his glasses and rubbed his eyes. "Patrick Banner, huh? You got him for sure?"

"He's just out of the army. Hasn't connected with a job yet."

Grabbing the ballpoint pen, the dealer resumed scribbling. He tore off the check and handed it across the desk. "I expect him to teach those kids every damn thing he knows."

Father John reached out to shake Beefer's hand as they both got to their feet. "The kids and I thank you," he said. "You realize they'll be outscoring Lander High School in a few years."

"I'll be there to see it," Beefer said. "'Course, I'm not gonna like it much."

As Father John started across the showroom, he spotted the blue van at the edge of the bay. "One more thing," he said, stepping back into the cubicle. "Since the kids will miss the school bus, I'll have to get them home after practice."

Big Phil looked across the showroom toward the expanse of plate glass and folded his arms across his chest. "Okay, you got the van. But only on loan for basketball season. I'll have somebody bring it over to the mission."

Father John started to thank him again, but the car dealer held up one hand, like a policeman stopping traffic. "You ever decide on another line of work, Father O'Malley," he said, "come see me. I can always use a damn good salesman."

The cowboy salesman walked over as Father John was about to back the Toyota away from the bay. He rolled down the window, and the goatee and mustache came toward him, along with the stale odor of cigarettes and garlic. "Say, Father, I been thinkin'. I could stop in at Herb's place and get that waitress's last name and telephone number. Talk to her for ya, if you want."

"No, thanks," Father John said, his boot resting lightly on the gas pedal. The Toyota began rolling backward. He would talk to her himself.

‹ 27 ›

Vicky fed a quarter into one of the phones lining the wall at the end of the hospital corridor and tapped out the number to the Arapaho ranch. The hospital was shrouded in silence. A lone nurse sat at the station, her head barely visible above the counter. "Pick up," Vicky said under her breath to the electronic ring. She'd been trying to reach Ben all day. He had the right to know about Susan.

Suddenly the ringing stopped. "Yeah?" It was a man's voice.

Drawing in a long breath, Vicky asked to speak to Ben.

The line went quiet for a few seconds. Then, "This his wife?"

"Former wife. It's important I reach him."

"He ain't here no more."

"What do you mean?" Ben was the ranch foreman. It was a good job, a natural for him. He wouldn't just leave.

"Ain't you heard?" Again, the silence. Vicky knew what he would say before he said it. "Ben took sick."

Sick. Why was it so hard for her people to speak the words? Ben was drinking again. He'd been sober six long years, and now . . . She felt her stomach curling into knots. "Where is he?"

"Don't know. His cousin's tryin' to find him. You ask me—"

Vicky replaced the receiver. She didn't care to hear what he and the other cowboys thought about her visit the other night. They would blame her. Maybe she was to blame. She leaned onto the phone, trying to recover her own bearings. She had a sick, drug-addicted daughter to look after, and she could not depend upon her child's father. She had thought she could depend upon John O'Malley, but now . . . Now she was alone. Woman Alone was the name the grandmothers had given her, and she realized it was a gift, a prayer-wish that she would have the strength to live her new life. She ran a finger under her eyes to stop the tears and walked down the antiseptic corridor to Susan's room.

The girl stood at the bed, stuffing a small bag with things Vicky had brought her—a couple of pairs of jeans, two sweaters, some underwear, shampoo and a hairbrush, a pale pink lipstick. The lipstick was still wrapped in plastic. Susan looked thin and fragile. Red circled her eyes, but her face no longer had a pasty look. A little while ago, she had agreed to enter treatment again, and Vicky had made the arrangements.

They would fly to Denver tomorrow. The place Father John had recommended was far enough away to give Susan some time—at least a few days—before she would have to talk to the police. She would feel better then, stronger. And who knew what might happen in the meantime? If the white men were linked to murder—even the thought made Vicky wince—Banner might find enough cause to arrest them without Susan's help.

Besides, Vicky wasn't sure how much help Susan could be. Susan claimed she didn't know Ty and his friends were selling drugs. But she admitted Ty had started her smoking a new drug, although she wasn't sure what it was.

"Heroin?" Vicky had asked.

Susan had shrugged. All she knew was that it didn't take much to get that floating feeling. Why had she started again? She didn't know. She'd met Ty, and they got high together, and he loved her.

Vicky sat down on the edge of the bed. Her shoulders sagged. This drug, whatever it was, could have killed Susan. Thank God she was alive and starting treatment tomorrow. And their evening together stretched ahead. Maybe they'd watch some TV, if Susan felt up to it.

"You talk to Daddy?" the girl asked.

Vicky moved slightly on the bed, considering her answer. She could cover up for Ben. She'd done that for years. *Don't be afraid. Everything's okay. Daddy's just sick right now.* Codependency, the psychologists called it. They had that right. Ben had been dependent on alcohol, and she'd been dependent on him. But half of the equation had changed. She was aware of Susan staring at her.

"He's not at the ranch," Vicky said.

Understanding shot across Susan's face, and she grabbed the little suitcase and tossed it off the bed. It made a *harrumph* noise as it slid over the floor. She started sobbing. "Why am I goin' into treatment, then? I'm gonna come out and go right back on drugs. Just like Daddy. What's the point? I should just die now."

Vicky placed both arms around her and reined her close. If that happened, she thought, then she must die, too. She said, "Susan, I love you. Your daddy loves you.

You are very important. You are necessary." She kissed the girl's forehead. It was moist and cool. They sat in silence a few moments. Then Vicky said, "We should go now."

The nurse insisted Susan ride in a wheelchair. Susan looked like a child with the small suitcase in her lap and the nurse stationed beside her. Vicky left them inside the front door of the hospital while she crossed the parking lot to the Bronco. As she drove down the row of cars and trucks, she spotted a gray Chevy truck at the end. Her breath stopped. Then she saw its cab was empty. She had to get a grip on herself. Weren't there dozens of Chevy trucks that color in Lander?

She set Susan's suitcase in back through the open tailgate and tossed her black bag on top as the girl climbed onto the front seat. Before she got in, Vicky glanced toward the truck again. It looked like any other vehicle in the lot. Harmless. Not until she pulled out onto Bishop Randall Drive did she see it start to move. It turned onto the street after her.

Vicky stepped on the gas. Her heart was racing, and she forced herself to take a deep breath. She had to stay calm for Susan's sake. She debated driving back to the hospital, but thought of the small, gray-haired woman at the receptionist's desk and the otherwise empty lobby. She continued north into downtown.

The truck stayed close behind. She could make out that the driver was Gary. She had an advantage over him—she knew Lander. She approached an intersection and, glancing quickly around, stomped on the gas, zooming through the yellow light. The truck came through on the red. Midblock, she jerked the steering wheel right and peeled into a narrow alley that bisected two large brick buildings. Snow and slush washed over the windshield.

"Mom. What're you doin'?" Susan cried.

In the rearview mirror, Vicky saw the pickup pass the alley entrance. Another few seconds and it was backing into view, starting down the narrow passage, tires squealing. Susan looked back. "Oh, God," she said, slumping into the seat.

Vicky prayed no one stepped off the sidewalk as the Bronco shot out of the alley and wheeled right. At the intersection, she took another right and glanced out Susan's window. The pickup was emerging from the alley. Gary would have seen the turn.

Her speedometer hit fifty, fifty-five. She was on Main Street now, weaving through traffic, the pickup still behind her. Horns honked, and people stopped on the sidewalks and stared. "Where are the police?" she said out loud. Susan gasped.

Another right turn, then down another alley. Coming out of it, she swerved into an office parking lot and cut across the block to the next street. The pickup was no longer in the rearview mirror. She'd lost it, but there weren't many blocks in Lander. The odds were great Gary would spot her again. She rolled into another alley. Halfway down, she pulled in alongside a garage and nosed the Bronco against a high wooden fence. She cut the engine. Either the Bronco was hidden from the street, or they were trapped here.

Vicky kept her eyes on the rearview mirror, forcing herself to breathe slowly, half expecting the pickup to pull in behind them. What if Gary broke the window and tried to drag Susan out? What would she do? She had nothing to protect them with. She had a jack. But she would have to open the tailgate and dig it out of its compartment, and if Gary happened down one of the streets at the ends of the alley, he'd spot her for sure. Then she remembered the flashlight. She groped under the seat until she found the round, hard plastic.

"Why's Gary after me?" Susan said. "I don't know anything about what they're doing. Me and Ty, we just wanted to get our business going so we could get married. I wish he never brought those guys here. They ruined everything."

Vicky said nothing. They'd gone over this earlier, after she'd told Susan about Father John's hunch—that Gary may have murdered Marcus Deppert, then murdered the girl who could identify him. Susan had been shocked. Slack-jawed. She had sworn by the spirits of her grandmother and grandfather, by all their ancestors, that she knew nothing about any murders. Vicky believed her.

They waited in silence. Five minutes. Ten. Fifteen. Finally Vicky started the engine. The roar sounded like an approaching jet. She backed into the alley and slowly started toward the street, her eyes on the rearview mirror.

She zigzagged through the neighborhoods, not daring to drive one street for long. She could not go home; he would be waiting. At the edge of town, she made a dash for the entrance to Highway 789 and sped north. There was no sign of the pickup.

"Where we goin'?" Susan asked.

"Trust me," Vicky said. The irony hit her. Why should Susan trust her? They wouldn't be in this position had she been a different kind of mother.

The highway lay open ahead, the asphalt streaked with snow. At one point Vicky glimpsed what looked like a gray truck behind. She tightened her grip on the steering wheel as the truck swerved into the oncoming lane and passed. It was the color of honey.

She turned left onto Seventeen-Mile Road, and, just past St. Francis cemetery, made another left onto Circle Drive. She could sense her pulse slowing.

Easing up on the gas, she turned the Bronco down the snow-rutted road that ran alongside the administration building and Eagle Hall. A quarter mile farther was the guest house. She parked on the far side, out of view from Seventeen-Mile Road. They were safe here.

As she and Susan got out, Walks-on came loping down the road, a red Frisbee in his mouth. Susan patted her thighs, calling the dog over. "Oh, how cute you are," she said, crouching down and rubbing his head. "What happened to you?"

Vicky explained about Walks-on as she grabbed Susan's suitcase and her own bag out of the tailgate. Her mind was on the key. What had John said about a key? Had he given her one? She riffled through her bag, searching for a small piece of metal. No, he'd given her the piece of paper with the information about the treatment center. He'd said he would leave the key under the rock by the door.

Please be here, she said to herself, stooping over to lift the large rock. The silver metal glimmered in the moist dirt. She jiggled the lock a few times before the front door swung loose.

"He looks happy," Susan said, stepping inside. Vicky had to refocus her thoughts to realize Susan was still talking about the dog, who didn't look so happy as Vicky slammed the door. She threw the bolt. The house was one room containing a bed, a sagging sofa, and an old upholstered chair. Lined against the far wall were a small stove, a refrigerator, sink, one cabinet, a small wood table, and two chairs.

Vicky dropped the suitcase and her bag on the bed. After removing her coat, she checked the cabinet. A box of crackers, a box of Cherrios, two cans of chicken noodle soup, a can of tuna, a jar of peanut butter, a tin of coffee. Inside the refrigerator were a six-pack of Coke, some milk, orange juice, bread, a hunk of cheese, a dozen eggs. A wave of gratitude washed over her. A man she could count on, who spoke the truth, who stood by his word—she wasn't accustomed to this, and she had lashed out at him, treated him as if he were like Ben.

She pulled out two Cokes and handed one to Susan, who had already settled onto the sofa, her jacket thrown over the back cushions. Sitting down next to her daughter, Vicky said, "We've got to go over everything again, Susan. You must know something important, something you don't realize you know. Otherwise Gary wouldn't be after you."

◆ 28 ◆

Amid the bars and package stores along Highway 789 about a mile south of Riverton sat Herb's Place, a one-story rectangle, plastered with green asbestos siding, listing toward the snow-packed parking lot. A spotlight fastened at the front corner carved a small circle of light in the darkness. Two or three trucks and a few sedans straddled the snow and ice. Father John parked the Toyota next to a brown truck outside the rim of light, in case somebody from the reservation happened down the highway. The mission pickup parked at Herb's place would set the moccasin telegraph humming for weeks.

He stepped out into the frigid air and started toward the front door as an eighteen-wheeler roared past. Behind the truck was a dark pickup. Was it green? He couldn't tell for sure. He was beginning to see green pickups everywhere. In any case, Nick Sheldon had already delivered the warning. Why would he still have him followed if indeed Sheldon had ordered someone to try to scare him off?

As Father John pulled the front door open, it gave out a loud screech on the cement slab. Smoke hung inside like a gray cloud. A few patrons sat in the booths that marched down the left wall: a man and woman side by side, a couple of cowboys, four or five people crowded into the end booth. A middle-aged couple occupied one of the tables in the center. In the room that opened off the right, two cowboys were shooting pool.

He made his way past the tables to the bar on the opposite wall and slid onto a stool, shoving his cowboy hat back. It had been a long time since he'd sat at a bar, but it seemed like yesterday. The slick, polished wood, the little rings of moisture, the smell of beer and whiskey and cigarettes were all so familiar. His eyes stung, and his throat muscles constricted.

The bartender was busy mixing drinks, his back turned. Three cowboys straddled stools at the far end of the bar, their hands wrapped around beer bottles, voices sharp against the din of other conversations. A waitress stood apart from them, tapping long red nails on a round tray. Catching Father John's eye, she sidled toward him, scooting the tray along the bar. "Well, hello there," she said. "Haven't seen you in here before."

She was tall, with long blond hair and dark eyes. Her smile revealed almost perfect teeth, except for the tiny space in front that, oddly enough, made her seem prettier. But there was an unfinished sense about her, a false note of bravado in the short, skin-tight black leather skirt, the pink sweater with shiny beads at the top, the scooped neckline that revealed the graceful arch of her shoulders, the bulge of her breasts. The pungent, sugary sweet smell of her perfume wafted toward him.

"Are you Jennifer?"

"I'm Marcy," she said. The breasts moved closer.

He tried to ignore them. "What time does Jennifer come in?"

The bartender set two whiskey sours on the tray. "Nobody here by that name," he said, his eyes fixed on the waitress. He was six feet tall with the neck and shoulders of a bull and a forehead that sloped upward into a receding hairline. Father John guessed his age to be about forty.

"Take it easy, Herb," the waitress said. Picking up the tray, she pivoted on her high heels, leaning toward Father John. "Catch you later," she whispered before moving away.

The bartender swished a white cloth over the bar, mopping up the moisture rings. "So, what's it gonna be?"

"Coffee," Father John said.

"Irish coffee?"

"Nope."

Stepping sideways, the bartender picked up a glass coffee pot from a hot plate and poured steaming brown liquid into a mug. He walked back and set it down. "I thought I knew all the cops around here."

"I'm a priest."

Inflating both cheeks, the bartender blew out a stream of air. "You don't say. That's how come you look familiar. You're that priest I seen on TV works with them Indians over on the reservation."

That was right. Father John asked where Jennifer was working now.

The bartender shook his head. "How would I know? Never heard of her."

"How about Marcus Deppert," Father John said. "You heard of him?"

"This ain't no Indian bar. You must be lookin' for that place up the highway, the Get-Along. That's where them Indians hang out." The bartender walked down the bar toward the cowboys, who, Father John noticed, had stopped talking and were looking his way.

Father John took a drink of coffee. How did the bartender know Marcus was an Indian? The bartender was lying. People lied for many reasons: to hide something, to protect themselves, to hurt someone, or just out of sheer perversity. What was Herb's reason?

Whatever the reason, Father John knew he wasn't going to get any information at the bar. He stood up, fished some coins out of the front pocket of his blue jeans, and set them next to the coffee mug. The cowboys swiveled around almost in unison, watching him. He felt their eyes on his back as he strolled to the pool room.

The pool table took up most of the space, allowing barely enough room for a small table at the far end. Cues rested in a rack hung on the wall, and a black-and-white television blared a hockey game from an overhead shelf in one corner. Cheers went up as the puck sailed past the goalie. Rangers, two; Sabres, zip.

The two cowboys playing pool ignored the television, their attention on the pool table. They looked like brothers, medium height, wiry, with brown hair combed straight back, pink cheeks, little mustaches. They both wore cowboy boots, blue jeans, and long-sleeved western shirts—one red, the other blue—like a hundred other cowboys from ranches nearby.

Red Shirt stretched low over the table, sighting the cue. Then his arm pulled back and quickly sprang forward in a smooth stroke. The loud *whack* gave way to the *clack-clack* sound of balls shooting over the table. The four ball and six ball spun into the side pockets. He took another shot and two more balls pocketed. He circled the table, studying the lays, calling each shot before sinking the balls. The last was the eight ball, which rolled into the corner pocket as he had predicted. He straightened from the table, a wide grin creasing his face.

"Jesus. You lucky son of bitch," said Blue Shirt.

"Pay up."

Turning sideways, away from the bar, the cowboys leaned together, hands touching briefly. Then Red Shirt whirled around. "You wanna shoot?"

Father John shook his head. "I'm looking for someone. A girl named Jennifer. She used to work here."

The cowboys exchanged a quick glance.

"Why you lookin' for her?"

"She knows a friend of mine. Marcus Deppert."

Blue Shirt laughed. "You must be one of them guys loves Indians. Yeah, I can tell by lookin'. One of them do-good, liberal types. Traitor to his own race."

"Do you know her?"

They both shook their heads, and Red Shirt turned his attention to chalking his cue.

Father John took off his parka, tossed it onto the small table, and lifted a cue out of the rack. Poking his index finger and thumb into the little pocket of his jeans, he extracted a folded bill. Ten dollars. It was the last money he had. He set it on the rim of the pool table. "If you win," he said to Red Shirt, "it's yours. If I win, you tell me what you know about Jennifer."

The cowboys stared at each other, a mixture of amusement and challenge in their faces. Then Red Shirt said, "Deal."

Father John chalked his cue, trying to remember the last time he'd played pool. Grace House. There had been a pool table in the rec room. But had he played? Much of his time in treatment was a blur. Before Grace House, he'd played at the prep school where he had taught. He liked to challenge the kids once in a while, and sometimes he got beaten, but not often. Before that, his uncle's saloon on the street level of the apartments where he'd grown up. He and Mike would wander in and shoot pool in the afternoons waiting for their mother to finish work—she had been the cook in the saloon. He had learned to play pool from the best sharks in Boston.

Red Shirt tossed a coin.

"Heads," Father John said.

"Too bad." The cowboy quickly pocketed the coin. He racked up the balls. Stretching his lanky body along the cue, he took a long stroke that blasted the balls across the table. The three ball banked off the rails before dropping into a corner pocket. He put a lot of English on the next shot—a beauty. Two balls in the side pockets.

Father John stood quietly watching. The cowboy could shoot the eyes off a ball. He was going to walk out of here with the ten dollars and anything he might know about Jennifer.

The next shot was easy. Red Shirt looked up and smiled as he drew back the cue. A mistake, Father John thought. The cowboy was showing off. You couldn't get cocky at pool. You had to stay focused.

The sharp *clack* of the balls sounded. The two ball spun toward the side pocket, caught the edge of the bumper, and jumped back. Too much draw.

Now it was Father John's turn. He walked along the table, eyeing the best shot. Red Shirt had left a bad lay. Finally Father John spotted the shot. He pointed to the pockets he intended to hit and leaned over. The heft of the cue felt natural, his swing loose and fluid, as if his muscles remembered what his mind had forgotten. There was the *whack* and the *clickety-clack* of tumbling balls. The ten ball found its pocket, then the thirteen went down.

He felt his confidence returning, the familiar focus and intent of all the times he had stood on the pitcher's mound, as if the game were all. He couldn't make any mistakes. If Red Shirt got back in, he'd clear the table. He called the next shot, then sank the fourteen ball, leaving a good lay for a double. Another stroke put two more balls in. Then he sank the nine ball.

Only the twelve ball remained—a tough shot. He would have to bank off the cushion to put on just the right amount of speed. Too much and the ball would spin off course. Not enough, it would stop short.

The cowboys were quiet. Cheers went up on the TV. Father John closed off the sounds and nodded to the pocket. *Whummp.* The twelve ball took the hit and careened sideways before dropping in. Now the eight ball. He indicated the center pocket and sank the ball. An easy shot.

Father John picked up the ten-dollar bill and stuffed it back into his jeans pocket. "What's Jennifer's last name?" He kept his voice low.

Red Shirt removed a cigarette package from his shirt pocket, shook one out, and stuck it in his mouth. "Smith."

"Smith?"

"Hell, that's what she said." The cowboy in blue shrugged. "She was a drifter. Drifted up here from Cheyenne following the cowboys after Frontier Days."

"Yeah," Red Shirt said. He had lit the cigarette, and smoke curled out of his nostrils. "Us cowboys got groupies just like rock stars."

"Where does she live?"

"She never took me home with her." Red Shirt faced his partner. "How about you? You get lucky?"

"Yeah. In my dreams."

"What happened to her?" Father John asked.

"Up and gone one day." The cowboy in red threw back his head and took another drag from the cigarette. "About two weeks ago. Maybe old Herb out there tried to get inside her little panties. Wouldn't blame him none. She had one tight little ass on her."

"Not to mention a couple of gorgeous bazooms." His partner cupped both hands on his chest and did a little jig. His boots snapped against the tile floor.

"Ever see her boyfriend around?" Father John asked.

The room was silent except for the static noise on the TV and a woman's laughter floating in from the bar. A curtain began to descend over the cowboys' eyes. The one in red stepped back, stubbed out the cigarette on the floor. "The deal was the girl. Debt's paid. Interview's over. Time for a beer." Swinging around, the two cowboys started for the bar.

Father John threw on his parka and followed. Silence fell over the bar as he threaded his way past the tables, almost all of which were now occupied. Outside, the cold air smelled new and clean. He took a deep breath. Innuendo, sly exchanges, and a lot of theory, that's all he had. He was getting nowhere. The police would have to find Marcus. But would they? In the meantime the Depperts, old and alone, were waiting, fearing the worst. He had to keep on. Before Sheldon succeeded in closing down St. Francis, he had to find out what had happened to Marcus Deppert. The problem was, he didn't know where to turn next.

He was about to get into the Toyota when, out of the corner of his eye, he saw a shadow flit across the side of the building. He spun around, adrenaline pumping, expecting a couple of cowboys to be on him. The figure darted in front of the pickup. It was the waitress. He felt his muscles relax.

"Wait," she called, picking her way toward him over the ice and snow, coatless, hunched forward, hugging her arms. "I heard Herb say you're that priest that works with the Indians." She moved close to him. "I'm sorry about in there." She nodded toward the bar. "You know, my comin' on to you like that. I didn't know you was a priest. I mean, you just look like this sexy guy." Gone was the shaky confidence. In its place, fear. He could sense it.

"That Indian guy you're lookin' for,"—she dropped her voice to a whisper, even though they were the only ones in the parking lot—"he might be dead."

Father John felt his heart sink. "What are you talking about?"

"Those cowboys at the bar, they beat him up real bad." The girl was shivering so hard, her teeth were chattering. Father John took off his parka and placed it around her shoulders. "Tell me about it."

"A couple weeks ago, Marcus come to pick up Jennifer, just like usual. They were . . . together, you know. Well, the guys inside was waitin' when him and Jennifer come out, and they grabbed him and took him over there." The girl's head flipped toward the back of the building. "Jennifer come runnin' back in screamin' for me to call the police, but Herb said if I did, I'd get the same. Then he pushed us out here and made us watch. Said that's what happens to Indians that sleep with white girls. After they got done, they tossed him in his truck. Herb told Jennifer never to come back. I'd have left too, if I didn't need this fuckin' job."

She glanced toward the front door, the spotlight reflecting in her eyes. They had the look of a deer caught in the sights of a rifle. She went on, "I shouldn't be talkin' to you, but I been so stressed out. I can't stop thinkin' about it, like maybe I'm some kind of witness to murder."

"Where does Jennifer live?" Father John asked.

The girl shook her head. It was like a shudder. "An old place over on Locust Street near Tenth. It's got a black picket fence in front. Only she's not there no more. I been by a couple times. I think she must've took off." Slinging the parka around, she handed it to him. "I gotta get back before Herb sees me gone." She turned and started running, the high heels skidding on the ice.

Father John sat in the Toyota thinking a minute. It was the worst he'd feared. Marcus was dead. But it hadn't happened the way he'd figured. He'd had it all wrong. The elaborate scheme involving Susan and the three white men—they had nothing to do with it. No wonder Vicky had gotten so angry. She'd had every right. Marcus had been beaten to death in the parking lot of Herb's Place. *Dear Lord.*

But then what? Had Jennifer panicked? Tried to dispose of the body in the ditch on Rendezvous Road, then returned for it? That didn't make sense. Why would the girl protect the thugs in the bar? Why hadn't she taken Marcus to the hospital? Neither hospital had any record of Marcus Deppert.

Father John flipped on the ignition. The engine whined as he turned onto Highway 789. Traffic was light. A couple of trucks and a semi thundered past, shooting snow and ice into the air. He drove north with the traffic, praying silently for the soul of Marcus Deppert, hoping the young man had lost consciousness early and hadn't suffered. There was nothing else Father John could do now, except notify Banner, who would notify the Riverton police and hope they followed up.

But first he intended to check Jennifer's house, on the chance she might be around. He wanted to know about Marcus's last moments in case the old people asked him. He found Locust Street and drove north to Tenth, not wanting to admit it was probably a wild goose chase. The waitress said Jennifer had taken off, and the cowboys had called her a drifter. She had probably drifted on, like a storm that blew across the plains.

The street lights formed a corridor of light ahead, making the black fence easy to spot. He pulled in next to the curb. The house was dark, except for a trace of light around the curtain at the front window. He might be in luck.

He walked up the snow-bordered sidewalk, his boots creaking against the black ice. A storm door stood slightly ajar. He pulled it open and knocked on the inner door. It was quiet inside, the quiet, Father John thought, of a still, human presence. He waited before knocking again. Slowly the door opened the width of a chain, creating a long sliver of half-light. A young woman's face peered cautiously around the edge. "Who are you?" Her voice was high-pitched, like a child's.

"Father O'Malley," he said. Then he explained he was a friend of Marcus Deppert's.

"You got the wrong place." The door started to shut.

"Let him in." The male voice came from somewhere inside.

There was a moment with the door closed, with the muffled sound of a chain rattling. Then the door swung open. Beyond the girl stood Marcus Deppert.

‹ 29 ›

father John stepped into the room. There was a loud
thud as the girl slammed the door. A lopsided lamp
next to the sofa cast a dim light over the cushions,
the wood block table, the dark upholstered chair, and
brown vinyl floor. The odors of stale food and perspiration—the smell of fear—floated toward him.

Marcus looked as if he'd just gotten out of the chair.
He wore a wrinkled blue-and-white-striped shirt, the
cuffs of which hung loose around his wrists, blue jeans
with the silver image of a buffalo at the belt buckle, and
cowboy boots with scraped toes. Father John felt like a
parent; he didn't know whether to hug the young
man—he was so glad to find him alive—or throttle him
for causing so much worry.

He'd already been throttled. The dark bruise along
his jaw and across one cheek, the abrasions around his
mouth, and the blood-red whites of his eyes were evidence of that. "Are you okay, Marcus?" Father John
asked.

Confusion came over the Arapaho's face a moment.
Then he raised one hand and patted his jaw. "Some
white sons-of-bitches worked me over. Messed up my
face. Cracked a couple ribs. Nothin' fatal. Lucky I was
wasted." He shrugged, and Father John sensed it wasn't

the beating that kept Marcus prisoner in this cavelike bungalow.

"Meet Jennifer," Marcus said as the girl sidled over and took his hand, lacing white fingers among the brown. She was almost as tall as Marcus—about six feet—and dressed in tight blue jeans and a black sweater that clung to the contours of her breasts. She was barefoot. Tossing back her long brown hair, she stared at Father John out of dark, scared eyes.

He said to Marcus, "Your grandparents have been worried."

The young man looked away, shifting from one foot to the other. "I been tryin' to figure a way to go see 'em, make sure they're okay, but I couldn't risk it. They're lookin' all over the rez for me."

"Who? Tell me, Marcus. Maybe I can help you."

"Nobody can help. I seen what they did to Rich. They're gonna do the same to me." There was a catch in the young man's voice. He sank down into the chair, pulling the girl onto his lap. She curled her body along his.

Father John perched on the edge of the wood block table. "Start at the beginning," he said.

Marcus kept his voice low, almost a whisper. Rich Dolby came to him with a deal. Just like Rich, always lookin' to score. Last time Rich got one of his big ideas, Marcus went to Leavenworth for three years. He should've told Rich to get lost, but he got sucked in. Besides, he wasn't up to any other kind of work 'cause of the fuckin' broken ribs. So what the hell. All he had to do was drive brand-new Jeeps to Denver and back for some nice money.

Father John interrupted. "Who hired Rich?"

Marcus shook his head. "He got orders from two

white guys. Gary and Ty, he called 'em. I don't know last names."

Father John drew in his breath. Whatever trouble Marcus and Rich were in, Susan's friends were involved up to their eyeballs.

Marcus went on. "They gave Rich a certified check, and we went over and picked up a couple new Jeeps at Big Phil's. We drove 'em back to Rich's house."

Jennifer nodded to confirm this fact.

"A few days later, Rich comes over, says the Jeeps are ready, and we gotta go." Marcus emitted a small, scared laugh. "I swear, Father, I thought maybe we was gonna drive some big shots to Denver or somethin', but there was nobody but us. Soon's we got to Denver, we went to some warehouse by the railroad tracks and parked inside. All of a sudden guys come from everywhere and start crawlin' all over the Jeeps, pulling out packages. There was packages everyplace—under the carpet and dashboard, taped in the compartment with the spare tire—real neat and tidy-like. I was totally shocked."

"You didn't know you were delivering drugs?" Father John found that hard to believe, given Marcus's history.

"I swear by my grandfather," the young man said, a solemn look in his eyes. "I was mad as hell. I wanted to kill Rich myself for handin' me a one-way trip back to Leavenworth. Then these guys at the warehouse throw in three big suitcases, make us sign for 'em, and we take off for the rez. We don't stop for nothin', not even gas, 'til we get to Cheyenne, and I say to Rich, What the hell's goin' on? Don't worry, he says. It's a real cushy deal. Gary and Ty produce the stuff, and all we gotta do is drive nice new Jeeps to Denver every week, and the boys in Denver ship the stuff around the country. Rich says Gary and Ty got the risk, but I figure, no way, we got the risk. Police stop us, we got the stuff. I say I'm out, but Rich says, oh no, you're in. 'Cause I've already made a delivery.''

Father John removed his cowboy hat and ran his hand through his hair, mentally filling in the blanks. Gary and Ty and Morrissey Porterfield, the man Vicky called "the professor," were operating a drug lab somewhere on Wind River Reservation. But where? Not at the ranch house. There had been no sign of anything like that. That meant the lab could be anywhere in about four thousand square miles—in some abandoned barn, in an arroyo, a cave in the mountains. Without the lab there was no proof, only the story of a convicted felon.

"What kind of drug are they manufacturing?"

"Heroin," Marcus said.

Father John blew into one fist a moment. That fit. It was probably heroin Susan was on. But heroin was a different matter from the kinds of drugs—the pot and amphetamines—that Marcus and Rich had been mixed up with in the past. Heroin was a big-ticket drug, controlled by outsiders, by powerful forces. Father John felt as if the air had been sucked out of the room. Who was Susan Holden involved with?

"Where are they processing it?"

Marcus was shaking his head. "Not processing. They're making it. Leastways, it's the same as heroin. Rich called it fentanyl. Users don't know the difference. The beauty is, it's cheaper to produce than heroin, but costs the same on the street. So the profits are way up there. 'Course, you gotta have a brain that knows how to make the stuff."

"That would be the professor," Father John said. The

pieces were clicking into place, like pool balls dropping into the pockets.

Marcus looked startled. "You know the professor?"

Father John ignored the question. "Where's the lab, Marcus?"

The Arapaho let out a loud snort. "Like they're gonna tell us? Me and Rich, we was flunkies. All we know was what they wanted us to know."

That was probably true. Get two Indians with experience in peddling drugs to be the errand boys. "What happened after you got back from Denver?"

"We parked the Jeeps at Rich's, and I got the hell out of there. A couple hours later, he comes to my place over in Easter Egg Village and hands me a thousand dollars. A thousand dollars for twenty-four hours' work!"

"How many deliveries did you make?"

Marcus shifted in the chair, and Jennifer traced one finger along the side of his face. "Go on, tell him," she said in the little-girl voice.

"One more. Last week. Same thing as before. We deliver the packages to the warehouse and load up some suitcases. Only when we stop for gas, Rich don't shut up about those suitcases being filled with cash. Jesus, I told him. Keep it down. We'll have every cowboy in Wyoming after us. I should've known he'd pull somethin' stupid."

Marcus glanced at the girl, then continued. "Like before, we take the Jeeps to Rich's, and I go home to wait. Only this time Rich don't come over. I'm thinkin' he stiffed me. So I go lookin' for him. I check out a couple parties, but he ain't there. I go back to his house. Out in front are two pickups. Somethin' about 'em made me kinda uneasy, so I parked my truck down the road a ways, and circled back along the creekbed. Soon's I snuck up to the back, I hear shoutin' inside, and Rich, like, he's cryin'. I slide open the kitchen window just enough so I can see straight into the living room." Marcus blinked, as if he were seeing it still.

After a few seconds, he went on. "There were these two white guys. One's got brown hair; the other's kinda blond with this stubbly beard. They got Rich tied to a chair, and they're hittin' him. The blond guy, he says they're gonna teach him what's his and what ain't. Rich is cryin' hard. He's got on that necklace he always wore, and the blond guy starts twisting it around his neck. When he let go, Rich is coughin' like he's dyin'. He tells 'em to go look on the closet shelf. The guy with brown hair goes into the bedroom and comes back with a box. 'Half of it's here,' he says. The blond guy yells at Rich, 'You motherfucker!'"

Marcus stopped talking and stared off into space, as if he were watching a movie. "Rich yells out, 'Marcus got the rest!' and that's when hell really breaks loose. The blond guy grabs a star quilt off the sofa—Rich's mom made it for him—and throws it over Rich's head. Then he pushes a pistol against Rich's head, like this." Marcus bent his head toward Jennifer. "The other guy's yellin', 'No, man. Don't shoot him!' Jesus, I knew what was comin' down, but I was frozen stiff. I couldn't do nothin'." Marcus dropped his head into his hands, and the girl slipped both arms around him, hugging him close.

After a few seconds, Marcus looked up. "I got the hell outta there. I must've run down the creekbed a couple miles. Then I circled back and got in my truck. But no way was I goin' home, 'cause they'd be waitin'. That bastard Rich told 'em I got the other half. He must've hid it somewhere, thinkin' if they got half of it, they'd come after me for the rest and leave him alone. So I drove over here. Next thing I hear, my old girlfriend's been killed. Jesus! What'd she ever do to them? She didn't know nothin' about it."

Father John could hear his own breathing, mingled with that of the couple scrunched together in the chair. Somewhere a faucet was dripping. His theory was almost right. The blond guy who had gone to Annie Chambeau's was Gary. He'd been looking for Marcus, hoping Marcus would lead him to Rich. Somehow he had found Rich, killed him, dumped his body on Rendezvous Road, and then retrieved it. And he was still looking for Marcus.

"What kind of pickups were in Rich's driveway?" Father John asked.

"What?" Marcus blinked. "Just pickups. I don't remember."

"Think, Marcus. It's important."

"You said one was gray, right?" Jennifer said softly.

"Yeah, a gray Chevy."

"The other?"

"I guess it was a Dodge. Yeah. A green Dodge."

Father John placed his palms together, as if in prayer. Dear Lord. Ty had been following him since Monday, ever since he'd gone to Easter Egg Village looking for Marcus. Ty must have been watching Marcus's house. He must have decided to follow the red Toyota pickup, hoping that sooner or later whoever had come looking for Marcus would know where to find him. But why had Ty rammed the Toyota on Seventeen-Mile Road? Out of frustration? Or had that been an accident? Had he just gotten so close, he'd slid into the tailgate when Father John had slowed down?

The next time he had spotted the green truck, it had

stayed a good distance behind, as if the driver wanted to remain inconspicuous. Like tonight, when the truck rolled north past Herb's Place. Had Ty backtracked, come through an alley, and parked where he could see the parking lot? Had Ty waited and followed him here? Was he outside now?

"We've got to call the police," Father John said.

"I thought you was gonna help us," Jennifer said, a whine in her voice. "And besides, I don't exactly have a phone."

"No way." Marcus managed to liberate himself and was on his feet, leaving the girl propped in the chair alone, like a mannequin. "They'll send me back to prison. I'd rather be dead."

Father John stared at the young man a moment. Nothing was worse for an Arapaho than to be locked up, confined to a small space. It was like death. Being alive meant being free to walk the earth, breathe the fresh air, and feel the wind sweeping over you. "A lawyer might be able to get you some kind of deal," he said finally.

Marcus emitted another tight, hopeless snort. "Last time some lawyer got me a deal, I went down for three years. I don't want no lawyers. You talk to Chief Banner for me, Father, okay?"

Father John's instinct was to insist they go to Fort Washakie right away, to insist on driving them there. But he knew that would lead to an argument, and there wasn't time to argue. Not when Ty might be waiting outside. He'd probably already called Gary, who might burst through the door at any moment.

Father John said, "You both have to leave this house now."

"Nobody knows Marcus is here," said Jennifer. "We hid his truck in the garage out back."

Father John ignored her. He was thinking where to send them. The guest house was a possibility, but he had already told Vicky to take Susan there. He prayed Vicky had taken his advice.

Suddenly the girl blurted out, "That's how come you want to know about the trucks. You seen them. They followed you here, didn't they?" She sprang to her feet, gripping Marcus's arm. He looked stunned, as if he'd had the air knocked out of him.

"We gotta get out of here," the girl said. "We can go back to the motel." She took a deep breath and said, "We was hiding at that motel out north on the highway after those cowboys beat him up, in case they came lookin' for us."

Father John got to his feet. His legs felt cramped and stiff. "You leave first. Go out the back door. They're watching for me to come out the front. I'll wait until you drive away before I leave. I'll call you at the motel as soon as I talk to Chief Banner."

Jennifer darted across the room and disappeared through a doorway. Marcus followed her. After a minute, they were back, wearing their parkas. The girl had one boot on and was hopping around as she pulled on the other, grasping a little pile of clothes under her arm.

Father John let them out the back door and watched as they disappeared around the dark hump of a garage. After a moment, a truck, headlights off, slid down the alley. He shut the back door quietly and waited about five minutes before going out the front. The street was clear, with tiny specks of snow fluttering in the hollow glow of the streetlights.

❮ 30 ❯

The Toyota crept through the streets of Riverton, empty except for the 4x4s and sedans parked alongside the curb. Almost invisible snowflakes, like dots of rain, touched the windshield. The clouds were breaking up. It might stop snowing soon. Father John kept one eye on the rearview mirror—nothing but darkness. He began to breathe a little easier as he swung out onto the highway and headed south. It was possible Ty had passed Herb's place earlier without seeing the Toyota pull into the parking lot.

Suddenly headlights appeared behind him. He pulled out to pass a semi, watching to see if the headlights also pulled out. They stayed back. Just short of Arapaho Junction, he turned onto Seventeen-Mile Road, darkness swallowing the space in the rearview mirror. Another mile and he wheeled into the mission. The grounds glistened with new snow, and the buildings stood out in ghostly relief against the faint moonlight.

He parked in front of the priests' residence and hurried inside. The hallway stretched ahead, silent and gloomy in the darkness. Somewhere beneath the floorboards the furnace was hissing, but the house felt almost as cold as outdoors.

He flipped the wall switch in his office, strode over to

the phone on his desk, and punched in 911. He waited, thumping his fist against the desk top. The instant the operator came on the line, he said, "This is Father O'Malley. Put me through to Chief Banner."

The operator began explaining that the chief was off duty. "This is an emergency," Father John interrupted. He could almost taste his own impatience.

The line went dead for a couple of minutes. Then he heard, "Jesus H. Christ, John. It's past midnight. Don't you priests ever sleep?"

Father John sank into the familiar chair behind his desk and related everything Marcus had told him. He had the chief's attention—he sensed the intensity in the silence at the other end of the line.

"Where's Marcus now?" Banner asked.

"He wants to come in, but he needs some assurance he won't go back to prison."

"He's violated probation, for Chrissake. The feds are probably gonna drop him down the prison hole and leave him there," the chief said. "But that kid doesn't have a choice. He can't hide forever. Those white men will find him eventually. If he wants to save his lousy skin, he's gotta get himself over to Fort Washakie."

"He won't do it, Banner. You know Marcus. He'll take his chances. Soon as he figures out how to leave the old people so they'll be okay, he'll take off." Father John felt certain of this. Otherwise Marcus would have been gone by now. There was good in him. "You need him, Banner. There are murderers and a synthetic heroin lab on the reservation."

Father John could hear the chief take in a couple of deep breaths before telling him, "I'll get back to you first thing tomorrow."

"What about tonight, Banner?"

"Jesus, John. Give me a break."

There was a click, followed by the dial tone, and Father John pushed in Vicky's number. He let it ring a long time, his anxiety growing. Finally he slammed down the receiver, pulled on his parka, and strode back into the frigid night. Crossing the center of the mission, he followed the rutted road toward the guest house. "Please be here," he said out loud into the cold air.

The small house looked as if it had drifted with the snow into the clump of cottonwoods, the leafless branches laced together above the peaked roof. There was no sign of Vicky's Bronco. He could hear his heart pounding. She wasn't at home. She wasn't here. Where was she?

As he got closer, he saw the churned snow outside the front door, the tire tracks running toward the far side of the house, and the glint of the rear bumper just past the corner. Thank God, Vicky's rational side had won out. He was about to knock, then decided against it. Vicky and Susan both needed their rest. First thing tomorrow, he would try talking to Vicky again. He had to convince her that Susan should go to the police, for her own safety.

The house where the Jesuits of St. Francis Mission had lived for more than a century groaned in the quiet. Father Peter was asleep upstairs, Walks-on in the corner of the kitchen. A few minutes ago the dog had pattered down the hallway, toenails clicking against the linoleum, and stuck his head through the doorway. Then he had pattered back, a sentry assured all was well.

Father John stood at the window in his study, sipping hot coffee and waiting for Banner's call. The moonlight outlined the humps and swales of the white landscape, while, in the distance, the black mass of the Wind River Mountains rose into the silver sky. He was trying to figure out the missing part of the syllogism. Locate the missing part and the conclusion is obvious, he used to tell his students. Somewhere on the reservation three white men had set up a laboratory to produce a drug called fentanyl, a synthetic heroin. They had hired two Indians to deliver the drug to Denver, from where it could be transported across the country.

Who had the capability to produce and distribute synthetic heroin nationwide? A drug cartel? The thought of a drug cartel moving onto the reservation sent an involuntary shiver down his spine. Yet it made sense. A drug cartel could handle the entire operation. And it would know how to handle the profits—run the cash through offshore banks, launder it through legitimate businesses. What was it, then, that bothered him?

He whirled around, spilling coffee onto the carpet, and started pacing in front of the desk. Marcus had said he and Rich brought the cash back to the reservation. Suitcases full of cash! That was it—the missing piece he hadn't been able to locate. How could anybody dispose of that kind of cash in the middle of Wyoming? Deposit it? Maybe, but banks would report any amount above ten thousand dollars. And a constant influx of large deposits into the area's small banks would attract a lot of attention. No, banks were too risky.

Maybe the cartel intended to ship the profits back to Denver or to Los Angeles. He imagined large semis stashed with money rolling down the highway. But if that were the case, why bring the cash back to the reservation? Unless . . .

Father John stopped pacing and stared out the window again. He could hardly believe what he was thinking; it was preposterous, but it could work. The cartel intended to launder the drug money right here by constructing a large recreation center that would eventually metamorphose into a casino. It would be a closed system on an Indian reservation—production, distribution, and money laundering. He'd heard about something like this on the big Navajo reservation a few years ago. He'd never imagined it would happen at Wind River.

Father John drained the last of the coffee and stared into the night. Maybe he was grasping at straws, hitching onto some outlandish theory to save St. Francis Mission. So far he'd batted .500 with his theories. It wasn't Marcus Deppert's body in the ditch; it was Rich Dolby's. But Gary was the killer; he had been right about that.

If this new theory came close to the mark, it meant Nick Sheldon, the Los Angeles lawyer, dispatched here to buy St. Francis Mission and build a recreation center, was in charge of the entire operation. He had purchased the two Jeeps under the name of Steve Nichols, his own initials reversed. And Sheldon answered to the cartel— the Z Group.

Father John debated about returning to the guest house to wake Vicky. He wanted her to know they were up against an organization more powerful and deadly than either could have imagined. Rich Dolby and Annie Chambeau had gotten in the way and had paid with their lives. The people who worked for the Z Group wouldn't hesitate to kill again.

He pulled back his cuff and checked his watch. Ten minutes past two. He'd wait until daylight. If he woke Vicky now, she'd spend the rest of the night worrying. Besides, it was still just a theory. He had no proof.

The jangling telephone broke into his thoughts. He crossed back to the desk and picked up the receiver, hoping the ringing hadn't awakened Father Peter. He knew the old man had taken the hall phone up the stairs with him when he went to bed.

"John, you there?" It was Banner.

"Yes." Father John was surprised. He'd hoped Banner would contact the FBI agent right away, but he'd been prepared to wait until morning.

"Radio call just came in from the Riverton police."

Father John closed his eyes, afraid of what Banner would say.

"They got a double homicide. Indian man, white woman, both about twenty-five. Night clerk at the Buffalo Motel on the north side heard the shots about thirty minutes ago and called the police. Looks like a real professional job. Perpetrator's long gone, as you might expect. No positive IDs on the bodies yet."

Father John's mouth went dry. His breath came in quick, burning gulps. "Marcus and a woman named Jennifer Smith," he managed.

"That's what I was afraid of," Banner said. "That poor son-of-a-bitch. He should've gotten his ass over to Fort Washakie like I told ya."

"I'm going to the motel."

Banner said, "Yeah. I thought you might want to do that."

◄ 31 ►

four black-and-white police cars stood at odd angles
in the snow-shrouded parking lot, circles of red and
blue lights flashing into the gray night. Yellow tape
enclosed most of the lot. A neon sign blinked BUFFALO
MOTEL, except the U was dark. White doors looking like
tombstones lined the side of the low brick building,
with knots of people huddled on the sidewalk, parkas
flung over their pajamas. A couple of uniformed police
officers stood guard outside the center door.

Father John nosed the Toyota into the yellow tape
and slammed out of the cab. Stepping over the tape, he
walked toward the policemen, one of whom came to
meet him. He identified himself, and the policeman
waved him on. Another opened the door, and he
stepped into the brightly lit room filled with uniformed
officers, two detectives in suits, and a photographer
who was weaving about. Everybody seemed to be talking at once, a chorus of rising and falling voices. Light
from the large lamp in one corner streamed like sun-
shine over the two bodies on the bed.

"Father John O'Malley," he said to one of the suits as
he stepped through the crowd. The room went quiet.
He had been to murder scenes before, but had seen
nothing like this. Marcus and Jennifer lay side by side,

naked, the white female body curled gently toward the slim, brown, male body, in the same attitude they'd taken in the chair a few hours earlier. Part of Jennifer's face was gone, as was the top of Marcus's head. Red-black blood as thick as jelly pooled around their heads and under their shoulders. She had a look of peace about her. Marcus's eyes were open, frozen in death. He must have heard the killer burst through the door.

Father John made the sign of the cross over the bodies. "May the Lord preserve you and lift you up," he said out loud. "May the Lord forgive you and show you His mercy and compassion and hold you in His arms. May you live forever in the House of the Lord."

"Amen." The voices were soft and reverent. Silence settled a moment. Then, "Is this Marcus Deppert?" a detective asked.

"Yes," Father John said.

"How about the woman?"

Father John told him what he knew: her name; that she had worked at Herb's Place; that she came from somewhere else, possibly Cheyenne. He was thinking she had a little girl's voice, and she and Marcus had been alive a short time ago.

A gust of wind swirled about, pelting the parking lot with little kernels of snow. Just as Father John was about to get into the Toyota, a white BIA police car skidded to a stop a few feet away. The driver's door flung open, and Banner jumped out. "The old people gotta be told," he said, his forehead creased in worry. "You wanna take care of that?"

"I don't think so," Father John said, sliding inside the cab and slamming the door.

*   *   *

The Toyota bumped over the ridge of ice at the edge of the parking lot. Father John hunched his shoulders against the cold and stared past the shimmering head-lights into the darkness. How could he tell Joseph and Deborah Deppert he'd led Marcus's killers straight to him? That the Dodge pickup had followed him all week looking for Marcus? That he'd seen it earlier tonight and should have known it was hiding in the shadows, waiting, waiting. That he'd done exactly what the killers had hoped? How could he ever explain?

He was shivering inside his parka; his hands were shaking, even though hot air poured from under the dashboard. How could this have happened? If he hadn't been so worried about losing the mission, maybe he would have realized Marcus had to be in serious trou-ble to disappear the way he did. Maybe he would have tried harder to find him. And when he did find him, why hadn't he insisted Marcus go directly to Fort Washakie? Why hadn't he taken him?

The snow and ice and asphalt blurred in the head-lights, and Father John ran one gloved hand across his eyes, wiping away the moisture. The highway skirted the edge of Riverton, past the ghostlike garages and restaurants, the automobile parts store, the supermar-ket. Everything seemed to be dropping away, leaving him alone with the thirst that burned inside like a laser beam. It was all he could think about.

He passed Herb's Place, his eyes searching for the brown frame building set back about fifty feet from the highway. After another half-mile he spotted the lighted sign between two posts close to the curb. FRIENDLY LIQUOR STORE. 24-HOUR DRIVE-THROUGH. WE NEVER CLOSE.

Father John took a sharp left, crossing in front of an

oncoming truck that came out of nowhere. He pushed hard on the gas pedal—a reflex—as a horn bleeped into the early-morning stillness. The Toyota jumped the curb, barely missing the lighted sign. Easing on the brakes, he managed to wheel into the driveway and stop at a glass box that glowed like a Christmas ornament on the side of the building. He rolled down his window at the same time the Arapaho woman inside the box slid back a glass panel and leaned onto a tiny counter. "That you, Father John?"

He must know her, this Arapaho woman selling alcohol to her people. Well, it was a job. He couldn't recall her name, his mind had collapsed into the burning light inside, the tremendous craving. He stretched back against his seat to extract the ten-dollar bill from the pocket of his blue jeans. Reaching through his opened window, he flattened the bill on the counter. "A bottle of whiskey," he said, dimly aware of the hoarseness in his voice.

The woman stared at the bill. "You sure, Father?"

"Just get whatever it buys."

She picked up the bill and disappeared into the dimly lit interior. Wind gusted between the building and the Toyota, blowing snow against his face. He concentrated on the woman's return. She was taking forever. Finally she stepped back into the glass box and set a bottle in a brown bag on the counter. She held out the change. He waved it away and grabbed the bag.

The weight of the whiskey bottle on the front seat beside him felt light and cool against his thigh as the Toyota followed the curve of the driveway around the building and pulled out onto the highway.

‹ 32 ›

father John drove through the grounds of St. Francis Mission, past the school and the administration building, past Eagle Hall and the guest house. He drove on, the Toyota rocking over the ice-rutted road until it ran into a wedge of snow. The tires churned and strained before finally grinding to a stop.

He turned off the engine and flipped off the headlights. Easing the bottle out of the paper bag, he twisted off the cap. The smell of whiskcy floated around him as he stepped out into the gray moonlight. Cottonwoods loomed overhead, a ghostly presence with snow tracing the leafless branches. Dipping his chin into his parka and pulling his cowboy hat forward, he started walking through the wind-sculptured snow, bending his knees with each step, as if he were climbing a steep mountain. The whiskey sloshed out of the bottle and bored little holes into the snow as he went.

He reached the bank of the Little Wind River and lowered himself onto the trunk of a fallen cottonwood. The soft swish-swish of the wind in the trees mingled with the sounds of water gurgling over the blue-gray ice. The river was streaked in moonlight.

It appealed to his sense of irony to get drunk here. The last pastor of St. Francis Mission would admit his

utter failure at the exact place to which the first pastor
had come: Black Night's camp. It was to this place the
Arapaho bands had straggled from across the plains
when they had nowhere else to go.

Father John glanced around him. The village was here
among the cottonwoods: the tipis arranged in a circle,
the campfire burning in the center, the pony herd cor-
ralled off in the clearings. He could almost hear the
sounds of ponies neighing, women keening over all they
had lost, children coughing and crying.

Come and help us, Chief Black Night had pleaded
with the Jesuits. Father John repeated the words out
loud: "Help us. Help us find the future." It was a re-
quest of hope, an affirmation that there would be a future. And the first pastor had come by train part of the
way, the rest of the way on horseback, guided by the
warriors. He had said Mass on the banks of the river,
had consecrated the bread, raising it toward heaven: the
body of Christ, the presence of God in the word. In
hope, he had prayed.

Father John set the bottle into the snow next to his
boot and dropped his head into both hands. He heard
the sounds of his own sobbing as he prayed. "*O God of
abundance and mercy, forgive me, forgive me. Give me
the grace to hope.*"

Straightening his shoulders, he gulped in the icy air,
feeling it crimp his lungs. Then he reached down,
grabbed the neck of the bottle, and tipped it sideways,
watching as the whiskey carved a brown trench into the
snow. The fumes wafted upward, engulfing him. He got
to his feet and walked to the edge of the river, where he
stood a long while, watching the water cut its narrow
channel through the ice. Finally he walked back, picked
up the bottle, and threw it as hard as he'd ever thrown

a baseball. His shoulder muscles burned as the bottle sailed through the cottonwood branches out over the river, into the darkness.

He retraced his footsteps through the snow until he realized he had walked to the river in circles, and now sighted a more direct path. As he neared the Toyota, he spotted a slight, dark figure coming down the road. He knew it was Vicky. He went to meet her.

"I heard an engine," she said. Her breath came in frozen clouds. "It woke me. I looked out and saw the Toyota headed down here. Are you okay?"

Father John said nothing. He put an arm around her shoulders and guided her back to the Toyota. He could feel her shivering through the downy layers of her parka.

He let her in the passenger side, then tramped through the snow and slid in behind the wheel. "You'll be warm in a minute," he said, turning on the engine and pushing up the heat lever. He knew it would take a few minutes before the old engine began cranking out any heat.

"It smells like a bar in here."

"Don't ask," he said, staring past the windshield at the cottonwood branches tangled against the gray sky. He could feel her watching him.

Vicky was quiet for a moment. Then she said, "Ben has started drinking again."

"I'm sorry," he said. "It can happen."

"But you didn't start." Her voice was low.

Father John was aware of the hint of warm air starting out of the vents now, the soft shuddering of the motor, the silence between them. He turned toward her. "Not this time."

"Tell me what's happened. What sent you here?"

"Marcus Deppert was murdered a couple hours ago," he said softly. "He and a white girl. At the Buffalo Motel." He drew in a long breath, then began relating everything, letting it all come out: the drug lab, Gary and Ty, the murders of Rich Dolby and Annie Chambeau. He stopped at relating his latest theory about Nick Sheldon and the plans to close St. Francis Mission and build a so-called recreation center. It was enough to comprehend just the facts. The hardest fact was the murder of Marcus and the girl, the murders he might have prevented.

Vicky hadn't taken her eyes away. "You mustn't blame yourself, John." She reached out and laid a hand on his arm. "They would've found Marcus eventually. It was a question of time."

"I should have taken him to Fort Washakie."

"Yes," Vicky said sarcastically. "You should have hog-tied him and thrown him in the back of your pickup. Because that's the only way he would've gone. He was a stubborn Indian." Vicky paused a moment. Then she whispered, "We don't control everything, and everything isn't the way we want it to be. I've had to learn that."

Father John felt the pressure of her fingers through his parka. The Arapahos believed there was a healing grace in the touch of human fingers. He knew the truth of it.

After a moment Vicky took her hand away and looked out her window. "If anything, I should have listened to you and had Gary arrested for menacing and trespassing. He was waiting for us outside the hospital this afternoon, but I was able to lose him. That's why we came to St. Francis."

Father John said nothing. It was some consolation. At least he had told her about the guest house.

"And I shouldn't have been so stubborn," Vicky said, sadness in her voice. "Of course you were right. I should have tried to convince Susan to go to the police."

"It's not too late," Father John said. "Maybe she knows something that will help."

Vicky turned back to him. Moonlight washed across her face, and he saw the worry in her eyes. "What can that be? Susan and I have gone over everything. She swears she doesn't know what Ty and the others are up to. They kept her drugged, fed her a story about starting a business. Some business." Vicky shook her head. "Anyway, Banner and the feds have enough for a search warrant based on what Marcus told you. They're probably all over Lean Bear's ranch right now."

"They have to find the lab, Vicky. There's no proof, nothing to tie the white men to Marcus without the lab."

Vicky stared out her window again. After a few seconds she said, "The lab is not in the house or in any of the barns out in the pastures. That would be too risky. Ben could show up at any time and discover it. It would be like him—when he isn't drinking—to check on how they're taking care of things. He's a stickler for keeping everything in tip-top shape. No, the lab is somewhere else, somewhere not Ben or anyone else would think of going to, especially in the winter."

Suddenly Vicky laid her head back on the top of the seat. "Oh, my God," she said, drawing out the words. "I know where it is."

◀ 33 ▶

Father John kept his eyes on the Indian woman beside him, staring up at the roof of the cab, a smile playing at her mouth. The last piece of the puzzle, and she had figured it out. "Where?" he asked.

Vicky raised her head and turned toward him. "Last Tuesday," she began, "when I drove up to the ranch to see Susan, the gate was closed. I was about to climb over when Gary came barreling down the mountain in a Chevy pickup. Down the mountain! I wondered at the time. There's nothing at the end of the road except the top of the mountain and probably twenty feet of snow. But about three miles up is the turnoff to the upper pasture. It's secluded, surrounded by mountain peaks. There's a barn and a couple of small buildings. The lab must be in one of them. That's where Gary had been. He must've come back to the ranch for something; maybe he forgot something. Anyway, he found me."

It could be, Father John was thinking. But how would Gary and the others know about the upper pasture?

As if she had caught the drift of his thoughts, Vicky said, "It was one of Susan's favorite places. It was where she learned to ride the gelding her father gave her on her eighth birthday. She probably told Ty all kinds of things about growing up on the reservation. She was in love with him, John. Women tell those things to the men they love. Unfortunately Susan fell in love with the wrong man." Vicky looked away again. "She's not the first woman to do that."

Father John leaned one shoulder into the window, took a deep breath, and blew it out. "Then it's over," he said. "Banner and the feds will find the lab."

"No," Vicky said, jerking upright. "They won't find it. It's not part of Lean Bear's ranch. It's a separate forty acres Ben inherited from his grandfather. A high mountain meadow good only for pasturing sheep in the summers. It was beautiful in the summers, filled with lupin and wild roses. We used to camp up there sometimes . . ." Her voice trailed off. "No one would know to look there. And anyway, a warrant for the ranch wouldn't cover the upper pasture."

"Banner has to be told," Father John said, jamming the gear into reverse. The tires screamed as they dug into the frozen earth. He shifted into forward, then into reverse again, rocking the Toyota free from the wedge of snow. As they began backing through the ridged tracks, he rolled down his window and stuck out his head to keep the Toyota in the narrow road. He backed all the way to the guest house.

"I'll call Banner and arrange to bring Susan in. She and I are supposed to fly out of here in the afternoon." Vicky grasped the door handle, then hesitated. "I called that Jesuit friend of yours who runs the rehab hospital in Denver, Jim McCarthy. Only I spoke with his wife. She said they had a long waiting list. When I mentioned your name, she agreed to admit Susan right away. Tell me, how is it Father Jim McCarthy has a wife?"

Father John was quiet a moment. Then he said, "Jim

was laicized. I guess he met someone he wanted to spend the rest of his life with."

"I see," Vicky said, opening the door and sliding out.

No, she didn't see, Father John thought, watching her disappear into the guest house. Jim McCarthy could no longer *be* a priest.

Father John punched in Banner's numbers again, trying to ignore the sounds of metal pans banging and cabinet doors slamming in the kitchen. Elena had arrived and was obviously registering her displeasure over the fact that he had trespassed on her domain to brew himself some coffee. He took another sip from the mug as the disembodied female voice on the other end of the line solemnly assured him the chief would return his call the minute he came in. She had said the same thing an hour ago.

He slammed down the receiver and glanced up from the desk, startled at the silent specter in the doorway: Father Peter in the oversized black coat that trailed along the tops of his boots, his black fedora squashed into the rim of fuzzy white hair. Just returned from saying Mass for the old faithfuls. He looked stricken.

"Leonard Bizzel, a reliable source of information, informed me about Marcus Deppert and the young woman. I offered the Mass for the repose of their souls. 'Confusion now hath made his masterpiece! Most sacrilegious murder . . .'"

Father John took another pull of the coffee. The gray light of morning filtered through the window, creating patterns of shadows over the walls and carpet, the wingback chairs. He had no patience for Shakespeare right now; he wanted Banner to call.

"*Macbeth*, act two, scene one," Father Peter said, sadness in his tone.

The jangling phone mingled with the sound of the old man's footsteps shuffling down the hallway. Father John pounced on the receiver. "Banner! What's happened?" He wasn't sure it was the chief until he heard the voice hoarse with tiredness.

"Listen, John," Banner said, "we've checked out Lean Bear's ranch. House, barn, outbuildings—totally clean. We didn't find a crystal of fentanyl, heroin, or anything else."

"What about the men?"

"Gone."

Father John felt his heart sinking. "What do you mean?"

"Cleared out. No sign of them. We've got an all points out. Meantime, the feds are runnin' the names through the computers, lookin' for priors. We're gonna get these dudes, don't worry."

It wasn't reassuring, Father John thought. The police hadn't ever located the gray Chevy truck after he had found the body—Rich Dolby's body—on Rendezvous Road.

"What about the buildings in the upper pasture?"

There was a pause on the line. "What upper pasture? What're you talkin' about?"

"The forty acres up the mountain."

"Jesus. You mean where Ben Holden used to pasture his sheep years ago?"

"That's where they're manufacturing fentanyl."

Father John heard the sharp jabs of breath. "You know that for sure? You seen it yourself? You know somebody who's seen it? You got any proof?" Anger mixed with incredulity in the chief's voice.

Father John admitted he hadn't seen it. There were no eyewitnesses, nothing except Vicky's hunch.

"Vicky and Ben been divorced a long time," the chief said. "What's she got to do with this?"

Father John ignored the question. Vicky would be bringing Susan in soon. She could explain it herself. He said, "It's there, Banner. Go back. You'll find it."

"What you're sayin' is the fed and I gotta go see the magistrate in Lander, who's real happy with us right now 'cause we roused him out of bed before dawn to get a search warrant which turned up nothing. Absolutely nothing. And now you're suggesting we ask him for another warrant? And on what evidence? That *you* know somebody who's got a hunch the drug lab's there."

"Trust me, Banner. I'm sure Vicky's right about this."

"Well, it's like this, John. We got a big problem. The magistrate was real reluctant to give us warrant number one. It's not like we had hard evidence to connect three white guys with last night's homicides. All we had was what Marcus told you—hearsay. And Marcus, poor son-of-a-bitch, wasn't the most reliable Indian in the world. However, because of the homicides, the magistrate went out on a limb and gave us the warrant, along with a little warning against racial harassment."

"What?"

"Harassing three white guys on an Indian reservation. After my boys went out there this week and had a discussion with Gary Rollins about where he was Sunday night when you spotted the body, he called an attorney and complained about harassment. And the attorney called the federal magistrate and said we were harassing whites for no reason. So, like I say, we were lucky to get one search warrant, and the magistrate's not gonna give us another without some hard evidence."

"Who is the attorney?" Father John stared out the window at the snowy grounds glistening in the morning light. He knew the answer. He was waiting for the confirmation.

"Some big shot out of Los Angeles. Just the kind liable to file a big harassment case against the tribe. Shaffer, Shelby."

"Sheldon?"

"Yeah. You know him?"

Father John's hand tightened on the receiver. The wild supposition, the preposterous theory—it was right. "Listen, Banner, the three men could be at Nick Sheldon's place in Lander. It's the large red brick house on the north end of Martin Drive."

The chief was quiet a moment. "This another one of your hunches?" he asked, then, hurriedly, "Okay. I'll put in a call to Detective Loomis in Lander, ask him to check it out. Soon's we get a chance to question those guys, one of 'em might decide to tell us about the lab. Then we'll have something to take to the magistrate."

Yeah, Father John thought as he replaced the receiver. *And if no one talks, you'll have nothing to take to the magistrate.*

He was struggling into his parka when Elena came down the hallway, the laces of her black shoes flapping against the linoleum floor. "I got your breakfast ready."

"Sorry," he said, brushing past the old woman. He hurried out the door down the sidewalk, into the rays of sun breaking through the cold air.

‹ 34 ›

Sage Canyon was divided into sun and shadow under the pale blue sky. Shadow washed over the snow-crested boulders on the mountainside, while sunlight danced in the abyss above the creek. The snow had not yet started to soften on the asphalt, and Father John could feel the rear tires slipping. He tried to concentrate on the road winding upward, but his thoughts were on Banner. He was a good policeman. He wouldn't sleep until he had closed down the drug lab and arrested the murderers. Eventually he would nail them. In the meantime—

In the meantime, Sheldon and the men he was paying were looking for Susan, and eventually they would find her. They might even trace her in Denver. As long as they were free, the girl and Vicky were in a kind of prison with no hope of release.

The mountainside sloped into a snow-covered valley as he passed Lean Bear's ranch. The gate stood open. Tire tracks cut through the snow to the house, but no vehicles were about. The house looked deserted, suspended in the white landscape. He glanced at the mileage. Three miles farther, Vicky had said.

The road narrowed as the Toyota climbed higher, skidding slightly around the sharp curves. He spotted the turnoff and wheeled toward it, but the Toyota balked and slid sideways. Suddenly he was spinning across the road in slow motion, making wide loops toward the rocks and trees, then out to the edge of the road. He pumped the brakes and turned the steering wheel into the spin. The rear tires shuddered as they sought a purchase in the snow. Finally they began to grip. The Toyota stopped. He rolled down his window and looked out. The tailgate hung over the abyss of the canyon.

He eased on the gas, willing the truck from the edge. Gradually it started across the road and up the narrow trail. It climbed through the shadows of ponderosas laden with snow, churning through tire tracks left by somebody else. About a mile and a half up, the road burst out of the trees into a wide clearing—the upper pasture. A blanket of white spread into the distances, surrounded by the snow-girded peaks of the Wind River Mountains.

Two small buildings stood off to the right. A rancher might care for orphaned ewes in one; a family could spend the cool summer nights in the other. Beyond the buildings, close to the rim of the trees, stood a barn. It had been painted at one time, and traces of green showed on the wood. Parked alongside it were three vehicles: the gray Chevy pickup, the green Dodge pickup, and a red Jeep.

Father John let out a low whistle. The lab was here, all right, and so were Gary and Ty when he'd just sent Banner and the Lander police to Sheldon's house. There was always the possibility Banner would find some excuse to check out the upper pasture, but he couldn't count on it. He threw the Toyota into reverse and started backing down, rounding a curve out of sight of the barn. He rammed the Toyota into a windswept clearing in the trees. The wind sighed in the branches and peppered his face with snow as he hiked back up the mountain, staying among trees, his boots sinking into the powder.

At the edge of the pasture, he heard loud, angry voices mingling with the wind that swished across the open spaces and a slow humming noise he couldn't identify. He moved sideways, staying close to the trees, then darted to the back of the barn and inched toward the small window. It was painted black inside, and he caught a glimpse of his own face. It surprised him: the prickly, unshaven chin, the flecks of perspiration on his forehead, his cowboy hat set back. Below the window stood a generator that emitted a sound like a hive full of bees. A faint antiseptic smell hung in the air.

"No murder!" a man shouted as Father John moved along the side of the barn toward the front. He heard another voice, low and calm, saying, "Unexpected problem . . . deal with it." It was Sheldon's.

Father John came around the corner. The barn door stood partly open. "You had no right to involve me in murder." The first voice again. The quiet, reasonable voice of the lawyer responded, "You have no reason to worry."

Father John moved slowly along the front, then bent toward the opening. The smells of chemicals—alcohol and ether and ammonia—stung his nostrils. The opening offered a clear view of half the barn. Long fluorescent bulbs dangled on black cords from the ceiling; light reflected off the stainless-steel table against the wall. Plastic and glass bottles, small glass dishes, flasks, and glass containers filled with liquids of various colors lined the tables, while the shelves above sagged under the clutter of boxes, packages, and bottles. On each bottle were white labels with large black letters that spelled out the words "Flammable" and "Explosive." At the far end of the barn stood a steel cabinet with glass doors. Behind the doors were still more bottles, all with black-lettered warning labels. Someone had stuck a red sign at the top of one door: DANGER. KEEP SPARKS AND FIRE AWAY. The cabinet itself seemed to fold upward into a hood, like a metal tipi, that, Father John figured, vented fumes from the bottled solvents to the outside.

Across from the cabinet stood a closet, its door padlocked, and on the floor next to it was some kind of fan encased in metal. It made a soft whirring noise. Father John had seen other barns on the reservation with this kind of rigged-up heating system, only here the boiler was locked in the closet away from the chemicals. He could feel the thin stream of warm air blowing across the barn.

Close to the fan stood Nick Sheldon, hands thrust into the pockets of his gray overcoat, black boots sunk into the red carpet spread across the dirt floor. He faced a stocky middle-aged man wearing a long-sleeved white shirt that strained against its buttons and blue jeans that sagged below his belly. A black beard wrapped around his chin and mingled with his curly dark hair. "Murder wasn't part of our contract, you S.O.B.," he shouted, reaching up a pudgy hand to push his plastic-rimmed glasses into place.

Sheldon bent toward him. "For a professor you can be very dense, Morrissey. I've explained that whatever happens outside this lab is no concern of yours. You do your job; we take care of ours."

The man with the beard reared backward, fists clenched. Father John thought he might slug the lawyer. Sheldon must have thought so, too, because he stepped back and took his hands out of his pockets.

The professor whirled around and brought both fists down hard on the stainless-steel table, sending a glass flask rolling toward the edge. He grabbed it, set it upright. Keeping his eyes on the flask, he said, "This was supposed to be a well-organized business enterprise.

You were supposed to be businessmen. Instead I find you are nothing but a bunch of bungling murderers." He turned back slowly, fists still clenched. "Well, I'm leaving here. Go find yourself another genius."

"You don't mean that, Morrissey." Sheldon placed one hand on the professor's shoulder. "Where would you go? Back to some dead-end job in some podunk college where no one appreciates you? This is your dream. A lab equipped to your exact specifications. Anything you want, we provide, just so you can work your wonders with no interference. Just to show you how much we appreciate your genius, Morrissey, I've been authorized to double the amount we originally agreed to pay you."

The professor seemed to relax; his shoulders rounded, he looked as if he might cave forward. Father John stepped quickly around the corner and darted again for the trees. He'd seen enough, heard enough, for Banner to get the warrant. He ran downslope a short way, then angled toward the road where he could make better time. He had to drive out of here before Sheldon started back. Most likely the lawyer had driven up here in the Jeep. And while the police were looking for the two pickups, Gary and Ty were probably using the other Jeep. But where were they? How long before Gary figured out where Vicky had taken Susan?

Just as Father John came around the curve, a gust of wind whipped the snow off the trees, engulfing him in a white cloud. He ran through it, then stopped in his tracks. Standing in the road ahead was Ty, wearing a dark parka, a knit cap pulled low around his face, and aviator sunglasses. He raised the blue-black barrel of a shotgun. "Turn around and keep walkin', Father," he said. "We gotta go see Mr. Sheldon."

ather John didn't move. "You don't want to do that, Ty. It would blow the only chance you've got." It was a gamble. He detected a hint of deference about the young man, even while his hands twitched on the gun, which was waving back and forth.

"What d'ya mean?"

"The police know about the lab. They're on their way here now." That was probably a lie, although Father John was praying Banner would find some excuse to get up here. He took a gulp of air and went on. "Four people have been murdered, Ty, and you're involved."

The young man's eyes widened; his head began shaking. "I ain't no murderer. I didn't kill nobody. I didn't even know about that Indian girl in Lander 'til after Gary shot her. Hell, I tried to stop him from shootin' Rich Dolby. And Mr. Sheldon just told me to find Marcus Deppert, and that's what I did. You was a big help."

Father John felt his stomach muscles constrict, as if he'd been hit with a fastball. The gun jerked upward, and the young man went on: Having figured that sooner or later Father John would lead him to the Indian, he had followed the Toyota. Last night he followed it to Herb's Place and then to the house. He was parked around the corner when Marcus and the girl drove out of the alley.

He followed them to the motel and called Sheldon. "I done my job, that's all. I ain't responsible for what happened next." Ty shifted from one foot to the other.

"Sorry," Father John said. "That's not how it works. You're an accessory to murder, and you're looking at spending the rest of your life in prison. But if you turn yourself in, things might go easier for you. We can drive to Fort Washakie right now. It's your only chance."

Ty's whole body began to shake. The shotgun moved back and forth erratically. "Nice try, Father. But I got other plans. I'm gonna collect what Mr. Sheldon owes me and, soon's Susan gets here, me and her are gonna cut out."

Father John made an effort to keep his voice calm. "What are you saying?"

A kind of smile crept into the young man's eyes. "Mr. Sheldon figured out you'd be hidin' Susan and her mom. So he sent Gary over to the mission to get 'em. He's bringin' 'em up here right now. And Mr. Sheldon's not gonna like you snoopin' around the lab. So start walkin', Father."

"Ty, don't you get it?" Father John heard himself shouting against the mountain stillness. "They're going to kill Susan and her mother."

The young man came forward jerkily, raising the barrel until it was pointed at Father John's head. "Don't try trickin' me. Mr. Sheldon ain't gonna kill my girlfriend. He knows we're gonna get married. Turn around and walk, or I swear I'm gonna have to shoot you. I don't want to, Father, so don't make me do it."

Father John turned slowly and started up the road, the muzzle hard against his back. Their boots scrunched the snow as they crossed the open space in front of the barn, and Father John heard the voices inside. Their tones were calm now, like those of two businessmen discussing shipments and packages. Ty kicked the door wide open, and he and Father John stepped inside. The voices went quiet as Sheldon and the professor whirled about. "My God," the professor yelled. "Get that gun out of here. This is a laboratory, you fool. There are highly volatile chemicals here. What are you trying to do, blow us to pieces?"

Sheldon seemed unfazed as he nodded toward Ty. "Wait outside," he said.

"I need my money, Mr. Sheldon."

"Get out! Get out!" The professor threw both hands into the air. His face had turned the color of rust, and his glasses slipped down his nose.

The lawyer stepped forward. "Wait outside," he ordered Ty. "We'll discuss the matter later."

Ty started backing up, eyes darting between Sheldon and the professor. His arms shook, and the shotgun danced in his hands. The professor watched him leave, then sank against the edge of the table. Extracting a folded white handkerchief from the back pocket of his jeans, he began mopping his forehead. "Idiot," he said, spitting out the word.

Sheldon turned toward Father John. "Well, Father O'Malley," he said. "I wondered how long it would take you to find our lab. The girl told you, right?" The lawyer shrugged. "That's unfortunate. And everything could have been so simple. You could be looking at a nice vacation on a white sandy beach in Antigua if you hadn't insisted upon meddling. I regret very much that matters have reached this stage."

"Here they come," Ty shouted from outside.

"Listen, Sheldon, Susan doesn't know what you're up to. Her mother is taking her to Denver this afternoon so the girl can enter treatment. None of this is any concern of theirs. Do something decent, and tell Gary to take them back to the mission."

"Decent?" The lawyer's eyebrows shot up in mock surprise. "I'll leave that to you, Father O'Malley. It's somewhat late for me," he said.

Father John heard the rustle of footsteps and turned around just as Vicky and Susan stepped through the opened door, Gary behind them. The girl's eyes had a dazed look behind her glasses, as if she were having trouble making sense of things, but Vicky's eyes flashed with rage. Then he realized Gary had a pistol jammed into her back. "Here they are, Mr. Sheldon," he said. "Just like you ordered. Anything you want, you can count on me."

"Shut up," Sheldon said. Gary's head snapped backward, as if he'd been struck. The professor flinched, one hand grabbing the edge of the table. "If it hadn't been for your stupidity," the lawyer went on, his eyes riveted on Gary, "we wouldn't have this problem. With hundreds of miles around here, you dump Dolby's body where any fool can find it, then you blow away a girl in her apartment, and shoot two people in a motel, for God's sake. Now we've got the FBI and the police swarming everywhere."

"Sheldon?" Vicky turned toward Father John, and he saw all the pieces come together in her eyes. She had grasped the whole picture. He shot her a warning look: *Don't say anything. Don't let them know what you know.* She stepped closer to Susan, as if to protect her, and Gary followed, the gun still in Vicky's back.

The professor inched forward, one hand outstretched. "Is that a gun? My God, another gun? Get out, you fool, you stupid bloody fool."

The lawyer ignored him and advanced on Gary, driving a fist into his arm. "You now have the chance to redeem yourself." He glanced around at Father John. "You like that, Father? Redemption? That's what life's all about, right?" Turning his attention back to Gary, he said, "You have created this problem, and you are going to take care of it. All three of these people will disappear out there in all that space. And nobody's going to stumble on the bodies. Not ever. Do you understand?"

Suddenly the professor bolted toward the doorway. He was nearly outside when Gary yanked him back with one hand, sending him sprawling onto the carpet, his chubby legs peddling the air. His glasses flew under the table. Slowly he twisted his bulky body around, crawled over and picked up the glasses, then got to his feet. He extracted the white handkerchief again and mopped his forehead. "I don't want to know what you're going to do," he said, looking from Sheldon to Gary, as if expecting to be thrown again on the carpet.

Susan started to cry, and Vicky slipped an arm around her shoulders. Father John stepped between them and the lawyer. "Let them go," he said.

"Now why would I do that?" There was amusement in Sheldon's eyes.

"I'll speak to the elders and the business council on behalf of the recreation center. The Arapahos will think that the Jesuits—that I—have abandoned them, and it will make it easier for them to accept your proposal. The Z Group should appreciate that, after all the problems you've had." Father John saw in the lawyer's expression he'd hit the bull's-eye.

Sheldon stared at him a moment. "I'd be a fool to accept your conditions. There won't be any opposition to closing St. Francis Mission after the pastor disappears,

along with his lady friend and her daughter. Run off together. Oh, my, the scandal." The lawyer straightened his
shoulders and nodded to Gary. "Take them outside. Walk
them over to that gorge where you brought Dolby's body."

"Listen to me, Sheldon," Father John said. "The police know about the lab. They're on their way here
now." He was stalling; the chances of Banner showing
up were becoming more and more remote.

The lawyer let out a loud guffaw. "If that were the
case, Father O'Malley, you wouldn't have come here."

"Let's go," Gary said, stepping behind Father John
and pushing the pistol hard against his back. He followed the two women through the doorway.

"Not Susan." Ty's voice came like a blast of cold air.
He moved into the doorway, blocking Gary. "Mr. Sheldon, you promised me nothin' would happen to Susan
if we brought you to the reservation. You said she
wouldn't never know what we was doin'."

"Get out of the way, Ty." Sheldon's voice came from
inside.

"I told ya, not Susan," Ty shouted. Father John
glanced around just as the young man raised the shotgun and leveled it through the doorway. Gary was coming toward him, arms extended, pistol aimed.

"Run," Father John shouted, stepping between the
women, grabbing them around the waist and propelling
them toward the trees. The frantic, hysterical voice of
the professor pierced the air, like the wail of a wild animal. *"Don't shoot!"*

Father John flung the women in front and pushed them
down, throwing himself on top, cradling Vicky's head
under his right arm. There was a sharp, sporadic popping
noise and then the roar of explosion, of wood and glass
shattering, of metal shredding. He felt the ground trem-

ble, the blast of hot air rush over him, and something as hard as a baseball thud against his arm. The noise reverberated through the air, as if they were inside a barrel. Then there was the sound of fire and the putrid, acrid smell of smoke. Someone was screaming—a woman. The sound was muffled in the snow, and from somewhere, floating as if in a dream, came the sound of sirens.

He struggled to get to his feet. It was as if they'd been welded together, he and Vicky and Susan. Chunks of wood and stainless steel and glass, pieces of plastic bottles, lay strewn in the snow around them. A thick beam lay a few inches from where his arm had sheltered Vicky's head. Then he saw the red streak, like a ribbon in Vicky's hair.

"Oh, God, no!" he heard himself shouting. He laid the palm of his left hand flat against her neck. He could feel her pulse, or was he imagining it? "Vicky, Vicky," he said.

She began moving beneath his hand. Slowly she turned her head and stared at him, shock and fear in her eyes. "I think I'm okay," she said, her voice hoarse as she tried to sit up. He placed his left arm around her waist and pulled her away from Susan, who was also starting to move. She was crying softly.

The sirens seemed louder as he helped them both to their feet, aware he could only use one arm, aware of the pain spreading like acid up his right arm, across his shoulder and chest. The sleeve of his parka was soaking up blood. Susan was weaving, and Vicky kept one arm around the girl's waist. He kept his good arm around Vicky's as they started for the road.

The barn lay flattened, as if it had been pulled into a crater with wooden planks strewn around the edge. Flames leapt from the center, expelling a cloud of blue-black smoke. Suddenly sirens drifted off into the air, and two police cars and a dark 4x4 jerked to a stop in the middle of the road. Banner slammed out of the lead car and ran toward them. There was the dark blur of other policemen, of a man in a topcoat running behind him, and then someone was guiding him into the front seat of a police car. He didn't resist. He knew he was losing a lot of blood.

He sat sideways with the door flung open, his boots planted in the snow. One of the policemen had attached a kind of splint to his arm and wrapped it with tape to keep it from moving. He couldn't move it anyway, but the gauze stuffed around the splint seemed to stanch the bleeding. He could see Vicky and Susan over by the body sprawled in the snow—Ty's body. Susan knelt beside it, and Vicky stood over her, a hand on the girl's shoulder.

Banner and the man in the topcoat leaned over the door. Father John recognized Mike Osgood, the FBI agent he'd met in Banner's office last Monday. It seemed like a year ago. The agent started firing questions: How many in the lab? How'd you and the women get out? What the hell happened?

Father John fielded them one at a time. Three in the lab, one outside. He listed the names, and both Banner and the agent nodded their heads, as if they had already figured that much. He wasn't sure why he and Vicky and Susan were still alive. They wouldn't be, if Ty hadn't stepped into the doorway, between them and Gary. What happened? A falling out of crooks. Glancing from the agent to the police chief, he asked, "How did you get the warrant?"

"Warrant?" Banner stepped back and stuffed his hands into the pockets of his parka. "Turns out we didn't need one. Soon's we got the FBI report on the names you gave us, we headed up here. There was nothing on Nick Sheldon, other than he got himself disbarred in

California a couple times. Nothing outstanding on Gary Rollins and Ty Jones, even though they got records from here to Lander. But Morrissey Porterfield . . ." The chief shook his head.

"A true genius," Osgood said. "One of the few chemists capable of producing fentanyl in a lab like this. We've been looking all over the country for him, ever since the L.A. agents raided a lab out in the San Bernardino valley. He was slippery. He managed to crawl through a window as the agents came through the front and back doors."

"And the Z Group?"

A sadness came into the agent's eyes. "We have an idea of who it might be. Unfortunately we can't confirm it. All our sources are dead."

Banner leaned over the door again. "One thing you don't have to worry about. The Z Group won't be closing down the mission."

Grabbing the door handle, Father John began leveraging himself to his feet. "You better stay put," the chief said as Father John walked past him and the agent and started for the body in the snow. He took a deep breath to steady himself. His legs felt a little wobbly. The acrid smell was still in the air, flames still lapped at the rubble of the barn, and in the distance the sound of another siren was coming up the mountain.

He knelt down beside Susan, aware of the girl's soft sobbing. Taking her hand in his, he said, "I'm sorry."

"I really loved him," she said.

"I think he loved you very much," Father John said. There was no greater love—the young man had given his life. He made the sign of the cross on Ty's forehead. Then he said the ancient prayers out loud: "Protect him,

Dear Lord Jesus; raise him up; show him Your mercy which is all encompassing, which you offer to us all."

He got to his feet, and Vicky walked beside him toward the road. The ambulance skirted around the police cars, stopping not far from them. The moment the siren cut off, there was only the soft crackling noise of the flames, the faint shushing of the wind.

‹ 36 ›

Howard Bushy was a natural, but so was Scott Nathan. Howard snatched the basketball and sprinted downcourt for a dunk, with Scott right behind, barely missing the block. Father John jumped up from the bench along the cement wall. Pain traveled along his arm, into his hand, to the tips of his fingers. He had to remember to move more slowly, with patience. It wasn't easy. The cast ran from his elbow to his wrist, a dead weight. His arm itched, and he wanted to rip off the cast and fling it into the winds. He forced himself to concentrate on the game.

Patrick had divided the kids into the Indians and the Warriors. They kept coming, always running, playing quick transition games. The Warriors had already run up a ten-point lead, but the Indians would never admit defeat. Howard made a three-pointer, and Scott took the inbound pass and headed downcourt looking for an opening, dribbling, one arm extended. The Indians moved in for an attempted steal.

"Where's the defense?" Father John yelled, jumping forward. He realized he had stepped onto the court.

The whistle screeched across the gym. The boys held their places, eyes on the coach, who came down the sidelines. "Father, do you mind?" Patrick said. "We're working out some tactical plays here."

"Oh, sorry," Father John said, backing off the court. It was hard to restrain himself. He loved coaching kids. He couldn't wait until spring when baseball season started and the Eagles suited up, but that was still three months away. He leaned against the cement wall, resolved just to watch. Patrick was doing a fantastic job.

Another field goal attempt by the Warriors. Then a turnover, and the Indians exploded downcourt. As Howard sank the ball, Father John heard a motor outside. He slipped through the door, wondering who the visitor might be. Not many visitors turned onto the narrow road that ran past Eagle Hall.

Reds, oranges, and pinks flamed across the western sky as the afternoon sun hovered above the dark ridge of the mountains. A Bronco stood in the middle of the road, silhouetted in the sunlight, and Vicky was walking toward him. She carried a package. He was surprised to see her—she had been in Denver the last couple of weeks.

"Father Peter advised me to look for you here," Vicky said as she came closer. Her brown coat flowed over the tops of her boots. The sun shimmered in her black hair.

"How's Susan?"

Vicky smiled. "That friend of yours and his wife run a very good clinic. I think Susan will make it this time, but . . ."

"It will always be a struggle." He finished her sentence. It wasn't just Susan he was thinking about. He was still struggling with the general anesthetic they'd given him to set his arm around a steel rod. The anesthetic had only whetted the thirst. It was like pouring gasoline onto a flame.

"It's over," Vicky said.

They were quiet a moment, then she went on, "It made the front page of the *Denver Post*. It looks as if you helped to thwart the plans of a major drug cartel."

Father John raised his good hand and pushed his cowboy hat back. "All the plans hinged on the mission, which, it turns out, the Jesuits never intended to sell."

"According to your Provincial?"

"According to some Scholastic in the outer office."

Vicky shook her head and laughed. "May the next economic development director work to preserve our traditions, instead of trying to destroy them. Eden Lightfoot had everything upside-down. Jobs rated first with him, no matter the cost. And he wasn't averse to accepting bribes along the way. He'll be facing charges at the Cheyenne Agency as well as here."

Father John drew in his lower lip. He had thought a lot about the economic development director. So much potential, so much waste.

Vicky was quiet, and he sensed something else on her mind. Finally she said, "I can't help thinking if I hadn't been so stubborn, if I had tried to convince Susan to go to the police right away, maybe she could have told them something that would have changed things. Maybe Marcus and the girl would be alive. Ty, also."

"Oh, Vicky," Father John said. "The world is full of maybes. Let's try not to torture ourselves. God is forgiving."

"Yes," Vicky said, but he knew she wouldn't let herself off easily. "It must be hard on the Depperts, and poor Loretta . . ." Vicky's voice trailed off.

Father John told her how he had been spending as much time as possible with the old couple, how the Arapahos had rallied around, and how Ike Yellow Calf had made it his business to look after them. In some ways, it might be easier for them than for Loretta. For her, it was very hard.

"At least her son has been properly buried now," Vicky said. "His ghost can be at rest."

Father John believed that was true. There had been the wake for both Rich and Marcus, and Thomas Spotted Horse had painted the bodies with the sacred red paint that would identify them to their ancestors. Father John had said the funeral Mass and blessed the graves at the St. Francis cemetery. And as the caskets were lowered, the elders had raised their voices in prayer, and the drums had pounded, the low, heavy sounds reverberating through the air, accompanying the ghosts to the spirit world where they would be at rest.

Vicky held out the package she was carrying. "This is for you. Because you kept the plank from striking my head and probably saved my life. And now you have that horrible cast on your pitching arm."

He smiled as he took the package. It looked like a birthday present, wrapped in yellow paper flecked with red balloons and tied with red ribbon. She had to help him undo it. They almost dropped the whole thing in the snow, but he made a quick one-handed recovery. "This isn't necessary," he said.

"Yes, it is," she said as he pulled back the last of the paper and read the black letters on the box: Stereo Cassette Player.

He felt like a kid, deliciously happy with an unexpected gift. Now he could listen to his opera tapes as he drove across the reservation. He couldn't imagine which opera he would listen to first. *La Bohème,* perhaps. Puccini, certainly. "You're right. This is absolutely necessary. *Hoho'u ho:3tone'3en.*"

Vicky threw her head back and laughed. "Oh, goodness," she said after a moment. "Arapaho is the most beautiful language in the world, but I wouldn't believe it listening to you. You mustn't let the elders hear you trying to speak it."

They walked the short distance to the Bronco, and he shut the door after she had slipped inside. Whatever had made him cradle her head against the explosion, he thanked God he had done so. He watched until the Bronco backed all the way to Circle Drive and began moving around the corner of the administration building. Until it disappeared into the sun.